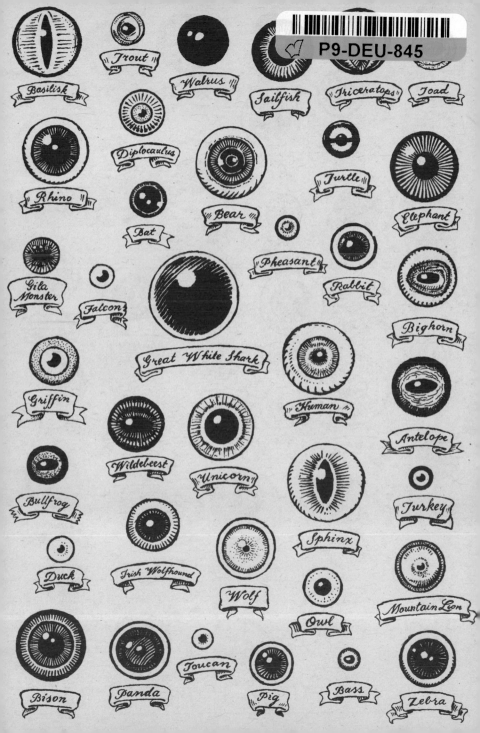

Basilisk

Trout

Walrus

Sailfish

Triceratops

Toad

Diplocaulus

Rhino

Bat

Bear

Turtle

Elephant

Pheasant

Gila Monster

Falcon

Rabbit

Bighorn

Great White Shark

Human

Griffin

Wildebeest

Unicorn

Antelope

Bullfrog

Turkey

Duck

Irish Wolfhound

Sphinx

Wolf

Mountain Lion

Bison

Toucan

Panda

Owl

Pig

Bass

Zebra

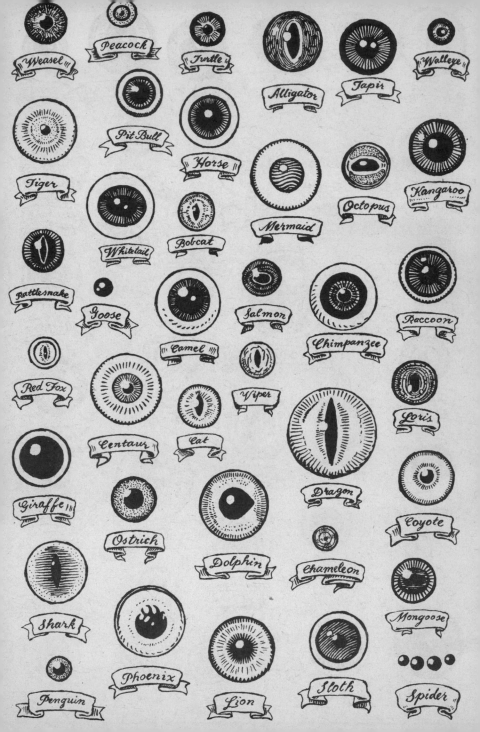

Weasel

Peacock

Turtle

Alligator

Tapir

Walleye

Pit Bull

Horse

Octopus

Kangaroo

Tiger

Mermaid

Whitetail

Bobcat

Rattlesnake

Goose

Camel

Salmon

Chimpanzee

Raccoon

Red Fox

Viper

Loris

Centaur

Cat

Giraffe

Ostrich

Dragon

Coyote

Dolphin

Chameleon

Shark

Mongoose

Penguin

Phoenix

Lion

Sloth

Spider

At first Leon couldn't figure out what he was looking at. Once he had, he reared back slightly. The contents of the drawer confused him. And embarrassed him. And grossed him out. The dull gray tangle wasn't as disgusting or fascinating as, say, teacher's spit, but it came pretty close.

"Mr. Zeisel," Miss Hagmeyer said.

Still puzzling over his discovery, Leon failed to hear his name.

"*Mr. Zeisel!*" Miss Hagmeyer repeated more forcefully.

"Huh?"

"Get your nose out of my PANTY HOSE!"

Leon
AND THE
Spitting
Image

A L L E N   K U R Z W E I L

Illustrations by BRET BERTHOLF

A Greenwillow Book
HarperTrophy®
An Imprint of HarperCollinsPublishers

HarperTrophy® is a registered trademark of HarperCollins Publishers Inc.

Leon and the Spitting Image
Text copyright © 2003 by Allen Kurzweil
Illustrations copyright © 2003 by Bret Bertholf

Printed in the United States of America. For information address HarperCollins Children's Books, a division of HarperCollins Publishers, 1350 Avenue of the Americas, New York, NY 10019.

Library of Congress Cataloging-in-Publication Data
Kurzweil, Allen.
Leon and the spitting image / by Allen Kurzweil.
p. cm.
"Greenwillow Books."
Summary: Leon, a fourth grader at the Classical School, tries to outwit the school bully and learn to sew for fanatical teacher Miss Hagmeyer, with unexpected help from his final project—a doll with magical powers.
ISBN 0-06-053930-5 (trade). ISBN 0-06-053931-3 (lib. bdg.)
ISBN 0-06-053932-1 (pbk.)
[1. Schools—Fiction. 2. Sewing—Fiction. 3. Magic—Fiction. 4. Single-parent families—Fiction. 5. Humorous stories.] I. Title.
PZ7.K96288 Le 2003   2002035325
[Fic]—dc21

First Harper Trophy edition, 2005
Visit us on the World Wide Web!
www.harperchildrens.com

For Max

Table of Contents

ONE

The Envelope

he night before the start of fourth grade, Leon Zeisel was on pins and needles. He lay in bed thinking about just one thing. An envelope.

Leon had first discovered the envelope one week earlier, while poking through his mom's desk. The envelope had attracted his attention for a simple reason. His name was written across the front in thick block letters. For a brief moment he had thought the envelope might contain a special surprise—tickets to a Yankees–Red Sox doubleheader would have been sweet—but that dream disappeared as soon as he noticed the school seal and a single word stamped in blood-red ink:

CONFIDENTIAL

That warning did the trick. Curious though he was, Leon shoved the unopened envelope back inside the desk.

But after a few days, curiosity turned into concern, and concern then turned into terror. Which was why, the night before school started, Leon slipped out of bed and made a beeline back to his mom's desk. Once there, he pulled the middle drawer halfway out. That released a catch on the slim side drawer.

Don't rush, he told himself. Mom's working late.

Leon squinched his eyes shut and clucked his tongue. Only after completing his good-luck routine did he remove the envelope, undo its clasp, lift the flap, and inspect the contents—three sheets of paper, each with the phrase HOME REPORT centered at the top. His fingers started shaking and his heart started thumping as it dawned on him that he was holding a top-secret history of his life at the Classical School.

Leon took a deep breath and began to read. Page one came from his first-grade teacher, Mrs. Sloat. She wrote: "Given the tragic loss of his father, it is not surprising that Leon is a tad delayed in the domain of manual dexterity."

Leon sighed. He didn't like being called delayed. And bringing in his dad—who had died in a freak accident at a fireworks factory when Leon was four—felt like a cheap shot.

He went back to Mrs. Sloat's assessment: "Leon's frustration most regularly expresses itself during craft time. He completed his macaroni necklace only with a great deal of assistance. And although a macaroni necklace might not seem important, it is. For here at the Classical School, our motto has always been, 'Nimble fingers make for nimble minds.'"

Geez! How many times had he heard *that* stupid saying!

Leon recalled only one thing about Mrs. Sloat, and the memory wasn't pleasant. He remembered her badgering him to stick his hands in Play-Doh and to *feel* the squishiness. Leon hadn't liked squishiness back in first grade, and he didn't like squishiness now.

He turned to page two. It came from his second-grade teacher, Miss Toothacre. Her report was just as grim. Miss Toothacre wrote, "Leon continues to be hampered by a troubling lack of fine motor skills."

That was another dumb thing he had heard a thousand times. Leon knew only too well that "lack of fine motor skills" had nothing to do with fancy cars. Teachers used the expression to avoid calling him a klutz.

The comment hurt. Suppose he was hampered; wasn't that Miss Toothacre's fault? *She* was the one cramming him into a bogus confidential report. Didn't that make *her* the hamperer?

Leon wiped his nose on the sleeve of his pajamas and braced himself for the third-grade report. It was now Mr. Joost's turn to get his licks in.

Mr. Joost wrote, "Leon's handwriting is *significantly* below grade level, and he is challenged by even the most basic manual tasks, such as tying his laces. At this juncture, I would seriously encourage corrective measures. One suggestion: Flute lessons might improve his finger movement."

Leon had always wondered why his mother forced him to take music classes with Miss Brunelleschi. Now he knew.

The home reports felt like strikes one, two, and three. And that made it all the more odd that the only nice words in the whole secret history came from Skip Kasperitis, the former minor-league pitcher who taught PE.

Coach Kasperitis wrote, "Leon is a real treat and a very special kid. His coordination needs work, but there's no question he's a champ. And if he ever learns to master his passion, I'll tell you this, Leon Zeisel is the kind of kid who could make magic."

Two

Trimore Towers

A dog barked from somewhere upstairs. Leon glanced out the window. The lights on the convention-center sign snapped off. It was late. He tucked the three sheets of paper back into the envelope and tucked himself back into bed.

Some home report, he thought as he built a tent with his blankets. I could have done a better job myself.

That was certainly true. And what's more, if Leon *had* written his own home report, he would have stuck to the assignment. There would have been no mention of macaroni necklaces, that's for sure. He would have focused his home report on his *home*—Trimore Towers, a wedding cake-shaped six-tiered hotel his mother called "the finest one-star lodgings in the city."

For a long time, Leon had assumed that the single gold star on the plaque near the key rack meant his hotel was tops. After all, *he* received a single gold star from Miss Brunelleschi only when he managed to make his flute do exactly what it was supposed to— and that didn't happen too often.

Then his mom set him straight about the whole star system. "Adults like getting *lots* of stars, sweetie," she said. "They're greedy that way."

Leon didn't care what grown-ups thought. He loved his hotel just as it was. Actually the lack of stars was a *good* thing, Leon decided. Because the Trimore wasn't snazzy, it attracted guests that snootier hotels turned away.

Elegant *five*-star establishments would never give a room to a seal act or a snake handler. The Trimore did.

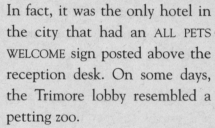

In fact, it was the only hotel in the city that had an ALL PETS WELCOME sign posted above the reception desk. On some days, the Trimore lobby resembled a petting zoo.

That didn't make Maria, Leon's favorite housekeeper, terribly happy, but over time, she had learned to take precautions. Along with her normal cleaning supplies, Maria relied on a highly effective product called Poop-B-Gone. Also, she kept the reception desk stocked with diapers in all different sizes. You never knew when a chimp or a llama might check in wearing a soiled nappy (or, worse, no nappy at all).

Obviously, animals weren't the only guests staying

at the Trimore. The hotel also booked humans, most of whom attended meetings at the convention center across the street.

Leon liked that, too. The convention center attracted all kinds of intriguing people: detectives, stuntmen, contortionists, potato-chip tasters. And the best part was, they often left behind stuff that couldn't fit into their suitcases.

That's where Maria came in. If she found an interesting freebie while cleaning a room, she'd save it for Leon. She'd presented him with blinking refrigerator magnets, penlights, a juggling pin, and a policeman's badge. Once Maria gave him a bag of potato chips the size of a pillowcase.

There were other matters Leon would have mentioned in his home report. For instance, how many places actually pay you to live there? And it wasn't just his mom, the Trimore night manager, who got that deal. Leon was on the payroll, too.

Every week the hotel bookkeeper would make out a check to Mr. L. Zeisel for the sum of three dollars.

It was Leon's job to maintain the lobby signboard. That meant fetching the daily VIP guest list from his mom, along with an old wooden letter box that had a sturdy brass latch shaped like a question mark. The box was divided into sixty-four compartments, ideal for separating the twenty-six letters of the alphabet—

upper- and lowercase—plus all the numbers from zero through nine. (Actually, that only adds up to sixty-*two*, but the weird thingamabobs—the &s, the $s, the #s, and the very useful !s—filled the two spare cubbies.)

Leon would use the letters, numbers, and thingamabobs to reproduce the VIP list on a signboard covered in black felt. Leon's penmanship might have been "*significantly* below grade level," but his signboard usually deserved an A+.

The day before the start of fourth grade, Leon had positioned the white plastic letters to read:

> **VVelcome VVest Coast**
> **Mime Company!!!**
>
> **Hovvdy Colorado**
> **Covvpunchers!!!**

Leon loved exclamation marks. He felt they turned VIPs into VVIPs. Another benefit of exclamation marks was that they drew attention away from a major signboard problem—the missing Ws.

No one at the hotel knew how it had happened, but all the Ws (both upper- and lowercase) had disappeared. This forced Leon to substitute side-by-side Vs.

(He experimented for a while with upside-down Ms, but they kept falling off the felt.) After diligently straightening the letters and punctuation marks, Leon would latch the wooden box and inspect the work that earned him his weekly paycheck.

Still, not everything about life at the Trimore was great. Actually, there were some things that were downright lousy. The Ice Queen, for instance.

The Ice Queen was an ancient ice maker that occupied an alcove on the far side of his bedroom wall. The noise it made drove Leon bonkers.

Leon *hated* the Ice Queen. Just thinking about her turned his blood to, well, ice. She reminded him of the fairy-tale witch of the same name. In the storybooks, the Ice Queen cast an evil spell that forced the entire village to sleep for one hundred years. But his Ice Queen, the one rattling in the hotel hallway, did the exact opposite. She *prevented* sleep.

Her spell was always the same. It began with three harsh clicks, followed by a long, obnoxious buzz. Then she would tease her victims by falling silent. The silence could last one minute, it could last ten. Yet the Ice Queen always revived her hex, creating a bed-rattling hullabaloo as she spat ice cubes into a large metal bucket.

Click-click-click-buzzzz . . .

The sound from the far side of the bedroom wall forced Leon deeper under his blanket.

Grind-groan-rumble-CRASH!

Leon reemerged from his dark, hot bunker and looked around the room. The ice maker's thunderous finale had been so intense it had knocked loose some of the pushpin flags stuck into the map of the world above his bed. Leon squinched his eyes and clucked his tongue, hoping a counterhex would silence the Ice Queen.

No such luck. Within seconds, she started up once more.

Click-click-click-buzzzz . . .

Leon couldn't stand it. Still in pajamas, he fled the hotel apartment and rode the elevator down to the lobby. He marched over to the reception desk.

"Mom," he moaned. "She's doing it again."

"I'm sorry, sweetie," his mother said, knowing instantly who "she" was. "I did make some calls. But that machine is so darn old I can't find anyone to quiet her down."

Leon ducked under the counter and planted himself near the key rack. "She won't shut up," he complained.

His mom nodded sympathetically. "It's the mimes, Leon. They've been whooping it up ever since they arrived. Maria just told me they've wiped out four minibars *and* the candy dispenser. Funny, I'd have expected the cowpunchers to be the rowdy ones, but they've turned out to be quiet as church mice."

"Mom? Can I . . ." Leon hesitated.

Emma Zeisel looked at her son's pale, anxious face. The dark circles under his eyes worried her. "Tell you what," she said. "Go fetch me a sandwich, and I'll fix up a bunk for you down here. How does that sound?"

"It's a deal," said Leon. He was already starting to feel better. "You want the usual, Mom?"

"I do," said Emma Zeisel before she had to turn away and help a cowpuncher change rooms because of a backed-up toilet.

The Trimore's coffee shop, like the hotel that housed it, was a small operation. Four booths, six stools of counter service, and one very plump woman who kept the whole place going.

"Hey there, Frau Haffenreffer," said Leon to the woman in question.

"Still up?" said Frau Haffenreffer with a look of concern. She knew he was starting school the next day.

"Can't sleep, and Mom needs a sandwich."

"The usual?"

"Yup."

"Ordering!" Frau Haffenreffer said to herself. "One tongue on rye! Extra hots! Extra mustard!" She then walked over to the sandwich station.

While she prepared the food, Leon kept himself busy by inspecting the pastry in the glass case near the cash register. There was a lot to inspect. Frau

Haffenreffer took baking *very* seriously. And even with fingers as fat as Twinkies, she had absolutely no trouble whipping up elegant pastries, cookies, and cakes.

"So, Leon," she said, returning with the tongue sandwich neatly wrapped in wax paper. "How should we top this off?"

"I'll have a sugar-dusted chocolate-chip cookie, and Mom will take one of those messy custardy things." Leon pointed to a pastry in the case.

"And a napoleon for your mother," Frau Haffenreffer confirmed.

Leon watched as she arranged the sandwich, cookie, and napoleon inside a cardboard box. After determining that everything was neat and tidy, she closed the lid and yanked some red string from a spool chained above the counter.

With a series of lightning-fast motions worthy of a ninja warrior, Frau Haffenreffer tied up the box. She completed her attack with a single effortless slice that severed the string from the spool.

For the longest time, Leon had wondered how she made that final cut look so easy. Eventually he had figured out the trick: Frau Haffenreffer wore a special ring fitted with a tiny hooked blade that looked like the horn on a horn beetle.

Leon took the food to the back office behind the reception desk.

"What do you think, sweetie?" said his mom, taking a bite of her sandwich. "Is the tongue tasting me while I'm tasting the tongue?"

Leon squelched a smile. Though he'd never admit it, he liked when his mom said goofy things. She pointed to a pair of battered leather armchairs she had pushed together to form a makeshift bed. "As soon as you've finished your cookie, I want you to get some sleep. You have a big day tomorrow. Got it?"

"Got it," said Leon. He curled up under a hotel blanket. It was scratchier than the ones upstairs, but he didn't care. He was happy to be far away from the Ice Queen and the confidential home reports—and happier still to be close to his mom.

Leon woke feeling exhausted and, because of the home reports, sad. He looked for his mom, only to discover that a hotel crisis involving a drunken mime had called her away from Reception. After getting dressed (in the school clothes thoughtfully laid out on top of a nearby file cabinet), Leon made his way into the lobby, where the signboard caught his eye.

Hotel guests were forever rearranging the plastic letters, sending private messages to one another, spelling out nasty words. And sure enough, the sign no longer welcomed mimes and cowpunchers. It now said:

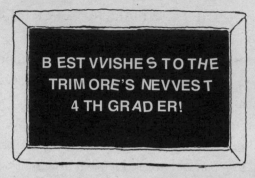

B EST VVISHE S TO THE
TRIM ORE'S NEVVES T
4 TH GR AD ER!

The announcement made Leon stop in his tracks. It didn't matter that his mom had used only capital letters and that she had messed up the spacing. And it didn't matter that she'd been chintzy with the exclamation marks. For just a moment, while he stared at the sign, Leon Zeisel felt a little better, ready to face fourth grade.

THREE

The Hag

t was raining heavily when Emma and Leon Zeisel pushed through the revolving door of the Trimore and walked to the curb.

"Did you remember your travel book, sweetie?"

Leon patted his backpack. "Right here, Mom."

"How about your milk and taxi money?"

"Check and double check," he said reassuringly.

"Oh, I almost forgot." Emma Zeisel handed her son a string-tied box.

"What's inside?"

"Dough balls. Frau Haffenreffer baked an extra batch just for you." Emma Zeisel gave Leon a quick motherly inspection. "Your laces, sweetie."

"They're fine," he answered, mildly annoyed. He craned his neck toward the street and looked for an available taxi.

Since the middle of third grade, Leon had been taking taxis by himself. He had no choice. The school bus didn't stop near the hotel, and his mom almost never finished work early enough to make the trip with him. After accompanying her son to school on a few trial runs, Emma Zeisel had handed Leon a blank notebook.

"What's this for?" he had asked suspiciously. He disliked anything that involved writing.

"It's to register the drivers' names," said Emma Zeisel. "You can get them off the hack license."

"Hack license?"

"The driver's picture ID," she explained. "It's always posted. It's the law. And if you start getting goosey, just ask the cabby where he comes from and add that to your notes."

Leon took the assignment seriously. He returned from his maiden voyage proudly announcing, "I got a guy named Cesar Viana. And you know what? He's from the Philippines!" A few seconds later Leon said, "Where exactly *are* the Philippines, Mom?" Almost before Leon finished asking the question, Emma Zeisel whipped out the atlas she stashed behind the reception desk and showed him.

On his second taxi trip, Leon flagged down Juan-Pablo Zapata from Mexico. And on his third, he hailed Push Singh from India. Each name and nationality went straight into the travel book.

And so began the taxi-driver collection.

For Leon's ninth birthday, Emma Zeisel bought her son a huge foam-backed map of the world and a box of pushpins tipped with colorful plastic banners. From then on, Leon recorded every country he "visited" on the map that hung above his bed as well as in his travel book. By the time fourth grade rolled around, he had collected thirty-seven nations and nineteen states.

* * *

Leon lifted an arm and expertly extended one finger toward the oncoming traffic. Despite the downpour, he managed to nab a taxi almost at once. (Drivers generally picked him over businessmen urgently waving briefcases.) He gave the cabby the address of his school, then squinched and clucked, hoping for an Alaska, or a Botswana, or—best of all—a Suriname. Suriname was the one country he still needed to complete South America.

Leon opened his eyes and looked at the name on the driver's photo ID: Ladislo Szekacs.

He recorded the name in his travel book and said, "Excuse me, Mr. . . . uh . . . "

"It is pronounced 'say catch,'" said the driver. "Like in your American baseball."

"Thanks," Leon said. "Could you tell me where you come from, Mr. Say Catch?"

"Why should you know?" the driver asked suspiciously.

"It's for my collection," Leon said.

"What collection?" the driver demanded.

Leon had his routine down pat. "Some kids collect baseball cards. I collect taxi drivers."

The cabby hesitated.

"Please," Leon said. He held up the travel book. "It's important."

"Hungary," the driver mumbled.

"Yes!" Leon exclaimed.

"Why are you so happy? This is good?"

"This is *great*," said Leon. "You're my first Hungary."

"And you, little boy," said the now smiling driver, "you are my first taxi-driver collector."

Leon closed the travel book and gazed out the window. A mail truck, idling at a traffic light, made him think of envelopes, which in turn made him think of the confidential report he had uncovered the night before. The memory prompted a sudden uncontrolled shiver. The assessments from Sloat, Toothacre, and Joost seemed so unfair. And it didn't help that the identity of his fourth-grade teacher was a total mystery.

Leon tried to forget about school, but he couldn't. When he struggled to break through the red string on the pastry box, a phrase from the home report popped back into his head. *Nimble fingers make for nimble minds.* What lamebrain thought that one up?

The only good thing about the first day of school was that Leon would see his two best friends, P.W. and Lily-Matisse. They had both been away all summer.

P.W. was called P.W. because his real name—Phya Winit Dhabanandana—tended to scare people off. P.W. was a short kid with a long name, whose parents came from Thailand. He loved math and building things. He hated spelling and keeping quiet. He had a reputation for being a bit of a smart aleck.

As for Lily-Matisse, she was lean and lanky (like Leon) and had buck teeth. ("Dentists must *love* that girl," Leon's mom had once conjectured.) She was an awesome jump roper, a gifted gymnast, and the daughter of the school art teacher, Ms. Jasprow, which meant she knew lots of stuff other kids didn't.

"Little boy, you hear me?" said the taxi driver. "We are arrived."

Leon paid the fare, and dashed out into the rain. He hadn't even made it up the limestone steps when he took his first tumble of the school year. He fell hard, face forward. Dough balls rolled down the steps and into the gutter. Embarrassed and bruised, Leon tried to pick himself up. He couldn't.

A very large army boot was pressing down on one of his untied shoelaces. Intentionally.

"Hey there, *Zit*-sel," a voice bellowed. "Welcome back." The owner of the boot completed his greeting with a brutal punch to the arm.

Leon winced, but said nothing. He knew his attacker would soon lose interest and seek out other targets.

The assault came from a beefy eleven-year-old named Henry Lumpkin. Henry Lumpkin had been torturing Leon nearly as long as teachers had.

Lumpkin's methods differed from theirs, however. To inflict pain, he relied on dead-arms and dodgeballs, not confidential reports. He was a thoroughly nasty life-form who picked up nicknames the way crooks acquire aliases.

Some kids called him Lumpkin the Pumpkin because of his bright orange hair and his pumpkiny shape. Others referred to him as Hank the Tank, in recognition of the armored body hidden under the olive drab army jacket he always wore to school. And still others identified him as the Lethal Launcher because of the force and accuracy of his dodgeball throws.

But to Leon he was just Lumpkin, a blockhead and a bully whose sudden and unpredictable attentions always spelled trouble.

Leon stayed put on the ground for almost a minute, even though it was raining. When the coast was clear, he darted into school. Lily-Matisse and P.W. were waiting near the water fountain.

"Hey," said P.W.

"Hey," said Leon.

"Hey," said Lily-Matisse.

"Hey," said Leon.

"You okay?" Lily-Matisse asked.

"Why shouldn't he be okay?" P.W. said.

"Well, for starters, he's limping," Lily-Matisse observed. "Plus he's rubbing his arm."

Leon glanced at the human tank rolling down the hall.

"Did Lumpkin do that?" Lily-Matisse asked.

"Yup."

"We'd better take cover," P.W. advised.

The three friends hung up their rain gear and entered the classroom.

"Holy cow!" said P.W.

"Geez!" Leon exclaimed.

"My mom told me our homeroom was going to be different," said Lily-Matisse.

"This is *so* weird!" P.W. said enthusiastically. He pointed to the back of the room, at a massive metal cabinet mounted on heavy rubber wheels. "Look at the lock on that thing! What do you think is inside?"

"And what about those!" Leon said, gawking at a series of wall posters featuring severed hands.

"Sure beats those poems Mr. Joost had on his walls last year!" said P.W.

"Don't count on it," said Lily-Matisse. "My mom told me—"

"Here it comes," P.W. interrupted. "Previews of upcoming attractions. Let's hear what your mom says."

"Well, my mom told me—"

DRRRRINNNNNG!

The school bell put a stop to Lily-Matisse's update.

A thin shadow darkened the frosted glass of the classroom door.

Leon squinched and clucked. *Please* make this teacher better than the last ones, he told himself.

The knob turned and the door opened.

When Leon unsquinched, he found himself in the

presence of a tall, thin woman wearing a long black cape. Not a Batman cape. More the kind of cape Florence Nightingale would have fastened around her neck before heading off to nurse the wounded.

Leon stared at the clasp on the cape. For

a moment, he thought the clasp was formed from two yellow marbles linked by a chain. But the more he looked at the "marbles," the more they seemed to look at him.

All of a sudden he understood why.

They're not marbles, he said to himself. . . . They're *eyeballs!*

Leon lifted his gaze from the glass eyes to his teacher's eyes—two dull black beads set deep into a narrow face framed by a helmet of unnaturally black hair. The severe hairdo exaggerated the thinness of the head and drew attention away from a mouth so pinched it looked as though it had been stitched in place by a doll maker who had pulled too hard on the thread.

The teacher hung up her long black cape and revealed a long black dress underneath. Not *everything* she wore was black. Between the bottom of her dress and the top of her precisely knotted lace-up boots (which were also black), there was a small stretch of leg covered by panty hose the color of cooked liver.

Leon wasn't the only one shocked by the new fourth-grade teacher. The rest of the class was equally amazed. They all watched in nervous silence as she marched over to her desk and began emptying her satchel. Leon made a mental list:

one clipboard
one container of cottage cheese (small-curd)
one box of chalk
one chalk holder
one metal pointer
one brass key

It didn't take a hotel detective to figure out that the key must go to the giant padlock on the cabinet. Leon observed his teacher insert a piece of chalk into the sleeve of the chalk holder and adjust it like a lipstick. She then wrote her name on the blackboard with terrifying neatness:

Miss Hagmeyer

P. W. leaned over to Leon and whispered, "*Hag* is right."

"Suspend the verbal games at once!" Miss Hagmeyer snapped.

P.W., lowering his voice to a murmur, said, "How'd she hear us?"

"Must have radar," Leon whispered back.

"I do," Miss Hagmeyer said. "So I advise all of you to keep quiet and concentrate on the matters at hand." She went back to writing on the blackboard.

"There," she said moments later, turning to face the room. "I would like all of you to read out loud what I have written."

The students dutifully repeated the phrase. "A place for everything and everything in its place."

"Louder," Miss Hagmeyer commanded.

The class said the phrase once again.

"Better," she allowed. "Those nine words will guide us throughout the year. There will be a proper place for books, a proper place for supplies, and a proper place for worksheets. There will be a proper place for study, a proper place for play, and a proper place for each of you to sit."

With that, Miss Hagmeyer put down the chalk and called everyone up to the front of the room. She then reached for her clipboard and pointer and began reading off the names of students—last name first, first name last. The roll call started with "Brede, Antoinette" and finished, inevitably, with "Zeisel, Leon." After stating each name, Miss Hagmeyer aimed her metal pointer at a chair.

Leon ended up at the very rear of the room, sandwiched between a desk assigned to Warchowski, Thomas, and the padlocked cabinet. Though the seat assignment separated Leon from his friends, it did have one advantage. It was beyond the range of Lumpkin's spitballs, noogies, and dead-arms.

Brede, Antoinette, wasn't so lucky. Because of the configuration of the chairs, she got stuck directly in front of the class bully.

The moment Lumpkin thought Miss Hagmeyer

wasn't looking, he reached forward to give Antoinette a poke with a brand-new highly sharpened No. 3 pencil (No. 3s being the ones with the extra-hard lead). But before he could complete his attack, Miss Hagmeyer whipped around.

"Stop that at once!" she barked. "Did you fail to register my earlier warning? I hear everything, Mr. Lumpkin—*everything*."

"But I didn't touch her," he protested.

"You were about to. I *heard* you leaning over, and don't bother denying it." Miss Hagmeyer lifted her unnaturally black hair to reveal a truly shocking pair of ears. "These little beauties never fail me."

Leon found himself gawking. Even from the back of the room he could see that the so-called little beauties were neither little nor beautiful. Quite the opposite. They were huge and gnarled, like the giant mushrooms one sometimes finds growing on rotten tree stumps.

It's never a good idea to praise your own body parts. It's an even worse idea when the body parts in question resemble a primordial fungus. Miss Hagmeyer must have sensed as much, because she quickly let go of her hair. "Now that we have established that I can hear *you*," she said to the class, "it is time to find out whether you can hear *me*."

She tapped her blackboard motto. "I did not invent this nine-word phrase. A medieval master who trained apprentices composed it. Which is fitting, since our year together will concentrate on the Middle Ages, that period between the fifth and fifteenth century that gave the world horseshoes, hard soap, and the horizontal loom. And as you will soon discover, the Middle Ages emphasized discipline and charity. That *I* shall supply. The Middle Ages also put stock in obedience and diligence. That *you* shall provide. And by stitching together *my* discipline and *your* dutiful diligence, we will create a glorious tapestry of learning. Do all of you follow what I am saying?"

A hesitant round of "Yes, Miss Hagmeyers" filtered through the room.

"Good. Now some of you might be wondering: How will we create this glorious tapestry of learning? I shall answer that question by quoting another medieval saying. Listen closely. 'I *hear* and I forget. I *see* and I remember. I *make* and I understand.' In this class you will *make*. And by *making* you will *learn*. You will exercise your fingers and, by doing so, exercise your brains. That is the Classical way. That is the way of all apprentices wishing to become masters."

Leon gulped. Mention of fingers never sounded promising.

Miss Hagmeyer walked over to her desk and grabbed the metal pointer. She held it up in the air and said, "In short, I will make your minds and your fingers nimble by teaching you how to use this!"

And that's when Leon learned the horrible truth. The metal pointer wasn't a metal pointer.

It was a giant instructional sewing needle!

FOUR

Coach Kasperitis

eon felt miserable as he left the classroom and headed for the gym. A whole year in the clutches of a teacher who threatened her class with a dagger-sized sewing needle? Something told him that Miss Hagmeyer's projects would be a lot more demanding than macaroni necklaces. And for a student who had trouble writing neatly and tying his shoes that did not bode well.

"Okay, here's the scoop," said Lily-Matisse as she, Leon, and P.W. made their way to PE. "Mom told me the Hag is a total maniac."

"No kidding," said P.W. "What clued you in? The glass eyeballs? The weird things she made us recite? Maybe it was her nickel-sized earlobes?"

"The Hag's earlobes are a lot bigger than nickels," said Lily-Matisse. "They're quarter sized at least."

"Could we argue about lobe size later?" said Leon impatiently. "What did your mom tell you, Lily-Matisse?"

"Well, for starters, the Hag is totally obsessed by sewing. She'll teach us math and English and stuff like that. But basically we'll be using needles and pins more than anything else. And you know those posters on the wall?"

"The surgery ones?" said P.W.

Lily-Matisse shook her head. "They're not about surgery. They're sewing instructions. And that big cabinet with the lock on it—the one Leon can touch from his desk? It's *crammed* with cloth and tools and other sewing junk."

"Great," said Leon despairingly.

"And that's not all," Lily-Matisse said as she entered the gym. "You know her hair? How it's super black and shiny? Mom says it's a wig!"

"A wig?" said Leon.

"No way," said P.W.

"Way," said Lily-Matisse. "Mom heard the Hag adjusting it in the teachers' lounge."

"What do you mean, *heard?*" said P.W. skeptically.

"Mom's pretty sure it's attached with *Velcro*."

"Velcro?" said Leon.

P.W. dropped to one knee and started pulling at his sneaker strap. *Sccritchh! Sccritchh!* "Did it sound like this?"

Lily-Matisse made a face. "Cut it out, P.W. That's gross."

A shrill whistle blast put an end to P.W.'s sneaker concert.

Coach Skip Kasperitis was a whistle-happy ex-baseball player with a great big heart, a great big behind, and a great big soft jowly face. But the most distinctive thing about the coach had nothing to do with any of those things. It had to do with a very unfortunate habit he'd picked up as a pitcher in the minor leagues.

That very unfortunate habit was tobacco.

Naturally the Classical School had a ban on *smoking* tobacco. But no one had thought to prohibit *chewing* it. And because of that oversight in the teacher handbook, Coach Kasperitis was able to indulge his unhealthy addiction.

Colleagues complained, of course, as did some parents. But the principal of the school, Hortensia Birdwhistle, turned a blind eye. She never liked raising a stink. Besides, she felt sorry for the coach. She knew he had cut back and that he was doing everything in his power to quit.

For a couple of months, when Leon was in second grade, the coach had tried gnawing on sunflower seeds instead of chomping on "chaw." But that didn't last. The wholesome substitute gave him headaches and drove the school janitor, Mr. Hankey, crazy.

"Hey, Skip!" Mr. Hankey complained. "It ain't no picnic sweeping up sunflower husks. My gym's *seedy* enough as it is, thank you very much!"

When Leon was in third grade, Coach Kasperitis had tried to break his habit by sticking tiny amounts of tobacco inside giant wads of bubble gum, a combination made famous by a legendary major league ballplayer named Rod Carew. That experiment also caused problems.

The janitor again blew a gasket. "Hey, Skip, this ain't called a *gum*nasium! Don't count on me scraping Bazooka off the bleachers, you got that?"

Mr. Hankey didn't have to worry. A couple of weeks into the gum-and-tobacco combo, the coach learned that the aforementioned legendary Rod Carew had spent a whopping $100,000 on dental work because of damage caused by the disgusting mix. So that was the end of that.

The coach eventually decided to chew his tobacco straight, in smaller and smaller amounts, less and less often. Still, no matter how much he cut down, his habit attracted attention. The reason, in a word, was *saliva*.

If you chew tobacco, you have to spit. There's no getting around it. And given how Mr. Hankey had complained about the sunflower seeds and the bubble gum, Coach Kasperitis knew he had to come up with a surefire method for spit disposal.

Spittoons, those little brass spit pots often seen in cowboy movies, were out of the question. With kids and balls flying around the gym, an open container of teacher's spit was an invitation to disaster. Nor could the coach expel his chaw into the gym's water fountain. The mesh on the drain was too fine.

After a bit of testing, however, he worked out a simple method of waste management. He turned an old pickle jar into a gob collector. Whenever the need arose, the coach would unscrew the jar and— *pffut!*—spit. This did wonders to get the students' attention.

Pffut! "Welcome back, guys!" Coach Kasperitis shouted as he resealed his pickle jar. "I hope all of you had championship summers! Guess how we're going to start off the year?"

"Dodgeball!" the whole class yelled.

"You guys *are* sharp!" said the coach. "That's absolutely right. Like I tell you every year, dodgeball teaches us an important life lesson. It teaches us that passion and practice are the secret to making magic."

The coach placed his jar on the gym floor and reached into a canvas sack. "Now that you've entered the big leagues, you're ready to handle this." He extracted a blue ball.

"The Rhino," he said. "A regulation-sized dodgeball just like the pros use. And in case you're wondering where the ball gets its name, I will tell you what you'll discover soon enough. Its skin is every bit as rough and tough as the skin on the genuine rhinos that stampede across Africa."

Coach Kasperitis bounced the Rhino on

the floor a few times. "Okay, everybody. Pay attention. We're going to ease back into things with a quick round of Team Multiple."

The fourth graders all hollered happily, Leon louder than most.

"It's your first day so I don't want anyone over-doing it. You got that?"

The tepid response of the class convinced the coach that he needed to reinforce the point. "Just in case you *don't* understand, I'm going to repeat the Kasperitis Code of Conduct. When you line up to choose sides there will be no backsies and no frontsies. Once play begins there will be no re-calls, no *re-re-calls*, no replays, no redos, no puppy guarding, and no time-outs—unless authorized by me. Another thing—*absolutely no headsies*. I don't want any bloody noses. They're a mess to clean up and Mr. Hankey rides me plenty hard as it is."

The coach bounced the Rhino. "Line balls are out," he continued. "Automatic sudden death after ten minutes of play. And the most important rule . . . anyone remember?"

"No trash-talking," said Antoinette primly.

"That's exactly right," the coach confirmed. "And no trash-talking means no teasing, no taunting, no insults of any kind. Right then. Let's get started."

He looked around the gym. "Jasprow. Lumpkin. Choose sides!"

Lily-Matisse put together her team based on friendship, which meant Leon and P.W. were her first- and second-round draft picks. Lumpkin took a different approach, giving preference to brute strength when assembling his squad.

Once the teams had lined up at opposite ends of the gym, the coach removed two more spanking new Rhinos from the sack and placed the three balls along the centerline. He then retreated with his pickle jar to the top row of the bleachers. With a short blast of his whistle, he started the first dodgeball game of the year.

It wasn't one for the record books. Play proved unusually sloppy. Almost everyone dropped easy throws, missed simple outs, aimed terribly, failed to cover teammates.

Seven minutes into the game, only two players remained alive—Leon, who controlled two Rhinos, and Lumpkin, who controlled just one.

Take it slow, Leon said to himself as he maneuvered around the court. He faked a few times, advanced to the centerline, and threw one of his two balls.

Lumpkin dodged it.

Leon beat a quick retreat. But while dashing to safety, he tripped over a sneaker lace and accidentally kicked his backup Rhino across the centerline.

"Hey, klutzo!" Lumpkin shouted as soon as he saw

that Leon was vulnerable. "Ready for complete and total annihilation?" (Lumpkin had a limited vocabulary, except when it came to blood sports.)

The coach blew his whistle. "Lumpkin! What'd I say about trash-talk?"

"Sorry, Coach," he said unconvincingly before returning his attention to Leon. Lumpkin plotted his attack slowly and methodically, clearly relishing the promise of public humiliation.

"Watch for his sidewinder!" P.W. warned from the bleachers.

Leon gave a nervous nod as he dodged about.

Lumpkin had a number of throws, but the most deadly in his arsenal was, without doubt, the low-flying waist-high toss called the sidewinder. When successfully launched, a sidewinder sent its victim straight to the school nurse. With the introduction of the Rhino, Leon speculated that it was probably safer to be charged by a *real* African rhino than to get in the way of one hurled by Henry Lumpkin.

For a few minutes Lumpkin forced Leon to jump and duck and twist by faking tosses this way and that. Then he stopped pretending and actually released one of the Rhinos.

I can catch this, Leon told himself as he tracked the surprisingly slow-moving ball.

He bent his knees and rounded his outstretched arms into a basket.

Bamm!

The incoming missile hit Leon's chest and ricocheted toward the sidelines in a soft, gentle arc.

To win the game, all Leon had to do was catch the
Rhino before it touched the ground. He took a few
quick steps and cradled his arms.

WHAMM!!!

Out of nowhere, a *second* ball pegged Leon in the
back.

Lumpkin's strategy suddenly announced itself. The
first, slow-moving toss had been nothing more than a
decoy, used to distract Leon from the patented, high-
velocity sidewinder.

The trap worked perfectly. The follow-up ball
slammed Leon to the floor. And that meant, of course,
he was out.

Leon felt like a total doofus as he stumbled off the
court. That feeling stayed with him for the rest of the
day, and it was still with him after dismissal.

Out on the front steps, Leon's thoughts only darkened.
Lumpkin *and* the Hag. Nine whole months of sewing
and sidewinders! An entire school year of needles and
noogies!

Leon felt so cruddy he didn't even want to catch
up with P.W. and Lily-Matisse. He waved good-bye to
his friends and dashed straight to the curb, where he
hailed a cab.

Once Leon flopped inside the taxi, he gave the driver the address of the Trimore and pulled out his travel book. A Nepal or a Tanzania might make things better, he told himself.

He read the hack license. It said NAPOLEON DE L'ANGE. The first name improved Leon's mood a little. Maybe Napoleon had a brother and sister named Muffin and Doughnut.

"Excuse me," he said to the driver, "but could you please tell me where you come from?"

"Haiti," the driver replied cheerfully.

Leon grimaced. Just great! I've already got *five* Haitis.

"You don't like Haiti?" said the driver, who had caught Leon scowling in the rearview mirror.

Suddenly Leon felt embarrassed. "Sorry, it's not that. It's just I was hoping you came from someplace else."

"Where?" the driver asked pleasantly.

"Well, Suriname would have been nice," said Leon.

"Oh?" the driver replied, obviously wanting to know more.

So as the taxi snaked through the city traffic, Leon described his collection. "I have all of New England— *including* Rhode Island. And Suriname's all I need to finish off South America."

"*C'est fantastique!*" Napoleon exclaimed, slapping

his hand delightedly on the steering wheel.

By the fifth traffic light, Leon was comfortable enough to complain about his first day back at school.

"How bad was it, from one to ten, with ten being the best?" the driver asked.

Leon considered the question for quite some time before answering. "I'd give it a two—two and a half, tops."

"I've had days like that," the driver said sympathetically. "The day I fled Haiti was a two and a half. I lost everything. My house, my car, my job. I had to say good-bye to my family."

"That sounds a lot worse than a two and a half, Mr. de l'Ange."

"Perhaps you are right," the driver said wistfully. "But please call me Napoleon. And your name is . . ."

"Leon," said Leon.

"A very grand honor to speak with you, Monsieur Leon."

The cab pulled up to the Trimore soon after the introductions. Napoleon jumped out to open the passenger door and revealed himself to be an immensely tall fellow wearing a snazzy pinstripe suit.

"Thanks a lot," Leon said.

"You are most welcome, Monsieur Leon," said Napoleon, tipping an imaginary hat chauffeur-style. "And do not worry. I am certain that tomorrow you will have a nine-and-three-quarters day!"

He punctuated his prediction by spitting on the sidewalk.

Leon gave him a look.

"Do you not know, Monsieur Leon? Spitting keeps evil far away!"

FIVE

The Stitches of Virtue

iss Hagmeyer strode into class on the second day of school just as the bell finished ringing. She looked pretty much the same as she had the day before. Black cape, black dress, black lace-up boots, liver-colored panty hose covering her skinny legs.

There was, however, one minor costume change. P.W. was the first to spot it. "Psst! Check out the glass eyes," he whispered to Leon, who in turn gave Lily-Matisse a nudge. The yellow eyes had been swapped for a snow-white pair that had silver flecks surrounding their slit-shaped pupils.

Miss Hagmeyer called the class to order with a wave of her instructional needle. After everyone was seated, she handed out *Medieval Readers* and said, "Let the apprenticeship begin. Turn to page sixteen and review the section titled Medieval Ethics."

There was a ruffle of pages and then silence. As the class worked its way through the assigned reading, Miss Hagmeyer unlocked her cabinet and removed a few supplies that she lined up on her desk.

Five minutes later, she said, "Okay, eyes up, readers down. Who can name one of the seven deadly sins that ruled moral life in the Middle Ages?"

Antoinette promptly raised her hand.

The metal pointer pointed. "Yes, Miss Brede?"

"Envy?"

"That's one," said Miss Hagmeyer. "Who can name another?"

"Murder?" Henry Lumpkin shouted.

"Don't yell, Mr. Lumpkin. And, no, murder is *not* a deadly sin."

"Greed?" said P.W.

"Yes, greed is good. What about you, Mr. Zeisel?"

Before Leon could respond, Henry Lumpkin caused another ruckus, this time by releasing a bodily noise that caused titters to spread through the room.

"Flatulence is not a deadly sin either," Miss Hagmeyer scolded. When she realized her word choice had confused some students, she went to the blackboard and wrote:

flatulence = fartyng

"This is the term well-mannered medieval folk would have used when breaking wind. Memorize it. It will be on your next vocabulary test."

Thomas Warchowski bent over and whispered to Leon, "She's wrong about farts not being deadly. If she ever ate my mom's brussels sprouts, she'd know those suckers can kill."

The radar beacons hidden under Miss Hagmeyer's possibly fake hair registered the remark. "That's enough out of you, Mr. Warchowski. Tell your mother to sprinkle some dill on her brussels sprouts if she wishes to reduce their gassy stink. That is what the monks used to do. Now can we get back to business? Mr. Zeisel, you were about to name another deadly sin."

"Anger?" said Leon.

"Good," said Miss Hagmeyer. "What sins are left?"

"Gluttony," said Lily-Matisse.

"Right. Can you name another?"

"Pride?"

"Correct. And what *is* pride?"

"Isn't it like boasting?"

"Not *like* boasting, Miss Jasprow. It *is* boasting. Who can give me an example of pride?"

Antoinette raised her hand.

"Go ahead, Miss Brede."

"Last year, for the third-grade Nimble Fingers Craft Fair, I made the *best* pot holders. Nanny bought me this real cashmere and I—"

"That's fine," Miss Hagmeyer said tepidly, "though let me assure you, cashmere pot holders will not be made in *my* class."

What a relief! Leon told himself.

Miss Hagmeyer looked at her watch and said, "Right. We have two remaining sins. Anyone?"

"Lust," said P.W., giggling.

"Correct. That leaves one more." Miss Hagmeyer looked around the room. When no one could name the last of the seven deadly sins, she said, "Sloth. The final sin is sloth, also known as laziness. And it is one sin this master will never tolerate."

Miss Hagmeyer put down her pointer and reached for a piece of cloth. "Now, let's move on to the seven heavenly virtues."

"But that's not in the reader," whined Antoinette.

"True, which is why I'm passing around this medieval sampler."

Leon's calm disappeared the instant the cloth arrived at his desk. It looked like this:

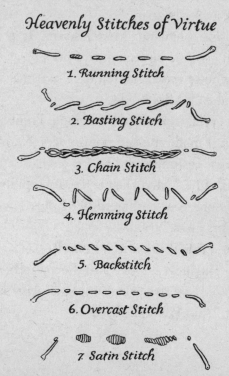

Heavenly Stitches of Virtue

1. *Running Stitch*

2. *Basting Stitch*

3. *Chain Stitch*

4. *Hemming Stitch*

5. *Backstitch*

6. *Overcast Stitch*

7. *Satin Stitch*

Ambushed! What kind of teacher thinks of sewing as *heavenly?* Leon wondered. He felt the deadly sin of anger surge through him as the implications of the sampler sank in.

"Can anyone tell me what a stitch is?" Miss Hagmeyer asked the class.

Thomas, still feeling bold, whispered to Leon, "A sharp pain in the—"

"Mr. Warchowski! This is your *second* warning. One more and you'll find yourself sitting in Principal Birdwhistle's office."

Thomas bowed his head. A trip to the Birdcage was not to be taken lightly.

Miss Hagmeyer scanned the desks for further signs of rebellion. Finding none, she answered her own question. "A stitch is a bond. A connection. An action that unites. In the Middle Ages, there were many kinds of stitches, but the seven listed on the sampler are the ones that you must learn."

She picked up a giant wooden spool she had retrieved from the cabinet. "For demonstration purposes I will be using my instructional needle, this yarn, and a specialized pair of yarn snips. All of you, of course, will be given regular needles and thread."

Leon stared at the spool. It was wrapped with thick orange yarn the color of Henry Lumpkin's hair.

"Now, please pay attention," said Miss Hagmeyer. "We will begin with the basics. Step one. Measure an arm's length of thread. Step two. Cut thread. Please take note of the verb—*cut*. I don't want to see any thread biting, which is a disgusting habit and entirely unacceptable."

So far, so good, Leon said to himself. He felt confident he could measure and cut.

"Step three," said Miss Hagmeyer. "With a firm, decisive poke, guide the thread through the eye of the needle."

That's when Leon started to get antsy.

"Notice how I pull *down* on my yarn once it is threaded. Doing so avoids slipping. Step four. Knot longer end of thread. For those of you who are a little clum—"

Miss Hagmeyer stopped midsentence.

"For those of you whose fine motor skills need some work, tie the two ends of the thread together."

Leon seethed. He knew what she had almost said. Why didn't she just stick a big fat KLUTZO sticker on his forehead?

With the threading portion of the exercise complete, Miss Hagmeyer called her students to the front of the room (individually, by last name). She presented each with a standard sewing needle, a spool of thread, and a handout that reproduced the stitches on her sampler. She also had everyone choose a piece of cloth from a colorful pile of scraps.

By the time she said "Zeisel" only one scrap

remained, and it was . . . *pink!*

For the rest of the period, the class threaded and stitched, consulting the sampler while Miss Hagmeyer moved between the desks like the shuttle of a loom. "Tighten up that backstitch, Miss Brede. . . . Mr. Lumpkin. Remove that needle from your thumb this instant! . . . Mr. Warchowski, watch the way you pull on the thread. You're making the cloth pucker."

Leon kept his head down, hoping to avoid notice.

"Mr. Zeisel. Haven't you threaded your needle *yet?*"

What do *you* think? Leon snarled back, if only in his thoughts. He gave a helpless shrug.

"Look around," Miss Hagmeyer said. "Most of the class has finished practicing their stitches. You have not started."

Leon surveyed the room. Lily-Matisse rolled her eyes. P.W. made a face suggesting their teacher was demented.

"What do you propose to do, Mr. Zeisel?"

"I don't know," Leon mumbled.

"Perhaps you might develop your skills by completing the assignment at home."

Leon nodded, only too happy to give needlework a rest.

Miss Hagmeyer walked over to the supply cabinet. "A place for everything and everything in its place," she said as she opened doors. After hooking the padlock onto one of the door handles, she returned the

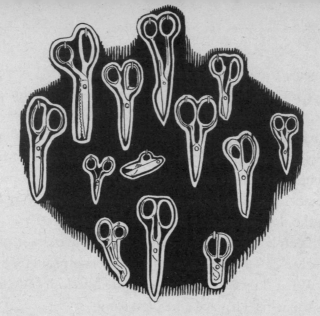

wooden spool and yarn snips, swiftly shutting the cabinet before Leon could get a peek inside.

But as she was walking back to her desk, the weight of the lock on the handle caused one of the doors to swing open, providing Leon a view of the cabinet's interior.

And what a view it was!

The top part of the cabinet was fitted with a piece of pegboard, from which hung dozens and dozens of tools, each labeled and outlined in black marker. Leon spotted the yarn snips Miss Hagmeyer had just used, along with twine nips, snappers, snapplers, zigzaggers, scallopers, pincers, pinking shears, and slishers. (And those were just the cutting tools!)

Directly below the pegboard there were racks of thread displaying a rainbow of colors. But it was the drawers dominating the lowest portion of the cabinet that attracted Leon most. One said CLAWS, another said FINGERS, a third said FLIPPERS AND FINS. There was a drawer marked ELEPHANT EARS—INDIAN and another (which was slightly larger) marked ELEPHANT EARS—AFRICAN.

Noses of various kinds (beaks, bills, trunks, snouts) filled one row of drawers. Eyeballs filled another two. There were drawers for smiles, grimaces, and smirks. Drawers for teeth and tongues, freckles and fangs. A section devoted to the body parts of mythical creatures included a compartment reserved for unicorn horns.

All the drawers were marked—with one exception. An especially large compartment lacked a masking-tape label.

Curiosity gnawed at Leon. He wanted to know what the unlabeled drawer contained, but resisted the impulse to sneak a peek. The unpleasant consequences of his last unauthorized investigation (of his mother's desk) were still fresh in his mind.

He distracted himself by glancing about the room. All his classmates were focused on Miss Hagmeyer, who was busily writing numbers on the blackboard and droning on about "bringing down the six."

Leon had no interest whatsoever in bringing down the six, so while Miss Hagmeyer generated remainders and dividends, he reached over and wrapped his fingers around the knob of the unidentified drawer. He gave the knob a gentle tug and peered inside.

At first Leon couldn't figure out what he was looking at. Once he had, he reared back slightly. The contents of the drawer confused him. And embarrassed him. And grossed him out. The dull gray tangle wasn't as disgusting or fascinating as, say, teacher's spit, but it came pretty close.

"Mr. Zeisel," Miss Hagmeyer said.

Still puzzling over his discovery, Leon failed to hear his name.

"*Mr. Zeisel!*" Miss Hagmeyer repeated more forcefully.

"Huh?"

"Get your nose out of my PANTY HOSE!"

It took a moment for the command to register. When it did, Leon felt the blood rushing to his head.

The whole class went berserk, laughing and hooting as he sank into his chair.

"*Silence!*" Miss Hagmeyer shouted. She marched over to the cabinet. "Next time I'll know better than to leave this open." She padlocked the doors and turned to Leon. "Students who can't thread needles shouldn't poke through their teacher's things, should they, Mr. Zeisel?"

"No, Miss Hagmeyer," Leon said abjectly.

"They should listen to their teachers, should they not?" she further chided.

"S-s-sorry," said Leon. He felt dangerously close to tears.

"Apology accepted—provisionally. However, in the future, I expect you to stay out of my drawers unless authorized. As it is, you have your hands full, what with the stitching practice and tonight's assignment."

"What assignment?" Leon asked.

Miss Hagmeyer released an irritated snort. "As I explained while you were rifling through my hose, I expect everyone to bring in a piece of cloth."

"What kind of cloth?"

Miss Hagmeyer shook her head in despair. "I answered *that* question, too, Mr. Zeisel. It doesn't make the slightest difference what kind. Bring in a dish towel. Bring in some upholstery fabric. Bring in a piece of old bedsheet, for all I care. Just so long as it's roughly the size of your desktop. And I'll answer your next question before you ask it," she added. "You will need the cloth for your first sewing project of the year."

Six

The Return of Napoleon

"*Panty hose!*" P.W. exclaimed as soon as class let out.

Leon nodded gravely and turned to Lily-Matisse. "Did your mom tell you why the Hag keeps her underwear in school?"

"Nope," said Lily-Matisse. "But she did see her changing glass eyes in the teachers' lounge."

"She stores the spares in the cabinet," said Leon. "There must be twenty different kinds."

"I'm pretty sure today's were snake eyes," said P.W.

"How do you know?" said Lily-Matisse skeptically.

"The slitty pupils," said P.W. matter-of-factly.

"I'll tell you one thing," Leon said. "I'd take a snakebite over sewing class any day."

"Ditto," said P.W.

"Double ditto," said Lily-Matisse.

The sound of a car horn interrupted them. Leon quickly spotted Napoleon de l'Ange, the cheery taxi driver from the day before.

"Need a lift, Monsieur Leon? No charge for friends."

Leon hesitated. He liked Napoleon. He was funny and nice. But there was a problem. Napoleon came from Haiti, and Haiti was already pinned on his map. Leon worried his taxi collection would never grow if he kept using the same driver.

"Go for it," P.W. urged. "That way you can spend your cab fare on candy."

"And potato chips," Lily-Matisse added.

Leon considered his options. "Sure," he said, accepting Napoleon's offer.

A few minutes into the ride, he tapped the hack license and said, "I've been wondering, Napoleon. Why are you named after a pastry? Were your parents bakers?"

Napoleon let out a deep-bellied laugh. "No, no, Monsieur Leon. I was named for a famous French general and so was the pastry. But the famous Napoleon was short, and I am tall. He was white, and I am black. He was powerful, and I am . . . well, I drive a taxi. And on top of all that . . . I *hate* napoleons."

"Me too," Leon admitted. "Too custardy." He was

Napoleon
(de l'Ange)

Napoleon
(the Emperor)

Napoleon
(the Pastry)

wondering about how he'd feel eating a leon (if such a pastry existed) when Napoleon said, "We do that in Haiti."

"Do what?"

"Name our children after important people. I have three brothers: Moses, Charlemagne, and Zeus—plus a sister, Cleopatra. You Americans are not interesting with your names."

"I guess not," Leon admitted.

"But tell me," said Napoleon, "did my prediction come true? Did you have a nine-and-three-quarters day?"

Leon sighed. "Hardly. More like a *negative* nine and three quarters."

"I'm sorry to hear that."

"It's my teacher," Leon complained. "All she cares about is sewing."

"But art class is a good thing, Monsieur Leon. Sewing can be very useful."

"I'm not talking about my *art* teacher. I'm talking about my *teacher* teacher."

"And she makes you sew?"

"Yup," said Leon glumly.

Napoleon shook his head in disbelief.

"Plus she has these disgusting-looking ears— they're like radar dishes—that she keeps hidden under her possibly fake hair."

"*Mon Dieu!*" Napoleon exclaimed. "You had better tell your mother about all this."

The cab pulled up to the hotel a few moments later. Napoleon parked and, as he had the day before, jumped out to open the passenger door. "Au revoir, Monsieur Leon," he said with a tip of his imaginary hat. "And let us hope tomorrow will at least be a seven."

"I'll settle for a five and a half," said Leon before he pushed through the revolving door. He negotiated his way past a drably dressed woman walking a peacock and headed over to the reception desk, where his mother clearly had problems of her own.

One of the guests, a rail-thin mime covered in white face paint, was shouting at her. "Look, lady! We didn't book this dump expecting a conference room with a broken microphone."

"I apologize, sir," said Emma Zeisel.

"Apologies won't get us our friggin' mike, will they?" the mime snarled.

"Again, I am sorry."

"Well, *sorry* doesn't cut it!" he yelled.

"Please lower your voice," Emma Zeisel said. "You are a mime, after all."

The observation rendered the man speechless. He stormed off in a (silent) huff.

Emma Zeisel turned to her son. "As group

bookings go, Leon, the West Coast Mimes are, without a doubt, *the* worst."

"What about those rattlesnake ranchers we had last year? Remember them?"

"At least they left me some antidote. Came in handy, too. Anyway, let's forget about difficult guests, sweetie. Tell me about your day."

Leon needed little encouragement. He provided a blow-by-blow account of the goings-on in his classroom, up to and including the business of the panty hose.

"*Panty hose!*" said Emma Zeisel. "Why on earth would a teacher store her old stockings in school?"

"I have *no* clue, Mom. All I can tell you is I need help with my threading and stitching. Plus I need a piece of cloth for tomorrow."

Emma Zeisel sighed. "You know my hours, sweetie. These double shifts are a killer. But I bet Maria can get you squared away. She's a demon with a needle."

After Leon updated the signboard (VVelcome Peacock Breeders of VValla VValla, VVashington!!!!) he sought out Maria. He found her in Housekeeping, funneling bright green shampoo from a large jug into dozens of tiny bottles.

"*Hola*, Leonito!" she said. "How you doing?"

"Not good, Maria."

For a third time since leaving school, Leon described his new teacher's behavior and the panty hose she kept in class.

"Is she *crazy* or something?"

"*Very* crazy, Maria. She expects us to thread a needle and to learn her seven dumb stitches. Take a look." Leon pulled the handout from his backpack.

"You need Maria to help?" Maria asked.

"Could you?"

"No problem," she said reassuringly.

After completing the shampoo transfer, Maria cleared a table and brought out her sewing basket. She reached for a spool of cotton and bit off a length of thread.

"Miss Hagmeyer doesn't want us using our teeth," said Leon.

Maria shook her head. "What harm can a little spit do?"

"Beats me," said Leon.

"Well, you show me what she taught you, this Miss Panty Hose," Maria said suspiciously.

Leon reached for the scissors and cut a length of thread. He tried poking the thread through the eye of the needle again and again but failed every time.

"See?" he moaned. "I'll *never* do it."

"Yes you will, Leonito," Maria countered. She expertly repositioned Leon's fingers on the scissors, like a baseball coach adjusting a batter's grip. "*Now* cut the thread," she said.

Leon held the scissors at a steep angle and sliced another length of thread off the spool. When it came time to thread the needle, he succeeded after just two pokes.

"Awesome!" he exclaimed.

"Sharp angle, sharp cut," Maria said with a smile.

"*Gracias,*" said Leon. For the first time since school started, he felt a small measure of satisfaction.

Threading became a breeze. Mastering the seven stitches of virtue, however, proved more challenging. Fortunately for Leon, Maria remained close at hand.

"No, Leonito," she corrected gently. "Watch me. For the hemming stitch you *slant* the needle."

Leon modified his grip and tried again. Eventually he hemmed three full inches of his practice cloth. "You're a much better teacher than Miss Mushroom Ears," he said.

"I've got a good student," Maria replied.

Good but not perfect. Leon only succeeded in replicating six of the seven stitches of virtue. One stitch eluded him—the overcast. According to his handout, the overcast was the stitch used when finishing off a seam. No matter how much Leon practiced, he couldn't get the needle to obey his less-than-nimble fingers.

He put his sewing away and was about to leave Housekeeping when he remembered the other assignment. "Oh, I almost forgot, Maria. I've got to bring a towel to school tomorrow."

"A towel? Why? Your teacher planning to give you a bath?"

Leon laughed. "I sure hope not."

Maria handed him a tattered Trimore hand towel just as Emma Zeisel stuck her head in.

"Sweetie, I'm on break. Frau Haffenreffer has some sandwiches waiting for us."

And so with his homework more or less done, Leon ended the day sitting across from his mom in the Trimore Towers coffee shop. He didn't want to gripe about school, but he couldn't stop himself. Over PB&J (extra J) and a bag of Zapp's Kettle-Cooked Mesquite Bar-B-Que Potato Chips (his current favorite), Leon complained about his needle-wielding teacher.

"Nine months, Mom. I'll have to deal with the Hag for nine months! That's two hundred and seventy days!"

"You'll be fine," said Emma Zeisel, sounding more wishful than confident. "And besides, there's no need to include weekends."

"Whatever," said Leon morosely.

Depressing thoughts about sewing gnawed at Leon long after he'd finished dinner. They were still with him when he climbed into bed. What had he done to deserve the Hag? Why'd she have to scream at him? Would his entire year be filled with pink scraps of material, terry cloth hand towels, and liver-colored panty hose? Would he be able to handle the work?

Click-click-click-buzzzz . . .

From the far side of the bedroom wall, the Ice

Queen started casting her evil spell. All hope of sleep disappeared.

Grind-groan-rumble-CRASH!

Leon rose from his bed and nervously paced around his room. The circuit took all of ten seconds to complete. He looked at his stuff. There was the fuzzy picture of his dad, taken a few months before the explosion at the factory. An empty fish tank that had, briefly, contained a piranha left by one of the guests. And of course the map of the world, with the pins marking the taxi drivers Leon had collected.

After six or seven laps, Leon returned to bed. He tried to muffle the grinding noises of the ice maker by burrowing deep under his covers, but that did next to nothing. The Ice Queen's mechanical hex lasted most of the night, spurred on by mimes whose loudmouth antics and desire for ice kept Leon awake.

SEVEN

Animiles

"Inspection time!" Miss Hagmeyer announced the next morning. "Fabrics out on the desks where I can see them!"

She swept through the room like a castle guard, her instructional needle taking the place of a pikestaff. Occasionally she would lower the business end of her pointer onto a piece of cloth that she deemed especially attractive. When she did, her manner would soften.

"This lacework is delicious, Antoinette. Belgian, is it?"

"No idea, Miss Hagmeyer," Antoinette answered. "Nanny told me to grab something from one of the guest bathrooms. She could care less what I took."

"You mean 'couldn't.' The proper expression is *couldn't* care less—Mr. Lumpkin!" Miss Hagmeyer's mood changed abruptly. "Remove that pillowcase from your head this instant!"

"Seems like an improvement to me," Leon said aloud, before he could stop himself.

"That's enough out of you, Mr. Zeisel," Miss Hagmeyer scolded.

Lumpkin removed his pillowcase, turned, and

gave Leon a look that made him instantly regret his quip.

Miss Hagmeyer continued her rounds. "Gorgeous piece of silk, Phya Winit," she cooed, rubbing his cloth between thumb and index finger.

"My dad told me silk comes from boiled worms!" P.W. said enthusiastically.

"Your father is correct—though technically it's a caterpillar, not a worm, that gets boiled."

Miss Hagmeyer next stopped at Lily-Matisse's desk. She reached for a piece of cotton tie-dyed in vibrant shades of purple, green, and yellow. "Did you make this, or did your mother?"

"My mom did," Lily-Matisse said, sounding a little embarrassed. "She tends to go for flashy colors."

"So it would appear," said Miss Hagmeyer neutrally. She moved on to Leon's outpost, where she found not one, but two pieces of cloth.

"I suppose it's a start," Miss Hagmeyer said of the pink scrap covered with after-school practice stitching. She then harpooned the hotel hand towel with her instructional needle and read out loud the faded blue words woven into terry cloth. "'Property of Trimore Towers.' How very *utilitarian*."

Leon kept his mouth shut. Exhausted from lack of sleep, he was nevertheless alert enough to know that asking the meaning of "utilitarian" would get the word tacked onto the weekly vocabulary test. His decision proved wise. Miss Hagmeyer ended her inspection and turned to the supply cabinet.

Leon cast his eyes on the blackboard as she removed the padlock. He wasn't about to get caught sticking his nose where it didn't belong a *second* time, thank you very much.

Miss Hagmeyer spent a minute or so retrieving a few sewing tools. She then secured the doors and returned to the front of the room. Once satisfied that the supplies were properly positioned on her desk, she picked up her instructional needle and said two words no student likes to hear: "Pop quiz."

Over the resulting groans, she aimed the needle at Thomas and said, "Mr. Warchowski. Stitch number three. Name it."

"Chain," Thomas managed.

"Correct. . . . Miss Brede, number one?"

"The first stitch of virtue is the running stitch, Miss Hagmeyer."

"Correct. . . . Mr. Zeisel, number six?"

"Umm, satin?"

"*Incorrect!*" snarled Miss Hagmeyer. "The answer is directly above your head." She pointed at a poster taped to the wall.

"Overcast?" Leon said sullenly after glancing at the picture of the severed hand stitching up a seam. He'd spent so much time struggling to master the stitch, he hadn't memorized its numerical rank.

"Bravo, Mr. Zeisel," Miss Hagmeyer said sarcastically. "For the future, I expect you to know all stitches of virtue both alphabetically and by number." She put down her needle. "Right. Let's move on to my worksheets."

As the handouts made their way around the room, Miss Hagmeyer registered some snickering.

"Miss Jasprow, does something amuse you?"

"No, Miss Hagmeyer," Lily-Matisse said, suppressing a giggle.

"Perhaps you would like to share your wit with the rest of the class."

"It's just that it says 'animiles' on the top of the page," said Lily-Matisse.

"It's *supposed* to," Miss Hagmeyer replied curtly. She retrieved her chalk holder and wrote the following word on the blackboard:

animiles

"It's a medieval variant of *animal* and shares a Latin root with 'animate,' as in living or making alive. All the creations sewn in my class will be called 'ani-*miles*'—*not* 'ani-*mals*.' Why? Because ani-*mals* tend to be smelly, uncontrollable beasts that bite and bray and refuse to show respect. On the other hand, ani-*miles* . . ."

Miss Hagmeyer turned and tapped the blackboard.

". . . ani-*miles* do *not* bite. They do *not* bray, and . . ."

She paused to glance at Lily-Matisse.

". . . they do *not* giggle disruptively. It is my expectation that by making ani-*miles* you will cease to act like ani-*mals*. Does everyone understand?"

A chorus of "Yes, Miss Hagmeyers" filled the room.

"Good," she said crisply. "Now begin."

Leon felt tense as he leafed through the handout, a nine-step project that was supposed to transform a scrap of material into a decorative stuffed snake.

Step one required Leon to measure a six-inch-by-ten-inch rectangle on the towel he'd brought from home. That was a snap. Step two—cutting along the marks—wasn't too tough either. The trouble only started with step three. That's when the actual sewing started.

Leon managed to make an okay-looking chain stitch down the middle of the towel, and he succeeded in backstitching the bottom and sides of his material. But then his fingers began to cramp.

He paused for a moment to look over his handiwork. It resembled a tattered tube sock more than a stuffed snake. The word PROPERTY ran up the side, with the last two letters hidden inside a seam.

Leon sighed. This snake is *not* proper, he said to himself. He wished Maria could help with the remaining stitches.

From the front of the room, Antoinette called out, "I'm up to step seven, Miss Hagmeyer. The handout says I'm supposed to see you about special supplies?"

"Excellent," said Miss Hagmeyer. "Come with me."

Leon and the rest of the class watched as teacher and teacher's pet went to the supply cabinet. Miss Hagmeyer unlocked the doors and pulled out the unmarked drawer that was cram-packed with panty hose.

"Dig in!" she said.

Antoinette balked.

"Don't be bashful. Go on, dig in!"

"Into . . . into your panty hose?" Antoinette stammered.

Leon looked down at his desktop. He knew that if he made eye contact with Lily-Matisse or P.W., he'd lose it.

"Well of course," said Miss Hagmeyer. "There isn't a better stuffing in the world than cut-up old panty hose."

One by one, students approached the cabinet to extract panty hose. Leon soon realized that he was *way* behind. His classmates had practically finished their animiles by the time he'd reached the stuffing stage. He caused himself further delay by refusing to handle his teacher's stockings directly. To minimize contact, he employed a pair of tongs as a panty hose injection device, a precaution that only made matters worse.

"That snake is looking *bloated*," Miss Hagmeyer told Leon on her next sweep of the room.

"It is?"

"Most definitely. It more closely resembles a football than a serpent. Thin it out at once."

"Yes, Miss Hagmeyer."

While Leon removed wadded-up panty hose from his snake, the rest of the class began submitting their snakes for final inspection. The procedure was the same for everyone. Miss Hagmeyer would survey the animile for loose threads, measure seams, and take extensive notes on her clipboard. If she liked what she saw, she would authorize a trip to the finished bin, a large bag-lined trash can located next to her desk. After that, students were free to practice their stitching or read the Fun Fact sections of their *Medieval Readers*.

Not long before the period was to end, Miss Hagmeyer reappeared at Leon's desk. "Well, I suppose the snake's shape is a tad better," she acknowledged. Her tone was one of mild disappointment. "But do hurry up. Skip the eyes. Just finish up the tongue and mouth."

"Yes, Miss Hagmeyer," Leon said.

Although his hands were cramping and his head ached from lack of sleep, Leon pushed on. A few minutes later, Miss Hagmeyer called him up to her desk. "The bell's about to ring, so show me what you have."

Leon plopped down his snake.

Miss Hagmeyer inspected it closely. "The stitches on the belly are all crooked."

"I know," Leon said miserably.

Miss Hagmeyer removed a tape measure she had draped over her neck and pressed it against the snake's mouth. "This overcast stitching is significantly below standard. It only registers *two* s.p.i.!"

"Two s.p.i.?" said Leon. He had no idea what Miss Hagmeyer was talking about.

"Stitches . . . per . . . inch, Mr. Zeisel—s.p.i. for short. An animile's seams should always register at least *four* s.p.i. Do you think you can tighten up the stitching?"

"I'll try," Leon said through clenched teeth.

"I certainly hope so," said Miss Hagmeyer. "And when you do, make sure the fabric doesn't bunch up. I don't want the mouth to pucker."

You mean like yours? Leon said to himself, looking at his teacher's pursed lips. "If I can't fix the problem, Miss Hagmeyer, I could call the snake Pinch."

"You will do no such thing, Mr. Zeisel. Animiles never get named."

"Why not?" asked Leon.

"If you named them, you'd get attached to them. And we certainly cannot have that."

"Why not?" Leon repeated.

"Simply put, I keep all animiles made in my class."

"Every single one, Miss Hagmeyer?"

"Yes," she said stiffly. "Every single one."

"But—"

"No ifs, ands, or buts, Mr. Zeisel. Go back to your desk and fix what needs fixing."

The recess bell rang. Leon gave Miss Hagmeyer a hopeful look.

She shook her head. "Repair your animile *now*."

As Leon worked on his overcasting, he could hear jump-rope songs and shouts of "You're it" coming from the playground. Tennis balls and basketballs flew past the window as he struggled to produce a thin, unlumpy, unpuckered snake.

"Let's see what we've got," Miss Hagmeyer said when Leon resubmitted his animile fifteen minutes later.

"Hope it's okay," he said.

"As do I," said Miss Hagmeyer. She picked up the snake and took a measurement. "I'm still not happy about your stitch count. Two s.p.i. is *entirely* unacceptable. The minimum, as I just told you, is four. Still, your mouth stitching does show some improvement."

I wouldn't mind stitching *her* mouth shut, Leon said to himself.

Miss Hagmeyer looked at her watch. "I'm feeling charitable. Deposit the animile in the finished bin as is and go catch the rest of recess."

Leon didn't have to be told twice. He binned the snake and hightailed it outside.

The Classical School playground was divided into

four areas. There was the wall ball section, the jungle-gym section, the place near the fence where the jump ropers jumped rope, and the basketball courts. Smack in the middle of these four distinct quadrants, bursting through the asphalt like a leafy geyser, was a hardy maple circled by a cedar bench.

Leon dashed over to the tree, relieved to be free of Miss Hagmeyer and her stitch counts. He jumped onto the bench that rimmed the maple's trunk and ran the circuit in search of his two best friends.

He spotted them on the jungle gym and rushed over.

"P.W. figured out about the eyeballs on the cape," said Lily-Matisse. She was hanging upside down by her knees when she made this announcement.

"What about them?" said Leon, clambering up to a crossbar one level below her.

P.W. said, "It's like some secret code. She chooses eyes to indicate future projects. Think about it. She came in with snake eyes yesterday, and look at what she made us do today!"

"I wouldn't be surprised," Leon said. "*Everything* the Hag does is sneaky."

"Yeah," said Lily-Matisse. "Can you believe she's keeping our animiles?"

"And she won't even tell us why," said P.W.

"Maybe not," said Leon. "But I know a way we might find out."

EIGHT
Parents' Night

You have to wonder how Miss Hagmeyer got away with it. How could she force her fourth graders to make animiles that she kept for herself?

Didn't the kids complain to their parents? Sure they did.

And didn't the parents complain to the school? Nope—not much, anyway.

Miss Hagmeyer knew just how to handle parents. She understood a fundamental truth: When it comes to school, parents are more easily fooled than children. Especially when those parents send their children to a place that believes nimble fingers make for nimble minds. (After all, if that motto were true, wouldn't it imply that every kid with a knack for video games was a certified genius?)

Miss Hagmeyer secured the support she needed during Parents' Night, two weeks after her class completed its first batch of animiles.

"If everyone will just grab any old chair," she said, suspending her ironclad rule about alphabetical seating.

The parents squeezed themselves behind desks intended for smaller bodies.

"Welcome *all*," said Miss Hagmeyer. "It is *such* a pleasure to meet the mothers and fathers of my eighteen extraordinary charges, each one *so* special in his or her own unique way. On the very first day of school, I told your remarkable children that there is a place for everything and that everything has its place. What I did not tell them, but what I wish to tell all of you tonight, is that *their* place—for me, as a teacher— is right *here*." Miss Hagmeyer tapped her heart.

"As you know," she trilled on, "I place a certain emphasis on sewing." She made a stitching motion in the air. "I do so because I believe strongly that learning about the life of fabric teaches us about the fabric of life."

Miss Hagmeyer reached behind her desk and grabbed a large metal bucket. "Behold the very first animiles of the year," she said, brushing her free hand over the snakes, which resembled a colorful bouquet of flowers.

"How extraordinarily divine!" said Mrs. Brede, Antoinette's mother.

"I couldn't agree more," Miss Hagmeyer replied, handing the matronly woman her daughter's Belgian lace snake.

"It practically *screams* to be worn as a boa!" Mrs. Brede

gushed as she wrapped the creation around her neck.

"That's because it *is* a boa . . . constrictor," said Miss Hagmeyer.

Antoinette's mother laughed hysterically.

"Hey, Teach!" a stocky man shouted rudely. "Hope you don't expect *us* to make stuff tonight!"

"You must be Henry Lumpkin's father," said Miss Hagmeyer.

The man guffawed. "Guilty as charged! What gave me away?"

Miss Hagmeyer glanced at the man's olive drab army jacket. "Let's just say I see where your son gets his military flair." She handed Mr. Lumpkin a snake. "I think you'll be pleased by Henry's pillowcase python. The racing stripes and fangs were entirely his idea. And to address your earlier concern, I *do* have a little exercise planned for you, but not to worry. I always go easy on grown-ups. No one will have to sew."

Miss Hagmeyer continued her flimflam as she strode through the room, handing out snakes. At each stop she made sure to say something tender. Even Leon's sightless terry cloth towel snake received a kindly assessment.

"Do you know, Ms. Zeisel, your son's handiwork measures the same length as a Texas blind snake. *Leptotyphlops dulcis* also grows to ten inches exactly. Isn't that marvelous?"

"I guess," Emma Zeisel answered coolly.

"And don't you love the way Leon's snake says PROPER right along the side of its lumpy little body?"

"I know he worked awfully hard on it. Could I possibly keep it?"

"Oh, I see," said Miss Hagmeyer, her voice hardening. "Leon must have told you about our conversation."

"Yes, as a matter of fact," said Emma Zeisel.

"Well, as I explained, I need to reclaim all animiles."

"You didn't tell him why."

Miss Hagmeyer tensed. "Didn't I?"

Emma Zeisel shook her head.

"I suppose not," said Miss Hagmeyer, grabbing Leon's towel snake and shoving it back into the bucket.

Before Emma Zeisel could press her further, Miss Hagmeyer turned away and headed for the supply cabinet. "So much for the handiwork of your children," she said. "Now it's time to see what their parents can do."

She undid the padlock and retrieved a pair of shears, which she presented to a thin woman with long black hair. "Ms. Dhabanandana, I hope you will assist me."

P.W.'s mother gave a tentative nod.

"Excellent," said Miss Hagmeyer. "The rest of you can follow along. This exercise is all spelled out on the blackboard."

There was some rustling in the room as parents glanced at the step-by-step instructions.

"Do we have to take notes?" someone whined jokingly.

"Will this be on the final?" moaned another.

Miss Hagmeyer forced herself to smile and waited for the parents to quiet down. "Okay, Ms. Dhabanandana. I want you to take your cloth and fold it like so. And so. And so. Then like this. Then like this. And then like this."

P.W.'s mother watched closely and repeated the multistep procedure flawlessly.

"Superb!" said Miss Hagmeyer, impressed by Ms. Dhabanandana's effortless dexterity.

"I fold all the napkins at our restaurant," P.W.'s mom explained.

"Well, your restaurant is lucky to have you," Miss Hagmeyer chirped. She reached into the pocket of her dress and pulled out her chalk holder. She gave it a couple of clicks and drew a dotted line across the material. "Now, I want you to take the shears and cut along the dots, Ms. Dhabanandana."

"Are you sure?"

"Yes. I'm sure."

Snip. "Is that okay?"

"Perfect," said Miss Hagmeyer. "Now unfold the material and hold it up for everyone to see."

P.W.'s mother displayed the material. With a single slice, she had produced a stunning five-pointed star.

"What *exactly* do our children gain by making

stars?" Emma Zeisel blurted out, over the oohs and aahs that spread through the room.

"Craft assignments are always tied to other subjects," said Miss Hagmeyer. "I can use stars to introduce concepts of geometry and astronomy."

"But—"

"Ms. Zeisel," Miss Hagmeyer said, cutting her off. "We really don't have time to discuss curriculum right now."

"Can you at least tell us why our kids spend so much time sewing stuffed animals?"

"Ani-*miles*," Miss Hagmeyer corrected. There was now a very obvious edge in her voice.

Emma Zeisel persisted. "Are pins and needles—and panty hose, for that matter—really as important as pencils and pens?"

"I believe they are," Miss Hagmeyer said strongly. "But if you wish to discuss this in more detail, I suggest a *private* appointment."

"Amen to that!" Mr. Lumpkin exclaimed. "How about us hitting those cookies I see over there?" He pointed to the front of the room, where the usual Hagmeyer desk set—small-curd cottage cheese, clipboard, instructional needle—had been replaced by a platter of homemade goodies and a pot of fresh-brewed coffee.

"A superlative suggestion, Mr. Lumpkin. As soon as everyone is done, that's exactly what we will do."

The parents tended to their projects—folding, chalking, cutting—for nearly half an hour. Despite some miscalculations (and at least one bloody thumb), they all completed the assignment, which Miss Hagmeyer called "Make Yourself a Star!"

Only two parents left the classroom unimpressed: Emma Zeisel and Regina Jasprow. They discussed Miss Hagmeyer as they exited the school.

"Boy, is that woman wound up tight," said Emma Zeisel. "Is she always like that?"

Regina Jasprow nodded. "You should see her in the teachers' lounge. If she's not adjusting her hair, or changing her eyeballs, she's off in a corner doing needlepoint. The woman is loony about sewing."

"It's hard to tell whether she's running a classroom or a sweatshop," said Emma Zeisel.

Regina Jasprow laughed. "I thought I'd lose it when she tapped her heart and said she keeps a place 'right here' for each child."

"Yeah, what a crock!" said Emma Zeisel. "She's always going on about a place for everything and everything in its place. I sure wish someone would put her in *her* place!"

Leon's mom needn't have worried. Someone eventually did put Miss Hagmeyer in her place.

Repeatedly.

NINE

The Three-Piece Dinosaur

When the first bell rang the next day, Miss Hagmeyer marched into class and hung up her cape, which Leon, P.W., and Lily-Matisse all instantly noticed was missing its glass eyeballs.

They gave one another puzzled looks but kept quiet. They knew not to ask questions while Miss Hagmeyer was arranging her desk.

She positioned her container of cottage cheese, clipboard, and instructional needle where the home-made cookies and coffee had rested the night before, then removed a stack of worksheets from her satchel.

Miss Hagmeyer shuttled between rows of the desks, handing out assignments. "The photocopier was broken, so the animile project we were supposed to start today will have to be postponed. Luckily, I unearthed these handouts from a previous year."

Leon, as usual, had to wait to receive his assign-ment. Even so, he had a pretty good sense of what to expect because of the classroom clamor.

"I got a T. rex!"

"Mine's a pterodactyl!"

"Miss Hagmeyer? This iguanodon *looks* funny. Can I make his spikes spikier?"

"Miss Hagmeyer? I thought hadrosaurs had *webbed* feet. That's what they said on the Dinosaur Channel."

"Quiet down, all of you!"

A worksheet eventually fluttered onto Leon's desk. It said DIPLOCAULUS and showed a picture of a fishlike creature with a head shaped like the point of an arrow. The list of materials indicated that the project required only three pieces of cloth, two of which were exactly the same shape.

The simplicity of the assignment surprised Leon. It almost seemed easier than the first. He decided to find out if his classmates' dinosaurs were as beginnery as his.

Pretending he needed to sharpen his pencil, Leon walked to the front of the room. As he did, he peeked about.

Lily-Matisse had snagged a triceratops that had *fourteen* pieces, including a nose horn, two side horns, and a jazzy neck frill.

Antoinette had received a complex ten-piece T. rex.

P.W. scored a duck-billed corythosaurus, a fantastic eight-piecer with terrifying body armor.

Lumpkin got a stegosaurus.

At least that makes sense, Leon told himself.

Stegosauruses, he knew, were the pea brains of the dinosaur kingdom. But his comfort disappeared when he spied that Lumpkin's dinosaur required *six* pieces of material—*twice* the number his animile demanded.

By the time Leon returned to his seat, he was feeling thoroughly down. Why couldn't *he* get spikes or horns or neck frills?

He read through the worksheet. It turned out his animile wasn't even an actual dinosaur. It was, according to the text, a "weak-limbed, bottom-feeding amphibian."

Leon knew what Miss Hagmeyer was up to. She had given the cool-looking, complicated dinosaurs to the coordinated students and had stuck him with the beginner's kit, a three-piece fake.

Miss Hagmeyer tapped the cabinet doors with her needle. "Since we do not know what dinosaur skin actually looks like, I'm allowing everyone to choose his own fabric."

In the general rush for the cabinet, P.W. tested his earlier theory. "Miss Hagmeyer?" he said. "What about the dinosaur eyes?"

"They're a mystery, too. That's why I didn't put them on the worksheets."

P.W. beamed. "And why she didn't put any eyeballs on her cape," he whispered to Lily-Matisse, who passed the info along to Leon.

This revelation did little to improve Leon's mood.

He hated that his dinosaur was so lame. In fact, Leon was so disappointed that when it was his turn at the cabinet, he settled for the first three scraps he touched: a blue-and-white striped cotton for the top of his diplocaulus, solid green corduroy for the bottom, and a piece of black-and-red polka-dotted material for the mouth.

Two weeks after the start of the second animile project, the finished bin started to fill. Lily-Matisse's triceratops was the trash can's first occupant. Antoinette's T. rex soon followed. P.W. deposited his corythosaurus a couple of days later. Even Lumpkin binned his pea-brained stegosaurus.

Leon lagged behind. Once again, everything seemed to go wrong. The first time he tried stitching the body together, he sewed the inside of the cotton to the outside of the corduroy.

Miss Hagmeyer made him start over.

The second time around, he matched the two halves correctly, but ripped through the head of the diplocaulus by pushing too hard with the tongs.

"What did you expect?" Miss

Hagmeyer said sourly. "Those tongs were never meant for that purpose." She took him over to the finished bin and tapped her boot against the side.

"I have a math problem for you, Mr. Zeisel. Are you ready?"

"I guess," Leon said.

"A class has eighteen students. Each student is required to make two animiles. If only thirty-five animiles have been handed in, how many students have *failed* to complete their assignments?"

Leon took a nervous swallow. He knew the answer without doing the math.

"Sorry, Miss Hagmeyer. If it's about my dinosaur—"

"Sorry will not do," she said harshly. "You need to pick up your pace. Perhaps my countinghouse tally will spur you on. Tallies were highly effective during the Middle Ages."

Even before he learned the nature and function of the countinghouse tally, Leon sensed he wouldn't like it.

Miss Hagmeyer confirmed his prediction later the same day.

"I want everyone to pick a medieval title," she announced just before recess. "Duke, prince, lady . . . the choice of title is up to you. Write it down, along with your name, on the gummed labels I'm handing out."

While the class worked on their labels, Miss

Hagmeyer placed an empty wooden spool on each student's desk. "Attach your labels to your spools, then pass them up," she said.

Once she had collected the labeled spools, she threaded them onto eighteen pieces of orange yarn and strung the yarn across a sturdy sheet of poster board. The handmade tally allowed the spools to move back and forth like beads on an abacus.

Top to bottom the tally went from QUEEN ANTOINETTE (Brede) to SIR LEON (Zeisel), stopping along the way to register MASTER DHABANANDANA, LADY LILY-MATISSE, LORD LUMPKIN, PRINCE WARCHOWSKI, and the rest of the class.

On the left-hand side of the chart Miss Hagmeyer wrote SEPTEMBER. On the right-hand side she wrote MAY.

"This countinghouse tally," she said, "will serve as an animile timeline. Nine months of school, nine animiles. Every time you finish a monthly project, I will push your spool one space to the right."

Leon recognized the evil implications of the chart instantly. It was a public record of everyone's standing. It advertised who was ahead and—much more worrisome—who was behind.

"Mr. Zeisel? Could you stay for a moment," Miss Hagmeyer said when the recess bell rang and the class stampeded toward the door. "When might we be able to advance Sir Leon?" she asked.

"Soon, I hope," came the woeful reply.

"Dinosaurs are supposed to help us *study* eons— not *take* them. You should be on to your *third* animile by now. Everyone else is."

"I *know*, Miss Hagmeyer," Leon said, his voice quavering. "It's just I can't seem to get the seams tight."

"Oh, for heaven's sake, let me see."

Leon retrieved his unfinished diplocaulus and offered it up for inspection. Miss Hagmeyer took a measurement. The results prompted her to shake her head. "You're *still* averaging two s.p.i.," she said disapprovingly.

Leon responded with a hopeless shrug.

"Are you getting enough sleep, Mr. Zeisel?"

"I think so."

"Maybe you should stay in during recess and work on your technique."

"What if I practice at home?" Leon said desperately. Miss Hagmeyer mulled over the counterproposal.

"I suppose we can try that. But remember, I want these seams tightened up."

"Oh, they will be," said Leon. "I promise."

He headed for the playground before Miss Hagmeyer could change her mind. As usual, P.W. and Lily-Matisse were perched on the jungle gym.

"Why'd she keep you back?" Lily-Matisse asked. She was hanging upside down by her knees.

"Guess," said Leon glumly.

"Your dinosaur?"

"Yup," said Leon, pulling himself up to the highest crossbar.

"What do you think about the medieval tally?" P.W. asked him.

"L-A-M-E," said Leon.

"I'll tell you what *I* think is lame," Lily-Matisse said. "The way the Hag holds on to what we make."

Leon swung down. "I got my mom to ask about that at Parents' Night. The Hag refused to answer. Probably she's keeping the animiles to monitor our progress."

"What makes you think she's *keeping* them?" said Lily-Matisse.

"What do you mean?" P.W. asked.

Lily-Matisse gave a coy shrug.

"Did your mom tell you something?" Leon demanded.

"Maybe."

"Start talking," said P.W.

"Yeah, out with it," Leon insisted.

"Swear you won't blab?" said Lily-Matisse.

"Swear," said Leon.

"Promise," said P.W.

"Crossyourhearthopetodiestickaneedleinyoureye?"

"I'm sick and tired of needles," said Leon.

"Say it," Lily-Matisse demanded. "Both of you."

After the needle oath was duly sworn, Lily-Matisse said, "Okay. Here goes. Did you notice how the first batch of animiles just kinda disappeared from the finished bin?"

"Yeah, so?" said Leon.

"What about it?" said P.W.

"Mom told me she saw the Hag carrying a big black plastic garbage bag out of school. Mom said she looked like the Grinch."

"The Grinch wears green, not black," said P.W.

"What difference does *that* make? The point is, the Hag is swiping our projects!"

"Maybe she's selling them," P.W. suggested.

Lily-Matisse swung into a sitting position. "Who'd want to buy animiles?"

"And besides," said Leon. "How much could the Hag make?"

"A lot," said P.W. "I mean think about it. Say each animile sells for five bucks. Twenty kids times—"

"There are only eighteen in our class," Lily-Matisse interrupted.

"Don't nitpick," said P.W. "I'm just guesstimating. Let's figure five dollars times twenty kids times ten animiles."

"We only have to make *nine*," said Leon. "One a month, remember?"

"Will you guys let me finish?" P.W. took a deep breath and started over. "Five dollars times twenty kids times ten animiles. That makes . . . "

The jungle gym turned silent. Then P.W., who was the fastest calculator of the three, screamed, "A THOUSAND DOLLARS!"

They were mulling over the staggering sum when someone beckoned from below.

"Yoo-hoo, Sir Panty Hose!"

Leon's stomach tightened. He recognized the voice. A quick glance downward confirmed his fears.

"Oh, please come down, Sir Panty Hose." Henry Lumpkin jumped up and smacked Leon on the thigh. "*Please!*"

Leon tried to stay put, but the smacking intensified until he had no choice. He had to hop off and face Lumpkin.

P.W. and Lily-Matisse dropped down, too.

"So you think I look better with a pillowcase on my head?" Lumpkin sneered.

"I was only kidding," said Leon, anxiously kicking the asphalt.

From inside his olive drab army jacket, Lumpkin

removed a pair of panty hose and pitched them at Leon's feet.

"He's throwing down the gauntlet!" P.W. exclaimed.

It was a phrase they all knew from their *Medieval Readers*. A gauntlet was a kind of old-fashioned glove that nobles tossed to the ground when demanding a duel.

News of the challenge spread quickly. Within minutes, a dozen or so classmates circled the two combatants, creating a human wall that screened the makeshift battleground from the teachers' bench.

It would be wonderful to report that Sir Leon summoned up some untapped power and that he trounced the evil Lord Lumpkin. Sadly, that did not happen. More predictably, Lumpkin dispensed a vicious array of punches, slaps, kicks, dead-arms, and bent-knuckled noogies that left Leon sprawled on the playground blacktop.

It took him a long, painful minute to shake off the daze and stumble away.

"Not so fast," said Lumpkin.

Something soft smacked Leon in the shoulder blade. Instinct told him to keep moving, but he couldn't. A powerful hand grabbed his shoulder and spun him around.

"Put them on," Lumpkin snarled. "Now!"

"What?" said Leon, pretending not see the "gauntlet" on the ground.

Lumpkin snatched up the panty hose and brandished them threateningly, inches from Leon's face. "I *said* put them on."

A couple of onlookers reinforced the command by chanting, "Put, them, on! Put, them, on!"

Leon looked around. There was no way he could break away.

Lumpkin closed in. Leon tried to duck, but Lumpkin was too strong and too fast.

"I hereby crown you 'Sir Panty Hose.'" Lumpkin shoved the stockings over his victim's head.

A gagging sensation rose up from Leon's stomach as the stretchy material flattened his nose and turned his lips into a pair of plump slugs. The two useless legs flopped to the sides like a pair of liver-colored rabbit ears.

"Now beat it," Lumpkin said.

That was one order Leon was only too willing to obey. As soon as he had broken free, he whipped off the panty hose and gasped for air.

Leon ran inside the school and headed straight for the boys' room, where he splashed some water on his face, hoping to wash off whatever invisible panty-hose residue might still be clinging to his skin. Once he had removed all trace elements of his defeat, he stormed back to the classroom, bent on revenge.

The room was deserted.

Leon went straight for Lumpkin's desk and looked inside. The desk contained a nearly complete animile—a unicorn made from camouflage material.

It's not fair, Leon said to himself. How come a bonehead like Lumpkin can make things I can't?

He gave the animile a long slow squeeze. Too bad I can't rip Lumpkin limb from limb as easily as this unicorn. . . .

Leon looked at the wall clock. Ten minutes remained until the end of recess. That gave him plenty of time.

He dashed over to the supply cabinet. As usual, it was padlocked. But a quick tour of the room turned up a pair of scissors next to the pencil sharpener. Leon took them back to Lumpkin's desk.

Snip. Snip. Snip.

In no time flat, Leon had amputated the horn from Henry Lumpkin's unicorn. Doing so removed what little magic the beast possessed. It now looked a lot like a donkey.

Perfect! Leon told himself.

Then, as he was cramming the horn and body back inside Lumpkin's desk, a *second*, more daring, idea presented itself.

Leon checked the clock again. Five minutes left. He could do it. There was still enough time.

He scrounged about for a needle. He took it as a

good omen that he found one already threaded. He grabbed the horn and body and briefly contemplated the two pieces before setting to work.

It was the first time all year Leon had actually *wanted* to sew.

A dozen basting stitches later, he had reattached the unicorn horn. Only he fixed it to a new location— a location where it absolutely did *not* belong.

A location better left unspecified.

TEN

The Birdcage

he instant Miss Hagmeyer learned of Leon's radical surgery, she went straight to the phone in the teachers' lounge and called Emma Zeisel.

The hotel operator answered the call after the fourteenth ring. "Trimore Towers— where we *try more* every day! How may I direct your call?"

"Finally! I wish to speak with Emma Zeisel."

"Sorry, ma'am," said the operator. "She has her Do Not Disturb light on. She's probably sleeping."

"At two forty-five in the afternoon?" sputtered Miss Hagmeyer. "Get her up at once!"

"I'm sorry, but—"

"At once!" Miss Hagmeyer repeated. "This is about her son."

"About Leon?" gasped the operator. "Hold on. I'll patch you right through."

Emma Zeisel sat bolt upright the moment she heard Miss Hagmeyer's voice. "Is Leon hurt? Is everything okay?"

"Your son is not hurt, Ms. Zeisel. However, everything is *not* okay. I believe you should come down to

Principal Birdwhistle's office immediately."

Emma Zeisel squinted at her watch. Her shift started at four, which didn't give her much time. "I'll be there in half an hour," she said, pulling herself up off the living-room couch, which doubled as a bed.

When Emma Zeisel entered Principal Birdwhistle's office, she was frothing at the mouth—or so it seemed, because toothpaste still clung to her lips. "Sorry," she said breathlessly. "It took ages to find a taxi."

Leon was tempted to ask what country her cab driver had come from, but he knew that the Birdcage was not the place to bring up his taxi-driver collection. In fact, the Birdcage didn't seem like a good place to discuss anything. Leon decided to keep his mouth shut.

"Oh, goodness gracious, don't apologize," Principal Birdwhistle said nervously.

"Can we proceed?" Miss Hagmeyer said impatiently, without so much as a hello to Emma Zeisel. "I'm on a very tight schedule."

"Very well, Phyllis," said Principal Birdwhistle. She turned to Emma Zeisel. "At Miss Hagmeyer's suggestion, I've been looking over your son's record. He is a bright boy, there's no doubt about that. But Miss Hagmeyer is concerned that . . . well, perhaps it's best if she explains."

Miss Hagmeyer got straight to the point. "I'll be

frank, Ms. Zeisel. We have a problem. A *serious* problem. Take a look."

She pulled the unicorn from her satchel, gingerly exposing its underside. "Your son is responsible for this—this—"

Emma Zeisel burst out laughing before Miss Hagmeyer could finish her sentence. "Excuse me," she said after regaining her composure.

"I want to be clear about this, Ms. Zeisel," said Miss Hagmeyer. "Animile vandalism is not to be taken lightly."

"If Leon did this, I'm sure he had a reason. Whose animal is it?"

"Ani*mile*," corrected Miss Hagmeyer. "It is Henry Lumpkin's unicorn that your son mutilated."

Leon's mother rolled her eyes. "I know all about Henry Lumpkin. The kids call him Hank the Tank. Maybe you should worry more about how he mutilates his classmates."

"We're not here to discuss Mr. Lumpkin. We're here about your son. The amputated unicorn is only a symptom of a larger matter."

Emma Zeisel sighed. "I'm all ears."

So is Miss Hagmeyer, Leon wanted to say.

"The Classical School," Miss Hagmeyer said, "places great importance on fine motor skills. And as you know, your son's capacities in that domain are seriously delayed. Here, take a look for yourself."

She reached forward and handed Emma Zeisel the unicorn, along with a tape measure that she pulled off her neck. "If you check the basting stitch at the base of the horn you will see that your son's handiwork barely averages two stitches per inch. At the risk of stating the obvious, two s.p.i. is entirely unacceptable."

"How do you know Leon did that stitching?" Emma Zeisel asked.

"I can spot your son's limitations a mile off. And besides, he doesn't deny it, do you, Leon?"

Leon shook his head.

"Let me get this straight," said Emma Zeisel, her outrage mounting. "I'm here because of my son's— what did you call it?—*stitch count?*"

"Correct."

Emma Zeisel again rolled her eyes. "I'm sorry if I don't put a whole bunch of importance on my son learning to sew stuffed animals."

Miss Hagmeyer bristled. "As I have already mentioned, here and at Parents' Night, the word is pronounced ani*miles.*"

"I'm not one of your students," said Emma Zeisel.

"More's the pity," Miss Hagmeyer muttered under her breath.

"Ladies, *please*," Principal Birdwhistle implored.

Miss Hagmeyer said, "I should also like to correct another misunderstanding you seem to have, Ms. Zeisel. Sewing *is* why you send your son to Classical. Whether you are aware of it or not, spool work is schoolwork. And from the very start of the year, Leon has not pushed himself."

"Seems to me he's been getting plenty of pushing from others," said Emma Zeisel.

Principal Birdwhistle again cut in. "Ladies, I beg you. We're not here to argue. We're here to see what can be done to keep Leon engaged in the business of learning."

"Well, I can suggest one thing," said Miss Hagmeyer. "He should get more sleep. Look at him. All raccoon-eyed and jittery."

"Maybe he's just bored," said Emma Zeisel defensively.

Miss Hagmeyer grimaced. "I've been called a great many things, but never boring. And it's not my teaching methods that are under review. It's the quality of your son's work."

Principal Birdwhistle said, "I don't mean to interfere, Ms. Zeisel, but your son does look a little tired."

Emma Zeisel tensed. Suddenly she felt attacked from two sides. "Look, I work afternoons *and* nights to keep us going. That means I can't sing my son lullabies, and I can't have cupcakes baking in the oven when he returns home from school. Heck, I don't even *have* an oven—just a hot plate we barely use." She looked at her watch. "Case in point. I'm expected at the reception desk in twenty minutes."

Miss Hagmeyer said, "However sympathetic I might be to your circumstances, Ms. Zeisel, the fact remains—your son is lagging behind. His reports and my stitch counts make that only too clear."

"As far as I'm concerned, Miss Hagmeyer, it's the teachers who should be getting the reports, not my son."

Now *there's* an idea, Leon thought. While the three women argued, he distracted himself by composing report cards in his head.

Report Card for *Principal Birdwhistle*

Absences	Conduct	Performance
0	*fair*	*B–*

Comments *A hopeless wimp. Should learn how to discipline nutso teachers.*

Report Card for *Coach Kasperitis*

Absences	Conduct	Performance
1	*good!*	*A+*

Comments *The best! Never forces his class to do jumping jacks. Knows tons about dodgeball. Plus he's an awesome spitter.*

Naturally, Leon lavished most of his mental energy on . . .

Report Card for *Miss Hagmeyer*

Absences	Conduct	Performance
O	poor!	F

Comments *Total loser! Tortures her class with sewing assignments. Weird hair (possibly fake). Mean temper. Big ears. Sells her students' schoolwork for big bucks.*

"Ladies, please!" pleaded Principal Birdwhistle. "Let's try to end this meeting on a positive note."

"I wish that were possible," said Miss Hagmeyer. "But even putting aside the unicorn incident, consider this. If Leon has had so much trouble with animiles one and two, how will he finish number three—the unicorn—before the upcoming field trip to the Cloisters?"

"Is that necessary?" Emma Zeisel asked.

"It is," Miss Hagmeyer said adamantly. "And taking the longer view, how will Leon handle the final project of the year—the master piece? How, in short, will he acquire the skills needed to enter fifth grade?"

Leon's cheeks started to burn. Where was *this* going?

"What are you saying, Miss Hagmeyer?" Emma Zeisel asked.

"Isn't it obvious? I'm *saying* there's a chance Leon and I may be reunited next year. Isn't that right, Principal Birdwhistle?"

The proposition seemed to catch the head of the school by surprise. "Yes, well, that could be beneficial, I suppose. It often proves helpful for the struggling student to repeat a year."

Leon broke his self-imposed silence. "No way!" he shouted angrily. "I'm not getting flunked! Forget it!"

"Don't worry, sweetie," said Emma Zeisel. "They're only saying it's a possibility."

"A very distinct possibility," Miss Hagmeyer muttered.

Principal Birdwhistle smiled at Leon and his mother. Neither of them smiled back.

"We've got to go," said Emma Zeisel, frowning at her watch.

"Okay, then," said Principal Birdwhistle, visibly relieved to put the meeting behind her. "I've made a note to myself to send you an update on Leon's progress."

As mother and son were leaving, Miss Hagmeyer said, "So long, Ms. Zeisel. So long, Leon." Her words would have seemed harmless enough if she hadn't ended the good-bye with a stitching motion, to clarify that what she *really* meant was "S-E-W long."

ELEVEN

The Ice Queen

Napoleon hadn't expected to see *two* Zeisels exiting the school. He broke into a broad grin the moment he noted the family resemblance.

"Is this your mother, Monsieur Leon? Bonjour, Madame!"

Emma Zeisel forced herself to smile, but Napoleon was sharp enough to sense she was in no mood to chat. He returned his attentions to Leon. "So, my friend, did you have a nine-and-three-quarters day?"

Leon jabbed his thumb downward.

"Seven?" Napoleon said optimistically.

Leon repeated the gesture.

"Five?"

"Lower," Leon said bitterly.

Napoleon shook his head. "No, we had better stop there."

During the drive to the Trimore, Napoleon resisted the impulse to talk. And when he pulled up to the hotel, he skipped his usual door-opening theatrics. He ended the ride with a simple, heartfelt good-bye.

"Au revoir, Monsieur Leon. Au revoir, Madame. *Bon courage!*"

But after the day he had had at school, the last thing Leon felt was courage.

Back at the reception desk, Emma Zeisel handed her son an updated list of VIPs. "Here you go, sweetie," she said. "The signboard awaits."

Leon looked at the sheet of names. "Who cares about some dumb plumbers?"

"I know your teacher is tough," his mother said consolingly as she pushed the wooden letter box across the counter. "But remember our motto." She tapped the words that ran along the bottom of her hotel badge. "We try more at the Trimore."

"Try, try, try," said Leon. "I'm sick of mottoes, and I'm *sick* of trying! What's the darn point? I'll just be *trying* to do next year what I'm already *trying* to do this year!"

"That's not definite. Miss Hagmeyer only said that repeating the year was a possibility."

"Yeah, right," said Leon. "A *distinct* possibility."

"Sweetie—"

"I don't want to talk about it anymore!" Leon grabbed the letter box and stormed off to the signboard. He stabbed two Vs into the black felt. They went in all crooked, but he couldn't be bothered to line them up right. His spelling was similarly sloppy. And as for his cherished exclamation marks—he skipped those altogether.

The signboard ended up looking like this:

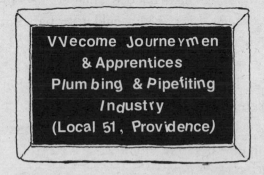

Later that night, after a coffee-shop sandwich that failed to make the grade (Frau Haffenreffer had forgotten the extra J on his PB&J), Leon let himself into his apartment and plodded into the bedroom. Without bothering to flick the light switch—he didn't have to; the neon glow from the convention-center sign lit up his small room—he flopped on the bed.

He felt as if he had weights tied to his arms and legs. It was a struggle just changing into pajamas. As he got under the covers, an annoying phrase started looping through his head: *Try more, try more, try more. . .*

Then another phrase, this one even more annoying, took its place: *Repeat the year, repeat the year, repeat the year . . .*

Soon the two phrases tangled together like twisted strands of thread: *Try, repeat, try, repeat, try, repeat . . .*

Leon sat up in bed and studied the map of the world. He hoped the pins marking his past achievements would temper his crummy mood. But they only made things worse. He hadn't added a new country in weeks and weeks. At this rate he would *never* nab Suriname.

He reached under his bed for the bag of Zapp's Kettle-Cooked Mesquite Bar-B-Que Potato Chips he kept on hand for emergency situations. But even potato chips failed to lift his spirits.

Just when he thought things couldn't get worse, the map pins began to vibrate.

Click-click-click-buzzzz . . . .

. . . *Grind-groan-rumble-CRASH!*

The Ice Queen was at it again, casting her odious spell.

Leon dropped the chip bag on the floor and shoved his head under the covers. He knew that the queen would repeat her hex.

And sure enough, she did. Only instead of the predictable clicks and buzzes, she now emitted an entirely new set of sounds.

Leon listened intently. An odd assortment of bangs, scrapes, and thumps replaced the usual three-click overture.

What is going on? he wondered.

Leon jumped out of bed and tiptoed into the hall. When he reached the alcove that abutted his bedroom wall, he discovered that the Ice Queen had company.

Two burly hotel guests had their shoulders pressed against the side of the ice maker.

"A little to the right, Sauly," one of the men said between gasps.

The man he'd addressed—Sauly—responded by rocking the massive machine. "How's that, Pauly?"

"Over more to the left."

The two men, Pauly and Sauly, were so focused on moving the machine they didn't notice Leon.

"What are you guys doing?" he demanded.

The men eased the ice maker back onto the carpeting and straightened up.

"What are *you* doing, kid?" said the man named Pauly. "Shouldn't you be home sleeping?"

"I can't sleep. And for your information," Leon added defiantly, "this *is* home. I live right next door." He tapped the wall.

"Yeah? Then I ain't surprised you can't sleep," said Pauly. "Not if you live near this baby." He gave the Ice Queen an affectionate slap and looked at his pal. "Are you surprised, Sauly?"

"Ain't surprised at all," said Sauly.

Pauly turned to Leon. "See, the bozo who did the install totally messed up on the clearance. Ice Queens ain't supposed to touch the wall."

"Don't forget about the venting," Sauly interjected.

"I ain't forgetting about the venting," said Pauly with mild irritation. "If you'd let me finish telling the kid. As I was about to say, the venting is whacked.

Also, something's wrong with the harvest bin. Plus, from what I'm hearing, I wouldn't be surprised if the compressor's out of alignment."

Sauly nodded respectfully.

"You guys sure know lots about ice makers," said Leon.

The two men smiled at each other.

"Hey, Pauly," said Sauly. "Do we know lots about ice makers?"

Pauly chuckled. "Enough to have earned the stars."

As if on command, both men patted the patches on their work shirts. Leon looked more closely. Their patches said MASTER PLUMBER, UNITED ASSOCIATION OF PLUMBERS AND PIPEFITTERS, LOCAL 51 (PROVIDENCE) and were rimmed with a circle of stars.

"They don't hand these out for looks, kid," said Sauly.

"Are you guys saying you can fix the Ice Queen?"

That prompted more chuckling. "Sorry, kid," said Pauly. "I know where you're going with this, but no can do. Sauly and me—we're here for the toilet-tank convention. Call your local refrigeration professional if you want this baby overhauled. We're done for the night."

"My mom's *tried* getting her fixed," said Leon. "She couldn't find *anyone*."

"Well, she *is* a relic," Pauly admitted. "The ice maker, I mean. Not your mom."

"*Please*," Leon pleaded. There was no way he was

going to let an opportunity like this slip through his fingers. "She keeps me up *all* night—the ice maker, I mean. Not my mom."

Pauly again let out a chuckle and rubbed the back of his neck. "Hey, Sauly," he said. "How'd you get down to the city?"

"How do you think, Pauly? Took the van."

"Got your tools with you?"

"You kidding, Pauly? I *always* got my tools with me."

"Well, go get 'em. And while you're at it, bring up some of that high-density insulation, a length of thread pipe, and ten feet of three-eighths-inch feeder line."

"You got it!" said Sauly.

"And don't forget the doughnuts," Pauly joked.

"Not so fast," said Leon. "Doughnuts are *my* department." He tore down to the coffee shop and arranged some goodies on a plate while Frau Haffenreffer poured out two cups of coffee to go.

Twenty minutes later the two repairmen had cracked open the Ice Queen. Coils, screws, wing nuts, tubes, and O-rings spread over the shag carpeting. (Along with doughnuts, napoleons, and cups of piping hot coffee.)

"See, kid," said Pauly. "Just like we told you. The compressor is all messed up."

"Don't forget about the harvest bin," said Sauly.

"Plus, like Sauly here says, some dimwit inserted the harvest bin backward."

Pauly and Sauly spent the better part of an hour unplugging, uncoupling, unscrewing, cleaning, lubricating, repairing, and realigning parts. Once that was done, they snapped everything back in place and repositioned the ice maker three feet from the wall.

"Go ahead, kid," said Pauly. "Test her out."

"She's awfully quiet," Leon said doubtfully. "You sure she's plugged in?"

"Is she plugged in, Sauly?"

"She's plugged in, Pauly."

Leon pushed the dispensing lever and braced himself for the usual racket.

It never came.

There were no clicks.

There were no buzzes.

There were no grinds or groans or crashes.

In fact, the Ice Queen dropped two ice cubes into Leon's cupped hand without making any sound at all. None whatsoever.

"Wow!" Leon exclaimed. "Wait till I tell my mom! That repair's been in the logbook for *years!*"

"Tell her tomorrow, kid. Right now, go grab some shut-eye."

Leon didn't argue. It was late, and he was tired.

That night he fell asleep thinking about the Ice Queen. She wasn't at all like the one in the fairy tale, he decided. She wasn't an evil witch. She was just a weird, cranky, out-of-date curiosity in need of special handling.

TWELVE

In the Belly of the Beast

The following night Leon conked out to the glorious sound of . . . *nothing*. The only *click* he heard came from the light switch near his bed. And in the silence that followed, he slept for eight full hours, three hours more than he had averaged during the Ice Queen's noisy, wall-shaking reign.

The next night Leon got *nine* hours of sleep, and he got *ten* the night after that.

If sleep is brain food, Leon's long-famished brain was suddenly served a feast. So was the rest of his body. The rings under his eyes started to fade. His pale skin gained some color. But most important, his fine motor skills slowly started to rev up. Shoelaces got a little easier to tie. Dodgeballs landed with greater accuracy. The stingy flute teacher, Miss Brunelleschi, stuck *two* gold stars in Leon's music book for deftly completing finger exercises she considered especially challenging.

Even Miss Hagmeyer tempered her usual criticism. "Not bad, Mr. Zeisel," she said when handing back a penmanship worksheet. "Your cursive Ms are actually beginning to look like camel humps." But then she spoiled it. "Pity," she added, "you can't show a similar turnaround in the animile department. I'm *still* waiting for your dinosaur *and* your unicorn."

Leon didn't respond—at least not directly. But he decided then and there to finish his overdue assignments and make Miss Hagmeyer eat her words.

That afternoon, back at the hotel, Leon zipped through his signboard duties—VVelcome VVinch Operators of VVisconsin!!!!—and set up shop in the office behind the reception desk.

Maria came by to clean while he was working on the diplocaulus. She waved her feather duster over the animile's arrow-shaped head. "Your project is looking *real* sweet."

"It better, Maria. I've got to hand it in on Monday."

"I'm not worried, Leonito. You'll show that Miss Panty Hose!"

Leon stitched through the weekend, fueled by Maria's encouragement, plus a steady supply of PB&J (extra J), Haffenreffer dough balls, and Zapp's Mesquite Kettle-Cooked Bar-B-Que Potato Chips.

When Monday rolled around, Leon handed in his second animile . . . *and* his third!

The double submission shocked Miss Hagmeyer. "My, haven't we been productive," she said suspiciously.

"Yup," said Leon with pride.

Miss Hagmeyer inspected and approved the dinosaur without comment, then turned to the surprise submission—the unicorn. She positioned it on the desk—horn down, legs up—and pressed her tape measure against its belly.

She gave Leon a sideways glance. "Is there something you wish to tell me, Mr. Zeisel?"

"Not really."

"Perhaps I should rephrase the question. How do you explain completing *two* animiles over a single weekend?"

"Discipline and diligence?" Leon said tentatively.

"That's terribly commendable," said Miss Hagmeyer. "However, it does not explain the stitch count on your unicorn."

"What's the matter with it?"

"It averages *five* s.p.i."

"Isn't that good?"

"Extremely—for a student who averages two. Must I schedule another meeting with Principal Birdwhistle?"

"Why?" said Leon anxiously.

"Why? Because this seam is too tight, too precise to be yours. Who helped you? Was it your mother? Someone from class?" Miss Hagmeyer scanned the room for accomplices. Her gaze locked on Lily-Matisse.

"I haven't *touched* his unicorn!" Lily-Matisse protested.

"She didn't," said Leon. "I did it all by myself. Honest."

"We'll see soon enough," Miss Hagmeyer said skeptically. She grabbed a pair of scissors.

Leon watched in horror as she cut open the stomach of his animile. His brain began to throb as panty hose popped out of the unicorn like guts from a wounded beast.

"How's it feel, Sir Panty Hose?" Lumpkin said with a snigger.

"Quiet down, Mr. Lumpkin," Miss Hagmeyer admonished before turning back to Leon. "If you sewed this well once, Mr. Zeisel, you can do so again."

Leon grabbed the unicorn and marched toward his seat.

"Halt!" Miss Hagmeyer commanded. "*This* will be your workbench." She tapped her desk with the instructional needle. "Redo that seam where I can watch you."

Lily-Matisse stood up and craned her neck to get a better view.

"Ms. Jasprow," said Miss Hagmeyer. "If you're *that* interested in your friend's handiwork, why not come up and join him?"

"Okay," Lily-Matisse replied, ignoring the sarcasm.

"Can I watch, too?" P.W. said in a daring show of solidarity.

"You can all come up, for all I care," said Miss Hagmeyer irritably.

Within seconds Thomas, Lumpkin, and the rest of the class had circled Miss Hagmeyer's desk. Only Antoinette stayed put, but that was because she already had a ringside seat.

As spectator sports go, sewing will never rival, say, baseball. Still, the showdown was pretty exciting for the fourth graders.

"Get going," Miss Hagmeyer ordered. She handed him a threaded needle.

Which stitch to use? Leon asked himself. A hemming stitch? No. A running stitch? No. A satin stitch? Definitely not a satin stitch. Panic clouded his thinking.

"Snap to it," said Miss Hagmeyer.

Leon continued to run through the options. Chain stitch? No. Overcast?

Overcast! That was the one he needed to fix the seam. It was also the one he had the hardest time getting right.

Leon poked the panty hose back inside the unicorn, folded one edge of the material over the other, like the flap of an envelope, and began to sew. Five minutes later he was done. He handed the unicorn back to Miss Hagmeyer and watched her inspect the repair.

As she remeasured the seam, her forehead wrinkled and her pinched lips tightened until they all but disappeared. Leon noticed a long blue vein, not unlike a running stitch, pulsing down her neck. Apparently something still troubled her.

Lily-Matisse peered over Miss Hagmeyer's shoulder as the teacher was pressing the tape against the redone seam.

"Four stitches per inch, Leon!" Lily-Matisse suddenly hollered.

It wasn't the best performance in the class—not by a long shot. But it did disprove the cheating charge, and it met the minimum s.p.i. requirement.

"The unicorn passes," said Miss Hagmeyer without apology or comment. "You may deposit it and the dinosaur in the finished bin. When you have, return to your seat. And that goes for the rest of you court jesters, too!"

As everyone dispersed, Miss Hagmeyer pulled Leon over to the countinghouse tally. "Don't think you're in the clear," she said. "I admit your sewing shows *some* progress. But can you sustain it? That's the question." She slid the Sir Leon spool two spaces to the right. "Remember this—to say good-bye to me at the end of the year, you will have to reach the end of the yarn."

Two weeks after the face-off with Miss Hagmeyer, Leon turned ten.

"The big one-oh," said Emma Zeisel, beaming. "We may not be able to afford anything fancy, but we can still throw you a real humdinger of a party!" To that end, she dug up some old Trimore stationery and wrote out five invitations that said, "Leon Zeisel requests your presents . . . And you should come, too!" She put three of the invitations in her son's backpack—for P.W., Lily-Matisse, and Napoleon—and gave Frau Haffenreffer and Maria the others.

The party took place at the Trimore coffee shop. Leon and his guests crammed into a booth piled high with baked goods and gifts. Frau Haffenreffer started things off by presenting Leon a box tied with her trademark red string.

"Can you cut it open with your ring?" Leon asked.

Frau Haffenreffer shook her head and hid her hands.

Her rudeness surprised Leon until he got the box open. "You're giving me your string ring?" he cried.

"*Ja*," said Frau Haffenreffer. "You're old enough now."

Leon slipped the hooked band onto his index finger and showed it off to his friends.

P.W. said, "I saw one of those in a kung fu film once. This guy used it to cut off another guy's—"

"That's quite all right, P.W.," Emma Zeisel interrupted. "Cutting thread would be a more practical application."

"Can we *not* talk about sewing?" said Leon.

"Sorry, sweetie. You're absolutely right."

Leon used Frau Haffenreffer's present to slice open a large gift-wrapped box.

"That's from me," said P.W.

"A Lego castle!" Leon exclaimed.

"If you want, I can show you how to make the drawbridge yank off the heads of the prisoners!"

Lily-Matisse groaned and then handed Leon a less military gift—a purple pouch. "It's for your travel book," she said. "And see, I personalized it."

"Thanks," said Leon. He wasn't sure about carrying his notebook around in a purple pouch that had LEON stitched across the front. But he didn't want any hurt feelings. "It's super."

"And who knows?" said Emma Zeisel. "Maybe it'll bring you luck with the taxi-driver collection." She handed her son a small, heavy parcel.

Leon ran his ring through the wrapping. "A remote-control dune buggy!"

"I pretested a few other models. This is the only one that makes it through the hotel's carpeting."

"It's great, Mom," said Leon.

Emma Zeisel pushed the old wooden letter box at her son. "And here's a little something extra."

"Why are you giving me this?" said Leon, puzzled.

"Open it and find out."

Leon undid the question-mark catch, lifted the lid, and peered inside. He noticed the change at once.

"Wow!" Leon exclaimed. "Upper- and lowercase Ws!"

"W-O-W is right," said his mom, extracting an O and two of the spanking new Ws to spell out her son's exclamation on the tabletop.

"You better save some of those wows, Leonito," Maria said. She presented him with a huge basket covered in cellophane.

"Potato chips!" he exclaimed. "One, two, three, four, five . . . *six* big bags. And all different!"

"And you'll be getting more," said Maria. "I signed you up for the Worldwide Chip of the Month Club."

P.W. inspected a bag of Golden Queen "crisps" from England. "These are wild!" he said.

"What about these?" said Lily-Matisse. "Fandangos. From Haiti!"

All eyes turned toward Napoleon, who gave Leon a sheepish look.

"I am sorry," he said. "I have come empty-handed. I will deliver my gift tomorrow, on the way to school."

THIRTEEN

The Hall of Unicorns

Napoleon never arrived the next morning. Leon waited and waited, pacing back and forth inside the lobby. Finally he had no choice but to give up and hail a cab to school. As luck would have it, one was idling right in front of the hotel.

"Where are you desiring to go?" the driver inquired.

"The Classical School," Leon said sadly. He provided the address and glanced at the driver's hack license. The photo ID pictured a scruffy man with a nasty scar that ran from cheek to chin.

Thwuck!

The lock buttons on the back doors suddenly dropped out of reach. Leon noticed moments later that the cabby was staring at him in

the rearview mirror. That made him nervous.

When the taxi stopped at a traffic light, Leon tested a door handle. It didn't work.

Trapped! Leon immediately switched into defense mode. Pulling his travel book from its brand-new purple pouch, he wrote down the full name and complete ID number of the driver: RAVI RAMPERTAB G63L.

He figured that if Scarface turned out to be a homicidal nutcase, the travel book might be the only way to link the driver to his body—after it washed onto a riverbank, riddled with bullets.

Wait a minute! Leon told himself. My travel book won't help. . . . Supposing Scarface *does* dump my body in the river, the ink will run. . . . Too bad Lily-Matisse didn't make the pouch out of waterproof plastic. . . . Maybe I could use my string ring on the driver, like that guy in the kung fu movie P.W. was talking about.

Leon's backseat terror lasted a full ten minutes until—*thwuck!*—the doors on the taxicab unlocked.

"Here we are," said the driver. "I am believing this is where you are needing to arrive."

Leon looked out the window. The sight of school made his whole body relax. As he was paying the fare, he asked the question that the kidnapping scare had almost made him forget.

"Excuse me, Mr. Rampertab? Could you tell me where you're from?"

"Why are you desiring to know?" the driver asked.

Leon told him about his collection.

"That is most interesting," said the driver without answering the question.

So Leon asked again, this time waving his travel book. "Could I know where you were born, Mr. Rampertab?"

The driver took his time responding. "South America," he said eventually.

"*Where* in South America?"

The driver turned around to look at Leon through the partition of the cab. "The north part of South America," he said.

Leon pressed further. "But where *exactly*? What *country* in the north part of South America?"

"You are wanting to know precisely what country in South America I am coming from?"

"Yes," Leon said impatiently.

Finally, as Leon was reaching for the door handle, Ravi Rampertab responded.

"Suriname," he said very softly.

"SURINAME?" Leon shouted. "Are you sure?"

The driver laughed. "Oh, most definitely. I was born in Paramaribo, and Paramaribo is most certainly the capital of Suriname. You may check in any atlas at all if you are not wanting to believe me."

Leon's whole body started shaking with joy.

"Are you feeling okay?" asked the driver.

"I'm feeling better than okay!"

"On a scale of one to ten, how might you be feeling?" asked the driver.

"Huh?" Leon gave Ravi Rampertab a funny look.

What were the chances *two* taxi drivers judged feelings numerically?

The driver said, "Would news of my birthplace perhaps allow you to be having a nine-and-three-quarters day?"

A lightbulb went on inside Leon's head. "Napoleon!" he cried.

"Indeed," said Ravi Rampertab.

Napoleon explained the whole glorious plot that same afternoon, on the drive back to the hotel.

"*Mon Dieu*. It is not a simple thing finding a Surinamese taxi driver in this city, Monsieur Leon. Not easy at all."

"How did you do it?"

"Ah, well," Napoleon said, grinning broadly. "I started with my dispatcher. He checked his list and said he could find me a driver from Senegal or Sri Lanka or Sierra Leone."

"But I've already got all those."

"I know, Monsieur Leon. I told him it was Suriname I required, and that no other country would do. So he gave me names of rival taxi companies. I called and called. Eventually I tracked down our Monsieur Rampertab. He lives thirty miles away, yet he did not hesitate to do me this kindness. He knows the importance of birthdays."

Later that evening, Leon triumphantly jabbed a

pushpin into the capital of Suriname and told everyone in the hotel about how Napoleon had helped him conquer South America.

"Sweetie, I believe the conquistadors got there before you," said Emma Zeisel.

"And some of *my* people were there before *them*," noted Maria.

The next morning Leon left the house lugging a gigantic box of pastries.

"Here," he told Napoleon as he shoved the box through the partition separating the front and back of the taxi. "This is for you."

"For me?" said Napoleon.

"Frau Haffenreffer baked you some napoleons for getting me Suriname."

"Napoleons for Napoleon?" Napoleon gasped.

"I *tried* to explain you hate them, but Frau Haffenreffer wouldn't listen."

"Keep them, Monsieur Leon! I do not want them! Give them out at school!"

The timing couldn't have been better. When the taxi pulled up to the steps of the school, Leon saw a yellow bus parked out front.

"The field trip!" he exclaimed. He boarded the bus with the pastries and headed to the back, where Lily-

Matisse and P.W. were saving him a spot. On the way, he passed Lumpkin, who was too busy teasing Antoinette to notice him or the pastry box.

"Your mom's chaperoning?" P.W. said to Lily-Matisse as Regina Jasprow climbed aboard.

"Looks like it," said Lily-Matisse. She sounded less than thrilled.

"What's that purple thing she's wearing?" P.W. asked.

"She calls that her place-mat dress," Lily-Matisse said with a sigh. "The seventh graders gave her some place mats for helping at the Nimble Fingers Craft Fair last year. Only Mom doesn't *believe* in place mats, so she turned them into a dress."

P.W. and Leon exchanged puzzled looks.

"And check out the handbag," said Lily-Matisse. "She made it out of an old velveteen glove. She's always complaining that her bus tokens get caught in the thumb."

"Well, she looks real colorful," Leon said graciously.

"Not as colorful as the coach," said P.W.

Skip Kasperitis climbed onto the bus sporting a bright green nylon tracksuit.

"Check out his pocket," said Leon. "I bet you that's his spit jar."

"Did you read chapter seven in the *Medieval Reader?*" said P.W. excitedly. "They had a Fun Facts box that talked about spit. There was this monk called

Jonas who figured out spit contains magic powers that can bring the dead back to life."

A large black cape darkened the front of the bus. "Quiet down, you knaves!" Miss Hagmeyer yelled, flicking her instructional needle in the air. "If you don't, I'll make you sit alphabetically."

"She looks like a witch the way she waves that thing," Thomas whispered.

"It's a pity this *isn't* a magic wand, Mr. Warchowski," Miss Hagmeyer shot back. "If it were, I would use it to remove your voice box! However, since I can't, adjust your volume control to low while we are driving to the Cloisters."

After performing a head count, Miss Hagmeyer sat down and told the driver he could go.

"What exactly *are* the Cloisters?" Leon asked as the bus rumbled uptown.

"It's this ancient castle place with a medieval museum," Lily-Matisse said. "Mom takes me there all the time."

"I hope they have a dungeon with torture stuff," said P.W.

"Why?" said Leon. "We just left a dungeon with torture stuff."

Ten minutes into the trip Leon held up the pastry box. "Good folk," he said loudly. "It is I, Sir Leon, wishing to ask how art thee?"

"It's not 'How art thee,'" quibbled Antoinette. "It's 'How art *thou.*'"

"Whatever," said Leon.

"You mean 'mayhap.'"

"Enough!"

"Enow," she corrected.

"Knock it off," said Leon. He gave the pastry box a gentle shake and said, "Anyone hungry?"

"What'd you bring?" someone shouted.

"A treasure beyond rubies," Leon answered, borrowing a phrase from the *Medieval Reader*. He pulled the birthday ring from his pocket and slid it onto his finger. With a quick, effortless tug, he cut through the string and said, "Behold!" as he lifted the lid.

Classmates peered inside the box at the custard delicacies. Antoinette immediately started pestering Leon whether people actually ate napoleons in the Middle Ages. He ignored her and offered P.W. a pastry, then turned to Lily-Matisse.

"And you, milady?"

Lily-Matisse blushed and bowed her head before grabbing a cream-filled dessert. Leon handed out a few more pastries before making his way to where the teachers were seated.

"No, thank you," Miss Hagmeyer said, barely looking up from her embroidery. "I brought my cottage cheese."

Regina Jasprow and Coach Kasperitis weren't so

restrained. They each took one. The driver of the bus, Mr. Groot (the same fellow who taught wood shop and served as the school photographer) would also have accepted a napoleon if Miss Hagmeyer hadn't intervened.

"A four-ounce pastry and a four-ton bus should not be handled at the same time, Mr. Groot. Satisfy your sweet tooth *after* we have parked. And with regards to the matter of safety, return to your seat at once, Mr. Zeisel."

On his way back, Leon hit a roadblock.

"Hey, Sir Panty Hose," said Henry Lumpkin. "You skipped me."

Leon tried to push through the muscled olive drab arm that now doubled as a tollgate, but he couldn't get by. Lumpkin repositioned his hand on Leon's shoulder and gave it a painful squeeze.

"Would thouest like to wear those desserts like you wore the Hag's underwear?" Lumpkin said.

Leon tried to pull away.

"What's going on back there?" Miss Hagmeyer asked.

"Nothing, Miss Hagmeyer!" Leon and Lumpkin both cried.

"Back in your seats," she admonished.

Lumpkin refused to let go. "So what'll it be?" he said in a dark, low voice.

Even with his bladed birthday ring, Leon knew he was no match for Henry Lumpkin.

"Now, Mr. Zeisel!" Miss Hagmeyer commanded.

"Here, help yourself," said Leon, suppressing the impulse to shmoosh a napoleon straight into Lumpkin's face.

It was a picture-perfect November day when the bus pulled into the parking lot of the Cloisters. A crisp breeze gave the air a pungent odor of wrinkled apples.

With Lumpkin temporarily bribed, Leon felt a brief sense of calm—until Antoinette started showing off, calling out architectural terms that she had plundered from the *Medieval Reader.*

TURRET

"Turret! I see a turret!" she squealed. "And those are *definitely* crenels. And look! One, two, three . . . *four* loopholes!"

"Maybe we'll get lucky and she'll find that dungeon I was hoping for," said P.W.

"And if we're really lucky," said Leon, "it'll have *two* empty cells. One for her highness and one for Lord Lumpkin."

"Aren't you forgetting the Hag?" said Lily-Matisse.

"Excellent point," said Leon. "Make it three cells."

At the museum ticket desk, Miss Hagmeyer quickly remedied the alphabetical chaos she had endured during the bus ride.

CRENELS (GAPS)

"Okay, pay attention," she said. "A through Gs

stay with me. Coach Kasperitis will take the H through Ns. Ms. Jasprow will monitor the rest of you rapscallions. We

LOOPHOLES

regroup at the tapestries in exactly one hour. Do not be late."

Leon was less than thrilled that his last name separated him from Lily-Matisse and P.W., but at least he hadn't gotten stuck with Miss Hagmeyer. Leading the O through Zs into the courtyard, Regina Jasprow explained to her charges how the museum's ancient stone buildings had been shipped from France and Italy. "Every brick, every stone, every roof tile was numbered in white chalk," she said breathlessly. "If you think your Lego constructions are complicated, try pulling apart a medieval church, complete with flying buttresses. Then try wrapping it up,

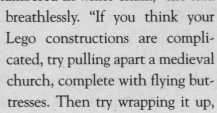

FLYING BUTTRESSES

sending it across the ocean, unwrapping it, and snapping it back together!"

At an archway, she stuck out her tongue at a carved stone monster that was making a similarly rude gesture. "See that gargoyle? What do you think caused the black stains on its teeth?"

"Didn't floss enough?" said Thomas Warchowski. "Nice try."

"Chewed too much tobacco, like the coach?" Leon offered.

"Getting warmer," said Ms. Jasprow. "The gargoyle did do a lot of spitting in its time. Any guesses what it spat?"

"Boiling oil?"

"No, that's *too* warm," Ms. Jasprow said. "Actually, it spouted harmless rainwater. But if you come with me through this arch, I can show you something more satisfyingly deadly."

Ms. Jasprow guided her group into an herb garden and spoke about plant poisons, then continued on, to a library gallery, where she provided an overview on toxic pigments.

"See the red paint in that illuminated manuscript?" Ms. Jasprow said, pointing at a peaceful castle landscape. "Artists call that color vermilion. Chemists, however, know it as mercuric sulfide. It's *highly* poisonous. And the yellow on the knight's banner? That's orpiment. Orpiment contains arsenic, which is the principal ingredient in rat bait. And farther up, that golden sun, any guesses what that's made out of?"

No one had a clue.

"Dried cow urine," Ms. Jasprow said matter-of-factly.

Thomas raised his hand. "Ms. Jasprow?" he said. "I think it's been an hour. Miss Hagmeyer is probably expecting us."

"And we certainly shouldn't keep the Ha—Miss Hagmeyer waiting," said Ms. Jasprow. But on her way to the meeting point, she had a change of heart. "I can't resist a quick detour," she said with a conspiratorial wink.

Ms. Jasprow hustled the O through Zs into a room dominated by a beautiful stained glass window. "Isn't it a joy to watch the light shine through this? It's like medieval motion pictures!"

She was just launching into a speech about the dangers of glassmaking when she was interrupted by a tooting sound.

The coach came running up, proudly displaying a clay whistle, shaped like a jester's head, that he had purchased in the Cloisters gift shop. "Uh, Regina? Phyllis is getting a little, well, you know . . . "

"Impatient?" the art teacher suggested. "Fidgety? Restless?"

"You got it," confirmed the coach.

"At last!" Miss Hagmeyer said as the O through Zs joined the A through Ns at the entrance to the tapestry room. "You're seven—no, eight—minutes late!"

"It's my fault," said Regina Jasprow.

"Of course it is," said Miss Hagmeyer. She leveled

a look of intense displeasure at her tardy colleague before marching everyone into a large stone hall.

"*These*," she said, waving her needle, "are the reason I arranged this trip."

"Rugs?" said Lumpkin.

"Not rugs—tapestries. Seven of the most exquisite tapestries in the world."

"And each one has a unicorn!" Antoinette blurted out. "That's why you had *us* make unicorns!"

"That is correct, Miss Brede. I gave you that assignment so that you could better appreciate the master pieces on these walls."

Guiding the group to a hanging on the far side of the room, Miss Hagmeyer said, "I would like you to focus your attention on that rose right there. It required no fewer than thirty-four stitches per inch— you heard me correctly, *thirty-four* s.p.i."

"I'd settle for six," Leon whispered.

Miss Hagmeyer neutralized Leon with a glower before continuing. "That exquisite rose is one of six hundred and twenty-seven similarly exacting flowers that blossom on *The Start of the Hunt*. I know because I tallied them up—twice. In addition to examples of the seven stitches of virtue that all of you should know, this master piece incorporates tent stitches, stem stitches, knot stitches—"

Miss Hagmeyer suspended her speech. "Did you wish to add something, Ms. Jasprow?"

All heads turned toward the art teacher, who was whispering to the coach. "What?" said Ms. Jasprow. "Add something? Me? Uh, no."

"You are quite sure?" said Miss Hagmeyer. "We wouldn't want to deprive the class of an *artist's* perspective." The snideness in her voice was unmistakable.

Ms. Jasprow turned red. "Sorry for the disturbance. Please go on."

"It's hardly a disturbance, Regina. *Enlighten* us."

"Well, if you insist," said Ms. Jasprow. "I was just telling Coach Kasperitis here that I find your perspective slightly"—she took a moment to choose the right word—"numbery."

"*Numbery?*"

"You know what I mean. This many knots. That many flowers. When I look at these tapestries I tend to see something a little more, well, *magical*."

"Perhaps you should share your viewpoint more fully," Miss Hagmeyer said icily.

P.W. whispered to Leon, "Let the joust begin."

"Quiet!" Miss Hagmeyer yelled. "I wish to hear what Ms. Jasprow has to say."

Everyone froze. Even the coach remained motionless, despite the wad of tobacco wedged against one cheek.

"Go on, Regina," Miss Hagmeyer goaded. "Educate us on the *magic* of medieval and Renaissance embroidery."

"Very well." The art teacher waved her hand around the room. "All of this is *not* about numbers, Phyllis. It's about adventure. It's about mystery. It's about struggle. And, above all, it's about *passion*."

Miss Hagmeyer gave Regina Jasprow the once-over. "This from a woman who wears place mats!"

"At least I don't turn my students into garment workers," Ms. Jasprow snapped. "Tell me, Phyllis, are the kids making quota? I swear, if the school didn't give me a break on tuition, I'd have yanked Lily-Matisse off your animile assembly line the minute I learned about the stitch counts and tally charts."

Coach Kasperitis stepped forward. "Ladies," he said nervously. "I think that's enough."

Miss Hagmeyer cut him off. "Butt out, Skip! Ms. Jasprow here is still telling us the *true* meaning of these hangings."

Ms. Jasprow took a deep breath and exhaled very slowly. She then gazed up at a tapestry that portrayed a slain unicorn and said, "The artists who made this extraordinary work employed their needles and thread the way an alchemist mixes potions—to restore, to resurrect, to transform. They believed that a slain unicorn could be brought back to life through a supernatural occurrence we call *art* but that they, wisely, never named."

"Oh, for goodness' sake, Regina!" Miss Hagmeyer

said derisively. "*Supernatural occurrence?* Do you honestly expect my kids to buy that piffle?"

"I do!" the art teacher replied fiercely. "Passion can reanimate the dead," she insisted. "Passion can make fabric come alive."

FOURTEEN

The Master Piece

A fter the unicorn animiles came greyhounds and after the greyhounds came
stallions. Once the stallions were cor-
ralled in the finished bin, lions had to
be made. Then lambs. Then falcons.
With each new project, Miss Hagmeyer
changed the eyeballs on her cape and moved the spools
on the countinghouse tally closer and closer to May.

Naturally she kept dishing out the usual fourth-
grade fare—math, English, social studies, science—
but none of those subjects pleased her as much as the
sight of a completed animile dropping into the finished bin.

Miss Hagmeyer monitored Leon with extra-special
attention. She was forever asking him to straighten a
crooked limb, thin a bulging belly, redo a substandard
seam. And still Leon's s.p.i.s remained borderline. His
promotion to fifth grade was far from guaranteed.

That wasn't the only thing bugging Leon. Where
were all his animiles ending up? This mystery drove
Leon and the rest of the class nuts. But try though they
did, Miss Hagmeyer's students never managed to
uncover even the tiniest detail about their teacher's

sideline business. Then one day in April, all that changed.

"I found out where the Hag's taking our animiles," Lily-Matisse told P.W. and Leon while swinging on the jungle gym. "Mom overheard her making arrangements in the teachers' lounge."

"What kind of arrangements?" Leon asked.

"Shipping arrangements," said Lily-Matisse. "She was on the phone talking about a shipment of animiles, and she was looking through a black binder that said SOV on the cover."

"What's SOV?" P.W. asked.

Lily-Matisse shrugged. "It's not like Mom could go over and ask her. She hasn't spoken to the Hag since the Cloisters blowup. But she did check the phone book. All she found was a number for the Society of Ventriloquists."

"A Society of Vampires would be a better bet," said Leon.

"Or a School of Victims," P.W. suggested. "I saw the Hag leaving yesterday with another garbage bag full of animiles. And when I checked the finished bin this morning—"

"It was empty, right?" said Lily-Matisse.

"Bingo," said P.W.

"Someone's got to stop her," said Lily-Matisse.

"Yeah," said Leon. "Someone should deposit *her* in the finished bin."

* * *

After recess, Miss Hagmeyer began class by writing
two words on the blackboard:

master piece

"Can anyone tell me what this means?" she asked.
"You may recall I used the phrase during our visit to
the Hall of Unicorns."

A forest of hands sprouted up.

"Miss Brede?"

"An awesome thing?"

"That's a start," said Miss Hagmeyer. "But what's
the *nature* of the awesomeness? What exactly makes a
masterpiece a *master . . . piece?*"

The forest of hands fell. Miss Hagmeyer had to
answer her own question. "A *master piece* is a special
object crafted by an apprentice to gain entrance to the
guild. I suppose you could call it a medieval final
exam."

The words "final exam" instantly made the whole
class antsy.

"Settle down and let me explain," Miss Hagmeyer
said. "Suppose you were a lad living in the Middle
Ages, and you were sent off to make wagon wheels.
Where would you go?"

Pencils twiddled and feet tapped, but no one
spoke.

"You would undertake an apprenticeship with a

master wheelwright," said Miss Hagmeyer. "And that master would teach you his craft much the way I have attempted to teach you mine. As an apprentice, you would start with the basics. Tend the fire. Fetch buckets of water. Sweep curlicues of wood off the ground. After a year of tending and fetching and sweeping, you might get to shave down the spokes of a wheel. After another year, you might actually begin to *make* wheels. And after making hundreds and hundreds—under the master's strict supervision—you might be allowed to strike out on your own."

"Why would you want to strike out?" Henry Lumpkin asked.

P.W. turned to Leon and rolled his eyes.

"Striking out on your own has nothing to do with baseball," Miss Hagmeyer specified. "It means you would become independent. You would start to work by yourself—and for yourself."

"Oh," said Lumpkin.

"But to earn that right you would first need to be declared a master. And how would that happen?"

Silence.

"I'll ask again. How does an apprentice become a *master?*" Miss Hagmeyer tapped the blackboard with her chalk.

"By making a master piece?" Leon guessed.

"Bravo, Mr. Zeisel," Miss Hagmeyer replied coolly. "To join the Company of Wheelwrights, an apprentice would have to make a *piece* worthy of a *master*. In other words . . . "

"A master piece," a few students muttered.

Miss Hagmeyer gave a nod. "Naturally, apprentice wheelwrights weren't the only ones creating master pieces. Apprentice bookbinders created them, as did apprentice goldsmiths and apprentice tailors. Now does anyone know where I might be going with this?"

Antoinette's hand darted forward. "You want *us* to make medieval master pieces, don't you, Miss Hagmeyer?"

"That is correct. Each one of you is to create an animile that confirms your command of the stitches of virtue. An animile that says, 'I am a nimble-fingered master ready to handle fifth grade.'"

"What do we have to make?" P.W. asked.

"Ah," said Miss Hagmeyer. "That is a crucial part of the challenge. Masters must have vision. They must create on their own, without guidance."

"You mean no worksheets?" said Lily-Matisse.

"I mean no worksheets."

"And no handouts?" said Thomas.

"And no handouts," Miss Hagmeyer confirmed. "You must design your final animile from scratch, by yourselves. Draw up plans for a goshawk, if that's what tickles your fancy. Stuff a quail. Piece together a patchwork pony. The choice is up to you. I will not intervene. In fact, I do not want to know about your projects until they are complete."

A buzz spread through the room. No worksheets! No handouts! No instructions! No surveillance!

"Just keep one thing in mind," Miss Hagmeyer said. "Master pieces, both in design and execution, must celebrate the skill of the master."

"When are they due?" Antoinette asked.

"The day of Carnival," Miss Hagmeyer answered. "That gives you a little more than one month."

Leon enjoyed his freedom—for a couple of days. But independence soon became a burden. With the possibility of flunking looming, he couldn't decide what to make.

Leon thumbed through an illustrated encyclopedia of imaginary medieval beasts. The book was filled with crocophants and dragons and other mythical creatures. It even pictured a rude gargoyle that looked just like the one grimacing on the Cloisters downspout. Yet none of the beasts, gargoyle included, inspired Leon. He asked for suggestions at the hotel.

"What about a llama, Leonito?" Maria said. (Maria had a soft spot for llamas—they recalled her native Peru.)

"Not medievalish enough," said Leon.

"How about a tiger?" Emma Zeisel proposed. "We've got the Amazing Lothar staying with us in July, and he's bringing his entire act. I could ask him for a

few whiskers. You could add them to your creature."

"July's too late," Leon moaned.

"Don't torture yourself, sweetie. I'm sure you'll think of something."

But Leon did not think of something. And worse, Miss Hagmeyer caught wind of his waffling.

"Have you at least drawn some sketches?" she asked one afternoon.

"No," Leon admitted. "I can't seem to come up with *anything*."

"One must exercise one's fingers to exercise one's mind," Miss Hagmeyer said unhelpfully.

"But—"

"No ifs, ands, or buts, Mr. Zeisel. If you can't complete your master piece *this* year you will have plenty of time to do so *next*. Is my meaning clear?"

"Yes," said Leon, feeling a terrible sense of despair.

"Now repeat after me. 'I *will* make Miss Hagmeyer a master piece!'"

"I will make Miss Hagmeyer a master piece."

Miss Hagmeyer shook her head. "Not good enough. Say it again. Only this time with feeling."

Leon forced himself to say, "I *will* make Miss Hagmeyer a master piece!"

And that's when it hit him.

While parroting his teacher's silly words, Leon suddenly figured out what he wanted to make. What he *had* to make!

"Got it!" he cried as he dashed back to his desk, dizzied by possibility.

His idea for a master piece emerged, fully formed, like one of those spongy toy sea creatures that burst out of tiny plastic capsules when dissolved in hot water. Except Leon's animile was a whole lot rarer than the octopuses and angelfish hatched inside a bathtub. It was also a lot more complex.

Although the *idea* for the master piece announced itself faster than a butterfly sheds its cocoon, actual construction took a good deal longer. Leon spent three full days working on preliminary sketches and another two tracing and cutting the patterns for the arms, legs, torso, and head. Once that was done, he drew up a list of materials.

Most of the items he needed— panty hose, cloth, yarn, eyes— came from Miss Hagmeyer's supply cabinet. But there were a few things Leon couldn't track down at school, and that's where Maria came in. She located all the hard-to-find stuff, like the special flexible wire coat hangers he used to make the animile's bones.

For six days Leon sewed like a demon. He had never worked so hard or cared so much. His effort was fueled by excitement, worry, determination, and Poore Brothers Salt & Cracked Pepper Kettle-Cooked Potato Chips (part of the April shipment from the Worldwide Chip of the Month Club).

And with that effort came a new sense of confidence. Leon discovered that his fingers behaved themselves in ways they hadn't when he was blindly following worksheet directions. Independence and conviction made the seven stitches of virtue easier to execute. In fact, Leon mastered every one, including the pesky overcast stitch needed when finishing off seams after the animile had been stuffed.

FIFTEEN

The Spitting Image

eon cut the loose threads from the last seam of his master piece and emerged from the back room behind the reception desk. He was bleary eyed but proud. Perching his completed animile below the ALL PETS WELCOME sign, he said, "Hey, Mom. What do you think?"

Emma Zeisel's jaw dropped. "If *that* isn't a master piece worthy of a master, I don't know *what* is!"

"Really?"

"Really! Let 'em try and say you lack fine motor skills now! Heck, you've got Rolls Royce motor skills!"

"Well, we'll find out in two weeks—at Carnival. That's when the Hag tells me if I pass."

"I wouldn't wait, sweetie," said Emma Zeisel. "Showing Miss Hagmeyer the master piece early might put her threats to rest."

Leon took his mom's advice. The following morning he left for school with his master piece snugly secured inside one of Frau Haffenreffer's pastry boxes. The choice of carrying case wasn't all that smart.

"No, it's *not* dessert," Leon had to tell Napoleon and P.W. and Lily-Matisse and everyone else who saw him clutching the tantalizing box. But despite the constant pestering, he refused to lift the lid. He wanted to show Miss Hagmeyer first.

Leon tried to catch her at check-in, but that plan was stymied because of a fire drill. He decided to take another stab after dismissal, when he could display the master piece more privately.

For the rest of the day the pastry box didn't leave Leon's sight.

He grasped it between his knees while practicing a Gregorian chant in music. He cradled it in his lap throughout art class, as he worked on his knight's costume. He even clung to the box during a pit stop at the boys' room, where he awkwardly squeezed it under his arm while taking care of business.

Lily-Matisse and P.W. cornered Leon during recess.

"C'mon," said P.W. "Best friends don't keep things from best friends. Show us what's in the box."

"I don't want to jinx things," said Leon.

"Just a quick look," Lily-Matisse pleaded. "We won't touch. Crossmyheart."

"After school. I *swear* you guys will be the first to see the thing once I get the Hag's okay."

"Thanks a bunch," said Lily-Matisse.

"Yeah," said P.W.

Leon felt guilty. "Okay," he said at last. "A peek—but just a quick one." He lifted the lid.

Lily-Matisse's eyes widened, and P.W. cried, "Whoa! Gruesome!"

The last class before dismissal was PE.

One hour to go, Leon told himself as he entered the gym. The wait was giving him butterflies.

"Coach," he said. "Can I sit out? I've got a stomach-ache."

"Sure thing," Coach Kasperitis told him. He knew Leon was no faker.

So while the rest of the class did laps and vaulted the pommel horse, Leon watched from the bleachers, the pastry box wedged safely between his knees. After ten minutes of warm-ups, the coach blew his whistle and shouted the single most potent word in the English language.

"DODGEBALL!"

"What type, coach?" P.W. yelled.

"Team Multiple!" the coach cried back. "You and Lumpkin to choose sides."

P.W. immediately turned to the sidelines. "Hey, box boy! Get over here!"

Leon hesitated.

"C'mon! I *need* you."

Leon waffled a bit before abandoning his precious cargo to join P.W.'s team.

Once the class was divided up, the coach walked onto the court carrying three spanking-new Rhinos. "Can anyone here tell me the object of dodgeball?" he asked.

"Elimination," a few kids called out.

The coach bent down and positioned the balls along the centerline, then stood up and cupped a hand around one ear. "Ex*cuse* me?"

"Elimination!" a few more kids called out.

"Say again?"

"ELIMINATION!" the whole class screamed.

"Right," said the coach. He settled his substantial rump on the top row of the bleachers, not far from Leon's pastry box, and gave a mighty blast on his whistle.

The fourth graders charged the Rhinos.

Plommm! "Missed!" *Blamm!* "You're out." *Boing!* "Gotcha!" *Zuftt!* "Missed me by a mile!" *Zzam! Wooomp!* "Busted, dorko!"

"Hey, Lumpkin!" the coach yelled from his perch. "Clean up your language! No trash-talking in my gym!"

The field of battle thinned pretty quickly. An unlucky ricochet—*pang!*—caught P.W. in the leg. A sneak attack from the flanks—*paff!*—winged Lily-Matisse.

When the clock ran out, only Lumpkin and Leon remained alive. A chant rose up from the sidelines: "Suh-din death! . . . Suh-din death!"

The chant grew louder: "SUH-DIN DEATH! . . . SUH-DIN DEATH!"

The coach blew on his whistle. "Go for it!" he cried.

"Yoo-hoo, Sir Panty Hose," Lumpkin said menacingly moments after the coach extended the game. "Get ready to be crowned!"

"Dream on," Leon replied.

The coach again shouted down. "Guys! You know the rules. No teasing. No taunting."

Lumpkin turned to the coach, as if to apologize, then whipped around and launched a ball, hoping to catch Leon off guard. His cheap shot failed. Leon darted out of the way.

A defensive pattern quickly emerged. Leon held on to one ball, and Lumpkin held on to another. Only the third and final ball moved between them.

Neither Leon nor Lumpkin was willing to find himself empty-handed.

But then, two minutes before the end of the over-time round, Lumpkin aimed a shot at Leon's backup ball and hit it with such force that both Rhinos bounced off the back wall and returned to Lumpkin's side.

A collective groan rose up from the sidelines, followed by the kind of somber, respectful silence that accompanies an execution.

Lumpkin, now in possession of all three balls, made Leon zigzag, lurch, duck, and jump with a series of fake throws. Throughout it all, Leon stayed alert. He wasn't about to fall for the slow ball/fast ball combo that had nailed him in the past.

From the bleachers P.W. suddenly screamed, "*Sidewinder!*"

But the warning came too late. Lumpkin had already recoiled and released his patented low-flying missile.

A split second later, the missile smacked Leon in the stomach with a brutal POCK! He ignored the searing pain. Only one thing mattered—catching the ball before it touched the ground.

The Rhino rebounded against his knee and sailed upward.

Leon stretched his arms forward and dove like a champion swimmer. At the very moment he felt the sandpapery texture of the Rhino against the tips of his fingers, the hard, smooth surface of the gym floor began burning the skin off his elbows and knees. But when at last the Rhino stopped defying gravity, it did so in Leon's battered hands.

He had caught the ball, which meant he had won the game and Henry Lumpkin had lost it!

The bleachers erupted in cheers. P.W. was the first to reach Leon and offer congratulations. "You pulpified him!" he cried.

"No such word," said Lily-Matisse, arriving a few seconds later. "Puréed him, maybe. Or made Lumpkin Pumpkin Soup out of him, but—"

Leon, still panting, cut them off. "Keep . . . your . . . voices down. . . . He . . . might . . . hear."

Lumpkin was standing all alone twenty feet away, scowling at his spare Rhino as the magnitude of the upset slowly penetrated his stegosauruslike brainpan.

Bruised and scraped though he was, Leon nevertheless approached his defeated archenemy. "Good game," he said, extending his hand. "That last toss really did a number on me!"

Lumpkin rejected the handshake and reached for the Rhino, angrily whipping the ball at the leather pommel horse on the far side of the gym. It hit the grip of the vaulting apparatus and ricocheted toward the bleachers, knocking Leon's pastry box into the air.

The box went in one direction, the contents in another.

Leon broke free of his friends and sprinted for the bleachers. By the time he got there, it was too late. Coach Kasperitis had already reached through the bench slats and retrieved the exposed master piece.

"Geez, Zeisel!" the coach gasped. "Did you *make* this?"

"Yeah," Leon said, out of breath.

"Amazing!" said the coach. "This is major-league work, kiddo. I mean it."

"Let's hope Miss Hagmeyer thinks so," Leon said.

"Are you kidding me?" said the coach. "She'll *have* to. I mean, what choice does she have? This doll, it's . . . well, it's her spitting image!"

SIXTEEN

A Supernatural Occurrence

The coach was right. Leon's master piece *was* the spitting image of Miss Hagmeyer. Everything on the doll matched its model perfectly. The long black cape. The black dress. The slightly droopy stockings the color of cooked liver. The pair of black lace-up boots that Leon tied just right—with double rabbit ears, plus the safety knot Miss Hagmeyer always added for good measure.

But far more extraordinary than the clothing was the expression on the doll. Leon had captured Miss Hagmeyer with eerie precision. The narrow skull. The pursed lips. And, of course, the eyes. All four of them—the dull ones set deep into the head of the doll, plus the glass pair clasped onto the cape.

Even the doll's hair, fashioned out of ordinary black yarn, looked like the shiny helmet of possibly fake hair on the head of the original. The coach lifted the yarn and revealed the doll's ears.

"You got the gnarls *exactly*!" P.W. said admiringly.

Leon smiled. "The lobes still need some work," he said humbly.

"How'd you think this up?" Lily-Matisse asked.

"Miss Hagmeyer kind of gave me the idea."

The coach shook his head. "I knew this kid was a champ. I *knew* it. And it's like I tell all you guys at the start of every season. Passion and practice. Combine the two, and you'll make magic every time."

Fear of flunking also helps, Leon said to himself.

Antoinette Brede pushed to the front of the growing crowd. "Where'd you get those boots?" she asked jealously.

"My friend Maria found them for me. There was a doll convention across the street from my building."

"She get you the hair, too?"

"No, I made the hair. It's yarn and shellac. I tested real hair, but it didn't look right."

"That's because the Hag wears a wig," said Lily-Matisse.

"We don't know that for sure," said P.W.

"Do, too. My mom *heard* her adjusting it."

Leon smirked. "Did it sound like this?" He grabbed a hank of the doll's hair and gave it a gentle tug.

Sccritchh!

"Velcro!" cried Lily-Matisse.

"Pretty slick," P.W. admitted. "But it still doesn't prove that the Hag's hair is fake."

After the bell rang and the crowd around Leon began to thin, Lumpkin approached him.

"Hey, Leon. Sorry about being such a spoilsport."

"No problem," Leon replied suspiciously. It was the first time he could recall Lumpkin using his actual name.

"Here, you'd better take this." Lumpkin handed Leon the smashed pastry box. "I found it near the water fountain."

"Um, thanks." Leon eyed Lily-Matisse and P.W. Understanding his cue, they headed off to find the coach, who was rounding up Rhinos at the far end of the gym.

"Can I see this dolly everyone's so wild about?" Lumpkin asked.

Leon froze. Now he *knew* something was up. "I don't think there's enough ti—"

Lumpkin yanked the animile out of Leon's hands and raced off.

"Hey! Give that back!" Leon yelled, running after him.

Lumpkin scrambled up to the top of the bleachers. When Leon confronted him, he was all set to toss the doll into the rafters.

"Stop!" Leon cried.

Lumpkin paused to draw out the agony. That's when he noticed the coach's pickle jar resting a few feet away. "Well, well," he said as he reached for the jar.

"No!" Leon screamed.

Lumpkin tucked the doll between his knees and unscrewed the jar lid.

Leon made a heroic lunge for the master piece, but Lumpkin scooted out of the way just in time. Leon took a nasty tumble. His foot went through a gap in the bleachers, and his ankle got twisted (that, in addition to the already scraped elbows and knees).

Wounded and helpless, Leon repeated his plea. "Stop. *Please!*"

Lumpkin smiled maliciously. Then, with terrifying calm, he tipped the jar and dribbled some of the tarry brown teacher's spit directly onto the master piece.

"Poor Sir Panty Hose," he said. "His master piece is all stained. Now he won't be able to hand it in."

"Give it back!" Leon cried.

"Sorry, no can do. You know what the Hag says about everything having its place." Lumpkin drew back his arm like a spear thrower. "Say good-bye to your—"

Thhhwomp!

A dodgeball smacked against the wall.

"LUMPKIN!" Coach Kasperitis hollered from across the gym. He was flanked by P.W. and Lily-Matisse. "You've got to the count of three to give Leon back his whatchamacallit. And if you don't, son, you're going to find out—*painfully*—how I made the all-star team two years running."

Lumpkin glowered at Leon, then grudgingly relinquished the doll.

Leon grabbed it and limped out of the gym.

By the time dismissal rolled around, Leon's ankle was throbbing, his knees and elbows were burning. His morale was battered, his animile damaged.

Sitting at his desk, Leon inspected the master piece. Spit had soaked through the cape and the dress, penetrating deep into the doll's panty hose–stuffed core.

One might think that the black cloth would have hidden the stain. But it didn't. A horrible blotch discolored a large expanse of torso. Lumpkin was right. There was no way the doll could be submitted in its current condition.

Maybe Maria can help, Leon told himself. She had all those special cleansers back in Housekeeping. Her Poop-B-Gone had worked miracles after a cheetah had an accident near the key rack. Maybe the stuff removed teacher's spit, too. It's worth a try, Leon concluded.

In the meantime, he did what he could to limit permanent damage. Not wanting to touch the spit directly, he rubbed the tarry blemish with the hand of the doll, failing to realize that his intervention would only spread the stain more.

As Leon brushed, the doll gave off a slight warmth. Then, for the briefest moment, a tiny sparkle of light seemed to enter the doll's dull eyes.

Leon stopped rubbing.

Giggles suddenly spread through the room. At first Leon thought he'd been caught cleaning the doll. But to his considerable relief, Miss Hagmeyer hadn't heard him and none of his classmates were looking toward the back of the room.

He returned his attention to the stain. But as soon as he did, more laughter erupted. He looked up and saw Miss Hagmeyer acting *very* oddly, even by her standards.

She was stony faced, as if in a trance. Yet she appeared to be strumming an imaginary guitar. Her gestures so startled Leon that he again stopped rubbing the stain. The moment he did, Miss Hagmeyer stopped flailing her arm and regained her normal expression. It was as if master piece and master were playing a game of Simon Says.

No way, Leon told himself. Not possible. Definitely not possible.

He decided to run a test.

"Leon says, 'Lift up your arms,'" Leon whispered to himself as he raised the arms of the doll. He watched and waited.

Within seconds Miss Hagmeyer was lifting *her* arms!

"Leon says, 'Lower your arms,'" Leon murmured, releasing the arms of the doll.

After a brief pause, Miss Hagmeyer flopped *her* arms to her sides!

Leon's heart began to race. Could his doll be controlling his teacher?

A more challenging test was in order. But what?

Leon initially decided to make Miss Hagmeyer stick her finger in her ear. But as he brushed back the doll's hair, he changed his mind. Here was a unique opportunity to resolve a dispute that had been lingering since the very first day of school.

Though getting the right hold proved tricky, Leon eventually managed to curl the tiny fingers of the masterpiece around its black yarn wig.

He did his good-luck squinch and cluck, then gave the wig a quick firm tug. A faint, scratchy sound of Velcro could be heard at the back of the room.

Sccritchh!

Leon watched his teacher closely. For a moment, he was concerned she might have heard the scratchy noise coming from his desk. But her hypnotic gaze quickly told him she had other things going on inside her head—and *above* it. . . .

A second sound, exactly like the first (only much, *much* louder) suddenly erupted at the front of the room. *SCCRITCHH!*

An eerie silence filled the room. Everyone was shocked by the sight of Miss Hagmeyer's exposed scalp, with its sparse outcroppings of snow white hair and the three strips of patented adhesive glued down in a perfect row.

Leon immediately let go of the doll. Once he did, Miss Hagmeyer awoke from her trance. Seeing her wig in her hand, she instantly turned the color of a red marking pencil.

"Class dismissed!" she yelled, fleeing from the room as her students began to squeal.

SEVENTEEN

Important News

Leon stumbled down the school steps with the master piece pressed against his chest. The powers of his doll so flustered him that he had fled the classroom nearly as fast as Miss Hagmeyer. In the race to escape, he had left his backpack behind.

Out on the street, he squeezed the doll tightly and stared fiercely at its features. How, he asked himself, could a spit-stained clump of cloth and panty hose *control* the actions of a teacher?

An ambulance siren prompted Leon to loosen his grip. As the ambulance zoomed by, he imagined the lifeless body of his bony, bald fourth-grade teacher strapped to a gurney inside. Could squeezing the doll squeeze the life out of the *real* Miss Hagmeyer? Suppose his careless clench had crushed her rib cage? Suppose his breathtaking power was exactly that— *breath taking*! Could he get sent to jail? And if so, what would he get sent to jail *for*? Telepathic suffocation?

Questions kept popping into Leon's head. What had activated the power? How long would it last? Had anyone seen what he'd been doing at the back of the room while the Hag was performing in the front? He didn't think so. And even if someone had turned around, it wouldn't have mattered. He'd kept the doll hidden under his desk.

A familiar voice pierced his panicked thinking.

"Hey."

Leon swung around. He was relieved to see Lily-Matisse. "Hey," he said.

"You tore out of class so fast, you forgot this." Lily-Matisse handed him his backpack.

"Thanks," said Leon. He quickly shoved the master piece inside.

"Can you *believe* what happened?"

Leon gave a distracted nod.

"What's got into you?" said Lily-Matisse. "You're acting weirder than the Hag—and that's saying something."

Before Leon could answer, P.W. bounded down the steps. "What do you mean, what's got into him? The Hag, obviously. She's wigged him out."

"Very funny," said Lily-Matisse. "And by the way, P.W., you owe me an apology. I *told* you that hair of hers was totally one hundred percent fake."

"Technically speaking, the Hag does have *some* hair," said P.W. "I saw a few strands."

"That's not the point," said Lily-Matisse.

"Fine," P.W. grumbled. "But I'll tell you one thing." He bent down and grabbed a sneaker strap. "From now on, this will always remind me of her." He gave the strap a yank.

Sccritchh!

"Stop it, P.W.!" Lily-Matisse cried.

P.W. turned to Leon for a reaction, but Leon had more pressing matters to consider. He had to figure out if his backpack now contained a time bomb or a treasure.

P.W. suspended the sneaker sonata and stood up. "Earth to Leon, Earth to Leon. Come in, Leon."

"I—I—" He was having a hard time threading words together.

"Spit it out," said P.W.

Leon grimaced. That was the *last* expression he wanted to hear.

"Don't push him," said Lily-Matisse protectively.

"It—It was *me!*" Leon blurted out.

"*What* was you?" said P.W.

"What happened—*inside.*" Leon tugged on his hair. "I did that to the Hag. *Me!* I wigged *her* out!"

Lily-Matisse and P.W. traded looks.

Leon was all set to spill the beans when a car horn intruded. Napoleon waved from the street.

"Hey, can you guys come over to the hotel?" Leon asked urgently. "I've got some important news."

The Trimore, with its unusual guests and on-site bakery, was an attractive after-school destination under normal circumstances. The added promise of important news only made his proposal more appealing.

"Definitely!" said P.W.

"Sure," said Lily-Matisse.

The hotel lobby was even more of a zoo than usual when Leon and his two friends pushed through the revolving door.

A tropical bird congress was leaving at the very moment the editorial board of *Weasel Weekly* was checking in. Squawks, honks, and coos (from the birds) competed with screeches, trills, and chirps (from the weasels).

"Hey there, kids!" Emma Zeisel yelled as she raced by with a broom raised over

her head. "Sorry. Can't stop. Red-billed toucan on the loose."

The fugitive guest dive-bombed a weasel before flapping back toward the reception desk.

Leon coaxed Lily-Matisse and P.W. into the coffee shop with the promise of his news (and some Haffenreffer dough balls). He sat down on one side of a booth and gave his friends the other.

"Okay, so what's so *important?*" P.W. said impatiently.

Leon looked around the coffee shop to make sure no one could hear. "Before I start, I want the pledge."

"Which one?" said Lily-Matisse, between bites of a dough ball.

"The crossmyhearthopetodiestickaneedleinmyeye pledge."

"But you *hate* that one," P.W. reminded him, fiddling with a glistening black toucan feather he had found in the lobby.

"Yeah, well, I've changed my mind."

After Lily-Matisse and P.W. swore the needle oath, Leon said, "And just so you know, if either of you *does* blab . . . the needle that does the sticking will be as long as the Hag's—and rusty."

"Sheesh, what's up with you?" said Lily-Matisse. "We get the idea."

Leon took a breath. "All right, Lily-Matisse— remember when your mom fought with the Hag at the Cloisters?"

"Hard not to," said Lily-Matisse. The memory clearly embarrassed her.

"Remember how she said something about a piece of cloth springing to life when stitched with passion?"

"Mom's *always* saying junk like that," said Lily-Matisse.

"Well, it's *not* junk. What she said is true."

"For like the ten millionth time, what are you *talking* about?" said P.W.

Leon took a moment to collect his thoughts. "Right. Here goes. When the Hag pulled the wig off during dismissal, you know why she did it? She did it because *I* pulled off *my* wig—well, not my wig, obviously, I mean my master piece's. *I* caused all the weird stuff the Hag did in the classroom—*all of it!* The strumming and the arm raising and the wig removing and the—"

"Slow down," P.W. interjected. "You're saying *you* made the Hag rub her stomach?"

"Yup," said Leon.

"Maybe she has a rash," Lily-Matisse conjectured.

"Lots of teachers scratch themselves," said P.W.

"This is *different*," Leon sputtered. "I did tests. The Hag raised her hands because I raised the doll's hands. And what about the hair? How do you explain *that*? How many teachers rip the hair off their heads?"

"You're telling us your doll has magic powers?" P.W. asked.

"You got it," said Leon.

Lily-Matisse and P.W. both burst out laughing.

"I'm *serious*."

P.W. gave Lily-Matisse a sidelong glance and twirled the toucan feather in circles near his ear. "I think our friend's gone totally bonkers."

"All those stitch counts must have pushed him over the edge," said Lily-Matisse. "The Hag's gotten to him."

"Wrong!" cried Leon. "It's the exact opposite. *I've* gotten to *her*. She told me to make her a master piece. Well, that's what I did. Only guess what? I'm the master of that master piece. *I* control *her*."

"The doll or the Hag?" P.W. asked.

"*Both!*" exclaimed Leon.

P.W. rolled his eyes. "Give. Me. A. Break."

"You guys don't believe me?"

"N-O," said P.W.

"That goes D-I-T-T-O for me," said Lily-Matisse.

"Okay, Mr. and Ms. Skeptical. I'll show you. Tomorrow. Recess. Meet me at the tree."

The following day at recess, Leon, Lily-Matisse, and P.W. gathered behind the giant maple.

Leon chose the spot because it provided a protected view of the whole playground: the teachers' bench, the jungle gym and jump-rope area, the ball wall, and the foursquare grids.

A creature of habit, Miss Hagmeyer was sitting where she usually sat (on the teachers' bench) doing what she often did (embroidery).

Leon reached for his purple pouch.

"Why did you bring the travel book?" Lily-Matisse asked.

Leon loosened the drawstring and removed his master piece.

"What happened to the pastry box?" said Lily-Matisse.

"Don't you remember? Lumpkin destroyed it with the Rhino. Besides, I can't exactly walk around school with a pastry box. And anyway, the master piece fits better in the pouch, and the pouch fits in my backpack."

"Can we skip the packaging instructions and get on with it?" P.W. said.

"Right," said Leon. He squinched and clucked, took aim, and began working the legs of the master piece.

Nothing happened. Miss Hagmeyer didn't budge.

"I swear it worked yesterday," Leon sputtered.

"Well, it's not working today," said P.W.

Leon flexed the legs of the doll with increasing desperation. Suddenly Miss Hagmeyer put down her needlework, rose up, and walked toward the maple tree.

For a brief, glorious moment Leon thought he had caused her to move. But it soon became clear that Miss Hagmeyer was responding to some jump ropers causing a disturbance.

Leon switched his grip and worked the arms of the doll, rotating them like helicopter blades.

Lily-Matisse abruptly cupped her hand over her mouth, and P.W. blurted out, "Holy mackerel! That thing you're doing, Leon. Keep doing it!"

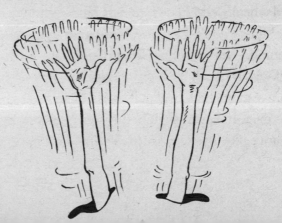

Leon continued to spin the arms of the doll.

"It's like—like she's trying to throw a couple of lassos!" said Lily-Matisse.

"Only without the lassos!" gasped P.W.

"I *told* you the doll controlled her!" Leon said.

"She must have been out of range when she was on the bench," said P.W. "This is incredible!"

"Shush! She might hear us," warned Lily-Matisse.

Leon shook his head. "Don't worry. Her radar doesn't work when I'm doing . . ." He struggled for the right word.

"Dollwork?" suggested P.W.

"Right," said Leon. "Dollwork puts the Hag into a kind of trance." He stopped the arm spinning.

"Keep going," said P.W.

"Cool your jets. My hands are cramping." Leon shook out his fingers and then bent the doll's legs. This time his efforts were rewarded. He was able to march Miss Hagmeyer across the blacktop and over to the deserted jungle gym.

"She's like a zombie!" P.W. cried enthusiastically.

"Maybe Lily-Matisse's right," said Leon. "Lower the volume. I don't want anyone to hear us or see what I'm doing. And it's hard to concentrate with you shouting."

Once Leon had "walked" Miss Hagmeyer to the jungle gym, he again switched his grip. Handling the doll's arms like joysticks, he made Miss Hagmeyer raise her arms straight up in the air.

"Reach for the sky, pardner," said P.W.

Lily-Matisse laughed. "It *does* look like she's been caught in a stickup."

Leon ignored the banter. He was too busy bending legs and curling fingers.

With the doll and teacher properly positioned, he performed a bouncy motion that made Miss Hagmeyer grab for a jungle-gym crossbar a few feet above her head. Then he flexed the doll's arms.

"Ohmigosh!" cried Lily-Matisse.

"Un-freakin'-*believable!*" P.W. exclaimed.

All of a sudden, skinny old Miss Hagmeyer was doing pull-ups like an army cadet. Up-down. Up-down. Up-down.

"Can you make her do those *one*-handed?" asked Lily-Matisse.

"I'll give it a shot," said Leon. He released one of the hands while continuing to pump the other. The result: Miss Hagmeyer performed a series of one-handed pull-ups worthy of an Olympic gymnast.

"How about a loop-the-loop?" P.W. proposed.

"There's no such thing as a loop-the-loop," said Lily-Matisse. An avid gymnast, she knew the proper names for all sorts of moves. "But you could try and get her to do a straddled Tkachev. No, wait, I've got a bet-ter one. A double twisting Yurchenko! And while you're at it, have her finish off with a full-twisting double layout dismount. Now *that* would be something."

"A double twist?" said Leon skeptically. "I don't think so."

"What about a single?" P.W proposed, in the spirit of compromise.

"That's still *way* beyond me," said Leon. "I'd need to practice to do stuff like that."

"Hey, can I give it try?" P.W. asked.

Leon wavered. "I'm not sure that's a good idea."

"C'mon," begged P.W. "I'm a level twelve grandmaster on Turbo Titan VI. If I navigated Zoltan through the Cave of Calamity, I'm pretty sure I can handle a few twists."

Reluctantly, Leon relinquished the doll. The instant he relaxed his hold, Miss Hagmeyer let go of the crossbar. Her lace-up boots landed against the blacktop with a thud, and her arms flapped limply to her sides.

P.W. yanked the doll this way and that, but his efforts had no effect whatsoever. Only Leon could move Miss Hagmeyer.

"What do you think's doing it?" Lily-Matisse asked.

"I bet you it's the spit," said P.W. "Remember the Fun Facts in chapter seven? Spit can contain magic power, just like Monk Jonas said."

"It's probably more complicated than that,"

said Leon. "There's also the Hag's panty hose to consider."

"Well, whatever's doing it, we'd better go easy on the dollwork," said Lily-Matisse. "I mean, *look* at her."

They stared at Miss Hagmeyer as she staggered to the teachers' bench.

"Go easy with the dollwork?" said P.W. "Are you kidding me? Do you realize the power Leon's got?"

The bell rang. Recess was over. Miss Hagmeyer struggled to pull herself up off the bench.

"Maybe Lily-Matisse has a point," said Leon as Miss Hagmeyer teetered toward the door. "We've got to take things slowly. We'll use the doll only when no one's looking. This could get me in serious hot water."

"You're not seeing the possibilities," said P.W.

"We can talk about possibilities at lunch," Leon said, slipping the doll into the pouch. "Meanwhile, no one says anything to anyone. Got it?"

"Got it," said P.W.

"Got it," said Lily-Matisse.

"Good," said Leon. "Now let's do a spit pledge and head in."

Lily-Matisse made a face. "But we already crossed our hearts yesterday, in the coffee shop. Remember?"

"I'm not taking any chances," said Leon. "Spit pledge. Now."

P.W. was perfectly happy to expel a sidewalk oyster, as a tribute to Monk Jonas and the miracle of the doll. Lily-Matisse proved harder to convince. But after some prodding, she made a spitting sound—an indifferent *ptooey*—which Leon, feeling charitable, accepted as legit.

EIGHTEEN

SPLAAAAAT!

After the pull-ups in the playground came the powwow in the lunchroom. As Lily-Matisse, P.W., and Leon snaked through the lunch line, they found it tough to keep quiet. Still, they knew better than to discuss the doll in public. They remained mum until they had set down their trays at an isolated spot behind the steam tables.

"I think your monk guy was right, P.W.," Lily-Matisse said excitedly as soon they were seated.

"You mean Monk Jonas?" said P.W.

Lily-Matisse nodded. "Take a look at this," she said, pulling a Xerox from her backpack. P.W. and Leon read the entry:

> **spitting image** *noun* [From Middle English. See *spite*. Date: circa 14th century] Perfect likeness of a person; exact image. Some experts think that "spit" is a corruption of "spirit." Others maintain that the phrase invokes magic—that armed with a sample of someone's saliva ("spit") and a doll made to resemble the person ("image"), a sorcerer could cast all-powerful spells on a hapless victim.

"Yeah, but we didn't use the Hag's saliva," P.W. said. "It was the coach's."

"I still think it's a combination of things," Leon said. "I bet the panty hose have something to do with the power, too."

P.W. rubbed his hands gleefully. "Well, whatever it is, the master piece is going to make the rest of the school year pretty darn interesting."

Leon chuckled. "What do you have in mind?"

"Can I go first?" Lily-Matisse interjected.

"Be my guest," said P.W.

"Okay, here's what I'm thinking," she said. "We have Leon force the Hag to sew animiles."

"That's not such a hot idea," said Leon.

"Why not?" Lily-Matisse said.

"Well, think about it. If I make the Hag make animiles, my doll has to make animiles, too—*teeny-weeny* animiles."

"Leon has a hard enough time with the normal-sized ones," P.W. noted.

"Any other ideas?" Leon asked.

"Yes, as a matter of fact." Lily-Matisse took a sip of milk. "We wait for the Hag to pick up her stupid chalk holder, right? Then, when she has it in her hand? When she's about to scribble some dumb vocab word on the blackboard? *That's* when you do your magic. I've written a list of things you can make her write."

Lily-Matisse flipped over the photocopy and

propped it between a milk carton and some lime Jell-O.
The back of the sheet said:

1. No more homework for the rest of the year.
2. Animiles are stupid.
3. Henry Lumpkin is a Loser with a capital L.
4. I promise never to argue with Regina Jasprow EVER AGAIN!

"That's some wish list," said P.W. "But you spelled
'capital' wrong."

"Did not," said Lily-Matisse. "You're thinking of
the *other* kind—like in the White House."

"Actually, it would be sweet to see the Hag make a
whole bunch of spelling mistakes," Leon suggested
diplomatically.

"Kid stuff," scoffed P.W.

"So what's *your* plan, Einstein?" Lily-Matisse said.

"You mean plans," said P.W., stressing the last letter. "First, we get the Hag to hose Lumpkin. That's
Plan A."

"I don't follow," said Lily-Matisse.

"Me neither," Leon admitted.

"It's simple," said P.W. "We have the Hag crown
Lumpkin with a pair of her panty hose. You know, give
him a taste of his own medicine."

"Now *that* I'd like to see!" said Leon.

"And Plan B?" said Lily-Matisse.

P.W. grinned broadly and cracked his knuckles. "Plan B is *my* master piece."

"If you do say so yourself," said Lily-Matisse.

P.W. ignored the sarcasm. Pushing aside his lunch tray, he removed a roll of graph paper from his backpack. "I drew this during study break." He unfurled the graph paper and weighed down the corners with milk cartons and juice boxes.

The sketch showed Leon's doll cuffed to the launching arm of a complex Lego contraption equipped with pulleys, chains, and counterweights.

"What *is* that?" said Leon.

"A trebuchet," P.W. answered proudly.

"Never heard of it," said Lily-Matisse.

"Well, you should have. They showed a picture of one in the *Medieval Reader*. Chapter fourteen. 'Arms and Armaments of the Crusaders.'"

"That was extra-credit reading," Lily-Matisse said defensively.

"So what does the thing do?" Leon asked.

"A trebuchet is basically your top-of-the-line catapult," said P.W. "*Highly* popular during the Middle Ages."

"You want to turn Miss Hagmeyer into a human *catapult?*" Lily-Matisse exclaimed.

"You got it," P.W. said.

Lily-Matisse gave him a challenging look. "Why do you need a machine to have the Hag launch stuff? Couldn't we just have her use her arm?"

"That's not as cool," said P.W.

Leon ran his finger over the design. It reminded him of a giant mechanical slingshot, with Miss Hagmeyer serving as the sling. "We could call it the Hagapult," he said, warming to the plan.

"Excellent!" said P.W.

"But we still have to figure out what to load her with," Leon added.

"Not a problem," said P.W. "I was thinking—"

"You guys are totally crazy!" cried Lily-Matisse.

"Hey, keep it down," Leon cautioned.

Lily-Matisse lowered her voice to an adamant whisper. "You *can't* turn the Hag into a giant human teeter-totter. If you got caught you'd get ejected from school!"

"Ejected for making a catapult?" P.W. said. "How perfect is *that?*"

"Ha. Ha," said Lily-Matisse. "I'm serious."

Leon looked over the design. "Maybe Lily-Matisse is right. I don't see how we could use the Hagapult without getting noticed. And it's not like I'm the teacher's pet."

P.W. abruptly smacked the milk cartons off the corners of the sketch. The graph paper curled up on itself.

"Hey, don't take it personally," said Leon, surprised by his friend's cranky response.

"Hag at eleven o'clock!" P.W. whispered urgently, as he shoved the plans into his backpack. Lily-Matisse quickly slipped her photocopy under a lunch tray. Leon dropped the pouch with the master piece into his lap.

Miss Hagmeyer suddenly was looming over them like a giant siege weapon. "You three are sounding awfully conspiratorial," she said. "I couldn't quite make out what you were talking about from the teachers' table. What is it you are hatching?"

"We were just discussing Leon's final project," P.W. said.

Leon kicked him under the table.

Miss Hagmeyer sucked her tooth. "You *still* don't know what you're doing for your master piece, Mr. Zeisel?"

"He's weighing his options," Lily-Matisse said sweetly.

Leon gave *her* a kick.

"Well, I wouldn't weigh them too much longer," Miss Hagmeyer said sternly. "Because *I* have options to weigh as well." She returned to the teachers' table and reclaimed her seat across from Mr. Groot.

"What a witch!" said P.W.

"Look at her, eating that cottage cheese," said Lily-Matisse. "We should use the doll to stick some of that disgusting stuff straight up her nose!"

"That is *so* lame compared to the Hagapult," P.W. said.

"I don't know," said Leon. "At least cottage cheese up the nose gets us instant results."

"Yeah," said Lily-Matisse. "Your thingy would take *years* to build."

"Not true," P.W. said. "Besides, the beauty of the Hagapult is that it's a twofer. It gets the Hag *and* its target."

"What target?" asked Leon.

"What target do you think?" said P.W. He scanned the lunchroom. "Target sighted. Location: thirty feet behind teachers' table."

Leon and Lily-Matisse quickly spotted the telltale fringe of orange hair.

"I still think cottage cheese up the nose is better," said Lily-Matisse.

"And let Lumpkin off the hook?" said P.W.

Leon considered his options. One friend wanted cottage cheese up the nose. The other was pressing for a more ambitious Hagapult contraption that could be aimed at Henry Lumpkin.

Which to choose? Hagapult or cottage cheese? Cottage cheese or Hagapult? Faced with this dilemma, Leon improvised.

"Block my sides," he said.

Lily-Matisse scooted in her chair.

"A little more," said Leon. "I'm still exposed."

"Want me to hold up a tray?" P.W. asked.

"No, that'll attract attention." Leon removed the master piece from its pouch and nestled it in his lap, safely out of view.

Miss Hagmeyer was just bringing a spoonful of cottage cheese to her mouth when Leon started working the hands of his doll like the levers on a crane.

"She's responding!" Lily-Matisse gasped.

"You're in range!" said P.W.

Leon did not speak. He was too busy pulling back and forth on the arms. He made Miss Hagmeyer jiggle a spoonful of cottage cheese inches from her mouth, then had her daub the cottage cheese on the tip of her nose.

Lily-Matisse and P.W. began giggling uncontrollably. Their outburst distracted Leon. He let go of the doll. Miss Hagmeyer snapped out of her daze and promptly used a napkin to wipe off the cottage cheese.

"That's it?" said P.W. disappointedly.

"It will be if you guys keep laughing," Leon said. "I told you in the playground—I need quiet to concentrate." He repositioned his fingers around the head of the doll and revived his efforts. Now each time Miss Hagmeyer attempted to eat some cottage cheese, he pulled her mouth away, instead of her hand. After a few such tests, Leon was satisfied. He reconfigured his grip.

Shifting his gaze between Miss Hagmeyer and the master piece, he tweaked the positions of the arm, hand, and fingers. "P.W.," he said, "you wanted a Hagapult?"

"That's a roger," P.W. confirmed.

"And, Lily-Matisse, you wanted a cottage-cheese assault?"

Lily-Matisse gave an eager nod.

"And we all want to get Lumpkin, right?"

"Oh, yeah," said P.W.

"Definitely," said Lily-Matisse.

"Well, then . . ."

Leon took a moment to fine-tune the angle of the spoon.

"Ready," he said.

He made a few minor adjustments.

"Aim."

He made a few more.

"Fire!"

He gave the doll's arm a decisive flick. . . .
SPLAAAAAT!

"Uh-oh," said P.W.

"You missed Lumpkin!" exclaimed Lily-Matisse.

"And hit Groot!" said P.W.

Leon groaned. "I can *see* that."

All three of them looked on as Mr. Groot blurted something at his presumed attacker.

Leon quickly bent the doll's head so that Miss Hagmeyer would turn away without responding.

Mr. Groot removed a shop rag from his pocket and wiped the cottage cheese off his ear. Then, apparently calmed down, he refocused his attention to the half-eaten open-faced grilled-cheese sandwich resting on his plate.

"I don't get it," said Leon. "I aimed perfectly."

"Remember what the coach is always telling us," said P.W. "Passion and practice make magic. Better try again."

"I don't know," said Lily-Matisse. "Maybe once is enough."

"Oh, c'mon," said P.W.

Leon grabbed hold of the doll's arms and shot a second spoonful of cottage cheese at Lumpkin. . . . *SPLAAAAAT!*

"Youch!" Lily-Matisse said.

"Not again!" moaned Leon. He couldn't understand why his aim was so off.

Once more Lumpkin escaped unscathed.

Mr. Groot was not so lucky. Miss Hagmeyer's cottage cheese hit his cheek, slid down his face, collected (briefly) at his chin, and then dribbled onto his shop smock, just above an oval patch that said MR. GROOT.

"He is *not* looking happy," P.W. observed with a smirk.

Lily-Matisse said, "Would *you* be happy if you got smacked in the face with cottage cheese?"

"Twice!" P.W. noted enthusiastically.

Leon was so annoyed by his misfire he didn't think to let go of the doll.

This oversight had significant, unexpected consequences. Mr. Groot was about to demand an explanation from Miss Hagmeyer. But he stopped short when he observed her pointing a discharged spoon straight at his head. It was clear he thought Miss Hagmeyer was taunting him, using the utensil to say "Gotcha!"

This misinterpretation prompted a change in Mr. Groot's normally mild demeanor. He again wiped the cottage cheese from his face, picked up his half-eaten open-faced grilled-cheese sandwich, looked Miss Hagmeyer straight in the eye, paused momentarily to take aim, and returned fire.

Regrettably, Mr. Groot's marksmanship was just as bad as Leon's. The half-eaten open-faced grilled-cheese sandwich missed its target and instead grazed the left shoulder of Mr. Rattles, an upper school English teacher.

Although the half-eaten open-faced grilled-cheese sandwich didn't make much of a mess when it winged Mr. Rattles, it did cause him to flinch. And in flinching, Mr. Rattles dropped the sandwich *he* was eating— a piping hot Sloppy Joe. It landed facedown on his (soon piping hot) leg.

Once Mr. Rattles had stopped howling and jumping up and down, he grabbed a bowl of lime Jell-O, leaned over, and deposited its contents on Mr. Groot's head.

After that, nature took its course. A full-scale all-out take-no-prisoners food fight erupted in the Classical School lunchroom. And it was the teachers—the *teachers*! —who had started it. (Or so it appeared.)

Leon, P.W., and Lily-Matisse sought refuge behind the steam tables.

"So much for keeping things quiet," said Leon as a hamburger bun bounced into his lap.

P.W. surveyed the lunchroom through the mists rising from the steam table. "It's just like castle defense in the Middle Ages."

"What are you talking about?" said Lily-Matisse.

"Simple," said P.W. "Take a look out there. There are the launchers and there are the pourers. Only instead of boulders getting tossed from castle walls, it's curly fries and Tater Tots. And instead of molten lead, it's milk and OJ that are poured."

A flying fajita forced P.W. to duck. "And I'll tell you one thing, Lily-Matisse. Your mom is *definitely* a pourer. Check out the salad bar."

Lily-Matisse poked her nose over the top of the steam table and saw Signora Pecora, the Italian teacher, ladling French dressing on Madame Pispartout, the French teacher. Madame Pispartout retaliated with thick gobs of Italian dressing. Suddenly

Regina Jasprow came into view and confirmed P.W.'s observation by squirting
the contents of a plastic ketchup
bottle onto the head of Mr. Joost, the third-
grade teacher.

A piece of chocolate cake caught P.W. in the
shoulder. "Position compromised!" he cried. "Fall
back! Fall back!"

"Where to?" yelled Leon.

"Over there," said P.W. He pointed to a row of
recycling bins.

The three of them zigzagged, under a volley of
chicken fingers and string beans, to the colorful bins, which were located near the
kitchen. P.W. took Mixed. Lily-Matisse
took Cans. Leon hunkered down behind
Plastics. (Thomas Warchowski had already
claimed Paper.)

P.W. peered over his lid. "Incoming!" he screamed.
Seconds later, a barrage of carrots pounded the containers.

"It's the coach!" P.W. cried. "And man oh man, is
he throwing heat!"

"Let's get out of here!" said Lily-Matisse. Using a
bin lid as a shield, she led the retreat into the hallway.

"Things got *totally* out of hand in there," she said.

"Out of hand is right!" said P.W. He imitated the
flicking gesture Leon had used to loft the first fateful
spoonful of cottage cheese.

Leon sighed. "I blew it. I wanted the Hag to nail Lumpkin, but I couldn't aim straight."

"Maybe it wasn't your fault," P.W. said.

"Then whose fault was it?" said Leon gloomily. "I had *two* chances, and I messed up both of them. Lumpkin was only a few feet away from the Hag, and I *still* couldn't hit him."

"Maybe something is disrupting signal reception," said P.W. He fell silent as soon as he made the suggestion. Leon and Lily-Matisse could practically *hear* the cogs turning inside his head.

"*Tests!*" P.W. suddenly blurted out. "We have to conduct tests. Meet me at the tree at recess. I'll bring everything we need."

NINETEEN

Interference

o sooner had the last of the carrots landed than the first of the rumors took off. Everyone was talking about the food fight. Mr. Hankey, the janitor, turned out to be the angriest commentator on the subject. He roamed the halls, mop in hand, grumbling and telling anyone who'd listen, "Next time my lunchroom gets turned into a *launch* room, I'm quitting, you can count on that!"

Principal Birdwhistle expressed her disappointment and outrage differently. She posted a memo.

Everyone ignored it. People were too busy trying to find out who had started the fight. No one seemed to know for sure.

Some thought it was Mr. Groot. Others placed the blame squarely on the wig-topped head of Miss Hagmeyer, since she'd been acting weird all week. A third contingent of rumormongers attributed the food fight to the coach, the ex-pitcher known for his fast-ball.

No one suspected the three fourth graders who met behind the maple tree that same afternoon.

"What's the raincoat for?" Lily-Matisse asked P.W. The sky was slightly overcast, but the chances of rain seemed slim.

P.W. slipped a hand inside his slicker. He withdrew a folded sheet of graph paper and a pencil.

"*Another* invention?" said Lily-Matisse.

"No," said P.W., mildly irritated. He handed the sheet to Leon, who eagerly opened it.

"A map?"

P.W. nodded.

"What's a Prooving Ground?" Lily-Matisse asked, pointing to the title that ran across the top of the sketch.

"That's the phrase NASA uses for a testing facil-ity," said P.W.

"Actually, I think it's sp—"

"The map is of the playground, right?" Leon said quickly, cutting in before Lily-Matisse could correct P.W.'s spelling.

"Affirmative," said P.W. "See, this is where we're standing at right now. And that, right there—that's the teachers' bench. And there's the jungle gym. And the jump-rope area." P.W.'s finger darted about. "I drew the map on graph paper so that we can plot test

results on a grid. It'll make it easier to mark the exact range of the doll's power."

"How do you want to start?" Leon asked.

"First we have to pace out distances," said P.W. "You check how far it is from here to the jungle gym. I'll do the same to the jump ropers." He took a couple of long steps to show Leon the standard unit of measure.

"What about me?" said Lily-Matisse.

"Think you can pace off the distance from the teachers' bench?"

"Of course," said Lily-Matisse. It was her turn to feel annoyed.

The three surveyors parted company and reassembled a few minutes later to share results.

"Forty-seven paces from the jungle gym to here," said Leon.

"Twenty-four from the bench," noted Lily-Matisse. "By the way, the Hag's grading our spelling quizzes."

"How do you know?" Leon asked.

"I saw when I was measuring."

"Guys, can we stay focused?" said P.W. "It's thirty-eight paces from the jump ropers. So figuring three feet per pace . . ." He scribbled a few numbers on the map and drew some dotted lines.

"What's next, Magellan?" said Lily-Matisse.

"We'll start our tests here," P.W. said, tapping a spot on the map. "And move in a few paces at a time."

Leon eased the master piece from the pouch and glanced around to see if anyone was looking. "All clear?"

"All clear," P.W. confirmed.

Leon took a bead on Miss Hagmeyer. She was hunched over a stack of paper. He aimed the doll and slowly lifted one of its arms.

Nothing happened.

P.W. scribbled some notes on the map. "We're too far away," he said, moving three paces closer to where Miss Hagmeyer was seated. "Try here."

Leon joined him at the new spot and again flexed the doll.

"Still nothing," said Lily-Matisse.

P.W. added the new data to the map and continued to close in.

After four moves and four tests, Lily-Matisse said, "I think I saw her twitch."

Leon leaned forward and jiggled the doll.

Miss Hagmeyer noticeably wiggled her bony rump.

"We have liftoff!" P.W. said in an excited whisper. He made further notations before turning to Leon. "Okay, here's the scoop," he said quietly. "By my calculations, you can't be more than about thirty or thirty-five feet away from the Hag. Beyond that she stops responding."

"So now what?" asked Leon.

P.W. again reached into his raincoat. This time he pulled out the black toucan feather he had picked up at the Trimore. He brushed it under Lily-Matisse's chin.

"Stop that, it tickles!" she complained.

"It's *supposed* to," said P.W. "How else can Leon wage a tickle attack?"

Leon's eyes widened. "You mean *on the Hag?*"

"Of course on the Hag," said P.W.

"You'd better be careful," Lily-Matisse warned. "You don't know how she'll react."

"That's the whole point," P.W. said.

Leon took a deep breath and brought the toucan feather against the parts of the doll he guessed would cause the most squirming. Under the arms. Behind the neck.

"She's not giggling," said Lily-Matisse.

P.W. gave a nod. "I bet you the master piece can make the Hag move, but it can't make her *feel.*"

"Makes sense," said Leon. "Dollwork definitely numbs her."

"That would also explain why she has no memory about the stuff she's made to do." P.W. said. He reclaimed the toucan feather and stuck it back inside his slicker. "Time to see if the master piece works through walls."

He pointed to a recessed doorway on the map.

"Leon, hide here and see if you can get the Hag to do a couple of jumping jacks through the wall."

Leon trotted off to the spot P.W. had selected. After flexing the doll so that its legs parted and its hands touched overhead, Leon glanced at the teacher's bench to see if "blind" dollwork prompted Miss Hagmeyer to do jumping jacks.

P.W. gave him the thumbs down.

The news comforted Leon. He no longer had to worry about crushing Miss Hagmeyer unknowingly because of something he accidentally did to the doll.

Lily-Matisse dashed over to the doorway with another piece of P.W.'s testing equipment. "Einstein wants to see if this will work," she told Leon.

He looked at the object in her hand. "A mirror?"

"I'm supposed to hold it up and you're supposed to aim the doll at it," Lily-Matisse explained. "P.W. thinks catching the Hag in the reflection might extend the doll's range."

"You mean like one of those cardboard periscope things?" said Leon. "I guess it's worth a try."

Lily-Matisse ran off to a spot halfway between the recessed door and the bench. She pressed the mirror against her chest and moved it back and forth until Leon could see Miss Hagmeyer in the reflection.

Lining up a bank shot off a mirror was harder than Leon imagined. The slightest movement (by him or by Lily-Matisse) jiggled Miss Hagmeyer out of view.

Eventually he managed to complete a couple of tests, which again turned out negative.

P.W. and Lily-Matisse joined Leon to go over the results.

"The mirror test proves that you can't extend or bend the signal," said P.W. scientifically.

"I guess dollwork needs a straight shot," said Leon.

"That might make my next test a little tough," said P.W. with a cryptic grin.

"Okay, I'll bite. What's the next test?" asked Lily-Matisse.

P.W. scrounged around in the pocket of his raincoat and pulled out a pair of panty hose. "Either of you see Lumpkin?" he asked.

"You're kidding!" said Leon. He understood immediately what P.W. had in mind. "You want the Hag to *crown* him?"

"We never did get a chance to execute Plan A," P.W. noted with barely suppressed delight.

"This is *not* a good idea," warned Lily-Matisse. "Besides, how'll you get Lumpkin and the Hag together?"

"Mr. Dhabanandana!"

Out of nowhere, Miss Hagmeyer appeared.

"Y-y-yes?" P.W. stammered as he shoved the panty hose and map under his slicker.

"Come with me!"

Lily-Matisse and Leon watched helplessly as Miss

Hagmeyer marched P.W. to the teachers' bench, where she flapped a test paper at him accusingly.

"Sorry, guys," P.W. said dejectedly when he rejoined his friends. "Plan A will have to wait. The Hag is pulling me out of recess. I have to go over my spelling."

"That's totally unfair," Lily-Matisse protested.

"Can't you stay a few more minutes?" said Leon.

"No, he cannot!" Miss Hagmeyer shouted from the bench.

After P.W. had headed back to the classroom, Lily-Matisse and Leon ducked into the doorway.

"So now what?" said Lily-Matisse.

Leon shrugged. Running tests without P.W. didn't feel right. "It stinks big time that he gets punished just because he's bad at spelling."

"Nothing we can do about it," Lily-Matisse said.

"Don't be so sure," Leon said. He glanced around the corner at Miss Hagmeyer. She was back to grading papers.

"Do you think you can isolate P.W.'s quiz?" Leon asked Lily-Matisse.

"What do you mean?"

"Can you sweet-talk the Hag and separate P.W.'s spelling test from the rest of the pile?"

"Why?"

"Don't ask why," said Leon. "Just tell me yes or no. Do you think you can do it? For P.W.?"

"I guess I could give it a shot."

Lily-Matisse approached the teachers' bench before she had a chance to get scared.

Leon couldn't hear what she said to Miss Hagmeyer, but he knew it concerned sewing because Miss Hagmeyer put down her grading and reached for the instructional needle in her satchel. She was soon waving the needle in the air like a conductor handling a baton. And as Miss Hagmeyer ran through her "piece"—Leon could tell it was part of her standard repertoire: *Stitches of Virtue, Variation No. 6, "The Overcast"*—Lily-Matisse started nodding as if she had a nervous tic.

What's she doing? Leon wondered.

Lily-Matisse continued to nod, and Leon continued to wonder. Eventually she pointed at the test papers and at the ground.

Leon understood. He grabbed the arm of the doll and jerked it to the side so that Miss Hagmeyer would smack the quizzes to the ground.

Lily-Matisse pounced while Leon held the doll (and Miss Hagmeyer) in place. She quickly gathered up the papers and placed them, in a reorganized pile, back on the bench.

Leon relaxed his grip on the doll only after Lily-Matisse was safely by his side.

"No wonder the Hag went ballistic," she said. "P.W. got a *D–*."

"Did you isolate his paper?" asked Leon.

Lily-Matisse frowned. "Wasn't that what I was *supposed* to do? It's on the top of the pile."

"Nice work," Leon said.

"Whatever you're planning, do it fast. The Hag will re-alphabetize as soon as she sees that the order is messed up."

"She won't while I have my little friend," said Leon. He aimed the master piece at the teachers' bench and started working the limbs.

Miss Hagmeyer snapped into action. With one hand she reached for the quiz that topped the newly ordered stack. With the other she removed the marking pencil tucked into her wig.

"Ohmigosh!" Lily-Matisse blurted out. "You're not going to—"

"Shush!" said Leon.

It took some doing, but eventually he managed to guide the marking pencil to a spot just inches above the D–. (The grade was a cinch to spot. Miss Hagmeyer had circled it twice and had underlined it for good measure.)

Leon forced Miss Hagmeyer to lower her pencil to the surface of P.W.'s quiz. Then, with a single downward stroke, he upped his friend's grade from a D– to a D+.

It wasn't a big improvement, but it would have to do. Telekinetic grade tampering demanded a lot more agility than a pull-up or a wig yank, since it required the use of a tool.

Unfortunately, P.W.'s good fortune didn't last. As soon as Leon let go of the doll, Miss Hagmeyer erased the downstroke.

The D+ was a D– once more.

"Doesn't look like your nimble fingers are going to change *her* mind," said Lily-Matisse.

"We'll see about that!" Leon said defiantly. He downstroked the hand of the doll a *second* time, forcing Miss Hagmeyer to *re*-revise P.W.'s grade.

The D– went back up to a D+.

"Amazing," said Lily-Matisse as her eyes pingponged between doll and teacher.

But she spoke too soon.

Miss Hagmeyer *re*-re-revised the grade to a D–!

So began a curious display of hand-to-hand combat in which the hands of the two combatants never actually touched.

D+ . . . D– . . . D+ . . . D– . . . D+ . . . D– . . .

And then disaster struck.

Leon made his fifth (or was it his sixth?) downstroke and waited for the minus sign to turn into a plus. Yet for some reason Miss Hagmeyer did not respond.

He tried again and waited. The grade remained unchanged. Miss Hagmeyer refused to budge.

"Get closer," Lily-Matisse advised.

Leon moved in and flicked the arm of the doll, still to no effect. Miss Hagmeyer had clearly regained control of her body. Within seconds she was re-alphabetizing the quizzes.

"Try the legs," said Lily-Matisse.

Leon moved one leg of the doll, then the other. "I've lost control!" he cried. "I've lost control!"

Miss Hagmeyer abruptly turned toward them.

"Be quiet," Lily-Matisse said in an urgent whisper. "She'll hear you."

For the remainder of recess Leon flexed the limbs of his master piece, hoping to revive the magic. But he couldn't.

The doll was powerless and so, it appeared, was Leon.

TWENTY

A Problem . . . and a Solution

It was at pickup, while everyone was standing on the school steps, that Leon and Lily-Matisse updated P.W. about the doll's malfunction.

"I'm getting *nothing*," said Leon.

"No response at all?" asked P.W.

"None," Lily-Matisse confirmed.

"Everything was working fine," said Leon. "Then about five minutes after the Hag sent you inside— *whammo!*"

"Maybe it's a range issue," P.W. suggested. "How far away was the Hag when the power died?"

"Probably around ten feet," said Leon.

"Fifteen, tops," Lily-Matisse said.

"So that's not the problem," P.W. concluded. "What about the sight line?"

"The sight line was fine," said Leon. "I had a clear shot."

"We'll find a solution," said Lily-Matisse, doing her best to sound hopeful.

Leon scoffed. "A solution? *How?* By waving some magic wand?" He reached into his pouch and retrieved the master piece. "*This* was the solution. *This* was the magic wand. And now the magic wand is broken!"

"Hey, don't get all snippy," said Lily-Matisse. "I'm just saying there's got to be a solution of some kind."

"Have you checked the doll thoroughly?" P.W. asked. "Maybe some of the stitching got loose."

Leon lifted up the arms and inspected the seams. He did the same with the legs. Then he scanned the cape and dress, the boots and the wig. There were no loose threads. Nothing seemed out of place.

In fact, the master piece was looking pretty good— the spit stain was beginning to fade.

Well, that's something, he told himself. At least I'll be able to submit the doll for final inspection. Then, all of a sudden, he cried out. "Hey, wait a minute! That's it!"

"What is?" said P.W.

"What Lily-Matisse just said!" Leon answered.

Lily-Matisse gave him a puzzled look. "What did *I* say?"

"You said I needed a solution!"

"Well, du-uh," said P.W.

"Don't you get it?" Leon exclaimed. "The solution *is* the solution!"

"What are you babbling about?" said Lily-Matisse.

"I'm *babbling* about the spit stain," said Leon.

"What about it?" said Lily-Matisse, mildly disgusted.

"Feel it!" said Leon, thrusting the doll toward her.

She recoiled. "No way, José!"

Leon turned to P.W. "Feel it!" he begged.

P.W. reluctantly reached over and prodded the spot. "It's dry, so what?"

"Don't you see?" said Leon. "*That's* why I lost power. It's just like a TV remote. The master piece needs recharging. Only instead of a couple of replacement batteries, it uses . . . " He waited for the lightbulbs to go on in his friends' heads. When they didn't, he gave the stained stomach a dramatic tap.

"Teacher's spit!" P.W. yelled at last.

Antoinette Brede, who was waiting for her limousine, heard the outburst. She turned and stared.

P.W. lowered his voice to an exuberant whisper. "Leon, you're a total, absolute genius! All we have to do is snag some of the coach's spit and we'll be all set!"

"Gross!" said Lily-Matisse. "There is *no* way I'm going anywhere near that goop. I like the coach and all, but that's, well . . . *forget* it!"

"C'mon," urged P.W. "It'll be cool. We'll be like those elite special ops forces that get dropped behind enemy lines."

"Let's not get carried away," said Leon. "We sneak into the gym. We take some spit. We leave. It's not *Mission: Impossible.*"

"Good," said Lily-Matisse. "If it's that easy, then you guys won't need me."

"You can't bail on us now," said Leon. "We're a team."

"How about being a lookout?" P.W. suggested.

"Would I have to get near . . . *it?*" Lily-Matisse asked.

"Of course not," Leon said reassuringly.

Lily-Matisse mulled over the proposal and agreed to be part of the team, just as Napoleon pulled up in front of the school.

They struck at noon the very next day, while Coach Kasperitis was at lunch. Lily-Matisse and P.W. posted themselves at the double doors of the gymnasium entrance while Leon slunk inside. He padded across the wooden floor, scanning the bleachers.

A door hinge creaked. Leon froze.

"Limburger, Egghead, Oreo, Noogie—do you copy? Over?"

Leon whipped around and spotted P.W. talking into his fancy wristwatch.

"Confirm your position. Over."

"Knock it off," said Leon. "Just guard the door and holler if you see someone coming."

"That's a roger," said P.W.

"Do me a favor," Leon said. "Skip the spy stuff. Do *you* copy?"

"Oh, all right," said P.W.

Leon tiptoed into the coach's office and peered about. The place was a sty. There was sports equipment scattered everywhere. A catcher's chest protec-

tor, a sack of Rhinos, dirty
socks, a leather pom-
mel horse . . .

Leon focused
his search on
the desk, which was piled high with catalogs,
late slips, whistles, and baseball memorabilia.
After a bit of scrounging, he located the pickle jar
underneath an ancient pitcher's mitt.

He set to work, removing an empty juice bottle
from inside his shirt and placing it alongside the pickle
jar. Before performing the actual transfer, he made a
tiny pencil mark on the side of the jar, at the level of
the spit.

Once that was done, Leon unscrewed the jar and
poured a small amount of the thick brown liquid into
the juice bottle. He then added a little more, figuring
it made sense to take extra, just in case. Cupping the
partially drained pickle jar with both hands, Leon
moved toward the water fountain at the opposite side
of the gym, like an explosives expert handling nitro-
glycerin. . . .

DRRRRINNNNNG!

The fourth-period bell so startled him that he
almost jumped out of his skin. Spit sloshed about
inside the pickle jar.

Should have sealed it! Leon told himself angrily.

He got lucky, however. Nothing spilled.

As Leon was refilling the jar at the water fountain, the door hinge creaked again.

P.W. stuck his head into the gym. "Spitter in view! *Repeat.* Spitter in view! Estimated time of arrival—*one minute!*"

Leon started to run to the office but soon realized he had to slow down. With the jar filled almost to the brim, the risk of spilling spit on the floor was even greater than before.

By the time he set the pickle jar down on the coach's desk, he was a nervous wreck. In fact, Leon was so discombobulated that he covered the juice bottle with the baseball mitt and shoved the pickle jar under his shirt, instead of the other way around. He was halfway out the door before he realized the mix-up, and only corrected it seconds before the coach entered the office.

"Looking for me, champ?"

"Y-yes," Leon stuttered.

The coach gave him a sideways glance. "You okay?"

"Um, fine."

The coach unzipped his tracksuit and sat down behind his desk. "What can I do you for?"

"Just came by to"—Leon racked his brains for a reason to justify his presence—"to say thanks for saving my master piece."

"Don't mention it, kiddo. Like I told you, it's major-league work." The coach pointed at the bulge under Leon's shirt. "Have you shown that to Miss Hagmeyer yet?"

Leon nearly had a heart attack until he realized that the coach was mistaking the juice bottle for his master piece. "Um, no—ah, not yet," he stammered.

"Well, when you do, I'm betting that doll of yours will really move her," said the coach.

"Move her?" Leon gave him a funny look. "I hope so."

Coach Kasperitis grabbed the pickle jar from underneath his mitt.

Leon suddenly noticed something troubling—the spit and water in the jar hadn't blended. In fact, the liquids had formed two distinct layers, like oil and vinegar. Leon held his breath and listened intently as the coach turned away to satisfy an urge. He heard the distinct, hollow sound of the metal jar lid rubbing against the glass, followed by an unmistakable *pffut!*

If the coach was going to notice anything fishy, it would be right now, Leon told himself—at the very moment the saliva was hitting the water.

It felt like an hour had passed before Leon registered the second scrape of metal on glass. He sighed deeply when he realized his spit theft had escaped detection.

The next phase of the restaining process took place at the maple tree, during recess. Leon proudly showed off the bottle to his friends.

"Gross," said Lily-Matisse.

"Excellent," said P.W. "This can't fail. Dried-out teacher's spit was *definitely* the problem. I did some research. The Crusaders moistened wounds with saliva to make them heal faster."

"Well, I did some research, too," said Lily-Matisse. "Spitting images sometimes need a magic spell to work. I made one up, just in case."

"Great," said Leon. "You can say it after we've applied the spit."

"Can we get going?" P.W. said impatiently.

Leon nodded and asked Lily-Matisse if she'd remembered to bring the drop cloth.

"Of course," she answered, producing a scrap of purple paisley left over from her falcon animile.

Leon tapped the ground with his sneaker. "Set it down here," he said.

As Lily-Matisse smoothed out the drop cloth, Leon turned to P.W. "Did you find an applicator?" he asked.

"That's a roger," said P.W.

"What'd I say about the dumb lingo?" said Leon.

"Fine," P.W. grumbled.

"Okay then," said Leon. "Let's see if the solution is the solution to our problem." He kneeled next to the drop cloth and placed the juice bottle on top. He then removed the doll from the pouch and gently rested it on its back.

"Anyone snooping?" he asked.

"That's a nega—" P.W. caught himself. "You're fine," he said blandly.

Leon reached for the bottle, giving it a vigorous shake before unscrewing the lid. He placed the lid next to the doll. "Applicator," he said decisively, holding out his hand.

P.W. slapped the requested instrument into Leon's palm.

"A pencil?" said Lily-Matisse. "Even a straw would have been better than that."

"Couldn't find any clean straws, okay?" said P.W. defensively. "And I didn't want to use a germy one from the trash. There's no telling what a milk molecule could do."

"And you think that's safer?" said Lily-Matisse. "News flash, P.W.—pencils have germs, too."

"Guys!" said Leon, shooting them both looks. He gingerly dipped the eraser of the "applicator" into the bottle and dabbed some spit on the spot of the original stain.

"All done?" said P.W. eagerly.

"I think so," Leon answered.

"What about my incantation?" said Lily-Matisse.

"Oops, sorry. Go ahead."

Lily-Matisse paused for a moment. "Drab, dribble, pour . . . Make Miss Hagmeyer soar!"

"Not bad," said Leon.

"Thanks," said Lily-Matisse.

P.W. abruptly resealed the bottle. "Can we hurry up?" he said. "I'm dying to see Lumpkin's face when the Hag crams a pair of panty hose over his head!"

"That's not going to happen," said Lily-Matisse. "Birdwhistle caught him trying to sneak out of school. He's birdcaged."

"All day?" asked P.W.

"No, but every single recess until Carnival," said Lily-Matisse.

"Guess we'll just have to concentrate on the Hag," said Leon, not sounding all that upset.

As they headed toward the recessed doorway to conduct further tests, P.W. couldn't resist whispering into his wristwatch. "Target in view. *Repeat*. Target in view!"

"Knock it off," Leon said. He took up position in the doorway. "Right," he said, sneaking a peek at the teachers' bench.

Miss Hagmeyer was, as usual, sitting alone. Less usual, however, was the object she had in her bony hands.

Leon said, "Lily-Matisse, take a look and tell me if that's what I think it is."

Lily-Matisse peered around the corner. "It is! It's the black SOV binder that my mom told me about!"

Leon reached for his doll. "I'm going to make her bring it to us! Maybe we'll finally find out who she's selling our animiles to!" He leaned forward and worked the legs to pull Miss Hagmeyer toward them. But the doll's eyes didn't sparkle, and its body didn't warm up. Nor did any telltale changes take place at the teachers' bench.

Lily-Matisse whispered, "What's wrong?"

"Beats me," Leon said. "It should've worked. I dabbed the exact same place Lumpkin did."

A frustrated silence filled the doorway.

"Maybe *that's* the problem," P.W. said all of a sudden. "You *dabbed*. Lumpkin *poured*."

"So?" said Leon.

"So . . . maybe the spit works like yeast," said Lily-Matisse.

"Right," P.W. continued. "Not enough and your cake won't rise! We've got to add more spit!"

The second time around, Leon didn't bother with the applicator or the drop cloth or the incantations. He pulled out the juice bottle right where he was standing, unscrewed the lid, and gave his doll's midsection a good thorough soaking.

Twenty-One

2520

Leon, Lily-Matisse, and P.W. ran halfway across the playground before they realized their plans had hit yet another snag.

The teachers' bench was empty.

They scanned the schoolyard. Basketball court . . . foursquare boxes . . . wall ball . . . jungle gym . . .

"There!" cried Lily-Matisse. "Over by the jump ropers!" They dashed toward their target and stopped just out of range.

Miss Hagmeyer was standing before a circle of girls, two of whom were linked by a pair of motionless jump ropes that reminded Leon of a suspension bridge.

"Repeat it!" Miss Hagmeyer barked at Antoinette Brede. "Do you hear me, Miss Goody Two-Shoes? Repeat that vile song!"

Leon and his friends traded looks. When was the last time Antoinette had gotten in trouble?

"I'm *really* sorry, Miss Hagmeyer," she whimpered.

Miss Hagmeyer kicked a jump rope with her boot. "Did I *ask* for apologies, Miss Brede?"

"No, but—"

Miss Hagmeyer cut her off. "No ifs, ands, or buts. You have a decision to make. Either you recite those horrid lyrics, or you join Mr. Lumpkin in Principal Birdwhistle's office."

Faced with that choice, Antoinette began to sing, and as she did, the two "enders" started twirling their ropes to mark the musical beats.

"Miss Suzie had a steamboat, the steam—"

"Stop!"

The ropes and the singing halted.

"That was *not* the version I heard," Miss Hagmeyer said angrily, tapping her ear.

Antoinette started over.

"Miss Hagmeyer had a hairpiece, the hairpiece had a smell,
The hairpiece went to heaven, Miss Hagmeyer went to—
HELLO operator, please give me number nine,
And if you disconnect me, I'll stitch up your—
BEHIND the 'frigerator, there was a piece of glass,
Miss Hagmeyer sat upon it, and cut her bony—
ASK me no more questions, tell me no more lies,
The boys are in the girls' room, sewing up their—
FLIES are in the meadow, bees are in the park—"

With each new line, Antoinette had a harder and harder time holding back the tears.

Miss Hagmeyer didn't seem to care. "Keep going!" she commanded. "I distinctly recall two more stanzas!"

"Do something," Lily-Matisse whispered.

"Yeah, start the retest pronto," said P.W.

"I can't," Leon told them. "Not here. We'll get caught."

P.W. glanced around the playground. He pointed. "There! By the wall ball!"

They rushed over and positioned themselves along the concrete wall, out of view. Leon placed himself between his friends and watched Miss Hagmeyer watching Antoinette choke her way through the song.

"Coast's clear," Lily-Matisse confirmed.

Leon unpouched his resaturated master piece.

"Prepare for retest," P.W. said.

Leon began bending the arms and legs of the doll.

"The spit's working!" exclaimed P.W.

"The Hag's responding!" Lily-Matisse whispered excitedly.

Leon didn't need their status reports. He could feel the heat emanating from deep inside the master piece. And though he couldn't see the doll's face—it was, after all, aimed away from his—he was sure its eyes were now sparkling.

"What are you going to do?" Lily-Matisse asked.

"Watch," said Leon. He guided Miss Hagmeyer toward the spinning ropes.

The teacher's trancelike approach so startled Antoinette that she stopped singing.

Leon began bending and unbending Miss

Hagmeyer's legs to the rhythm of the spinning ropes.

"D-d-do you want to jump rope, Miss Hagmeyer?" Antoinette stammered.

Leon gave the doll's head a couple of swift nods.

"Are you sure you can handle this?" Lily-Matisse asked him.

Leon nodded his own head, all the while monitoring the action taking place some twenty feet away.

"Just remember to keep the Hag in the center of the ropes," Lily-Matisse advised. "That's where the loop is the biggest."

"Thanks," said Leon. He fiddled with the doll until Miss Hagmeyer's shoulder lined up with the shoulder of the nearest ender. It took especially fine motor skills to synchronize the movements of the doll with the motion of the ropes, which were spinning in opposite directions, like eggbeaters.

"Her cape!" Lily-Matisse warned urgently. "It'll get caught."

Leon deftly wedged the doll's miniature cape between its fingers so that Miss Hagmeyer would do the same.

"Nice move," said P.W.

Leon had no time for compliments. "Lily-Matisse, tell me when I can send her in."

"Are you sure about this?" she again asked.

Once more Leon nodded.

Lily-Matisse stared fiercely at the spinning ropes.

"Get ready . . . three . . . two . . . one. . . . *Now!*"

Her timing was perfect. She helped Leon inject Miss Hagmeyer into the vortex without a snag.

"Incredible!" said P.W. "She's doing it!"

"You mean *we're* doing it," Lily-Matisse said proudly.

News traveled quickly. Students rushed from all over the playground to see Miss Hagmeyer's command performance.

"Way to go, Miss Hagmeyer!" yelled Thomas Warchowski. "Can you show us some tricks?"

Leon tried to get Miss Hagmeyer to say no. But given all the motions he had to sustain—the pumping, the swaying, the clamping, the flexing—he couldn't spare the fingers needed to make the doll shake its head.

"Can you do mumbles, Miss Hagmeyer?" Antoinette asked tentatively.

The crowd started to chant, "Mumbles! Mumbles! Mumbles!"

"What are mumbles?" Leon asked Lily-Matisse.

"That's when you put both feet together and do super-small hops." She demonstrated the move.

Leon decided to give it a shot. He brought the doll's legs together and bent them up and down as the ropes *thwapped* against the ground.

"That's it!" said Lily-Matisse.

"Sweet!" said P.W. "She looks like a tap-dancing bat."

"What about doing some kick-bys?" Antoinette said more daringly.

Leon again turned to Lily-Matisse. "*Kick-bys?*"

"Don't sweat it," said Lily-Matisse, gaining confidence. "You can handle 'em. All you have to do is kick one foot out and one foot in, one foot out and one foot in . . . "

"Like this?" said Leon as he worked the doll.

"That's pretty good," said Lily-Matisse. "Just try to keep her legs down."

Leon made some adjustments.

"Perfect," said Lily-Matisse.

But no sooner had Leon mastered kick-bys than someone shouted out a new challenge: "Peppers!"

"*Peppers?*" Leon gasped.

"Peppers are about speed," Lily-Matisse explained. "Keep your eye on the enders."

As predicted, the two girls holding the ropes started to pick up the pace.

"Bring it on!" Leon said gleefully as he moved the doll faster and faster. Soon he was shaking his masterpiece like it was a can of spray paint. As a result, Miss Hagmeyer bounced her feet on and off the asphalt with the speed of a sewing-machine needle.

"Sizzlers!" someone cried.

"What's a sizzler?" said Leon, his worry returning.

"Beats me," Lily-Matisse told him.

Leon was trying to figure out how to respond when

Miss Hagmeyer began crossing and uncrossing her legs.

"I-I-I'm not d-d-doing that," he sputtered.

"What do you mean?" asked Lily-Matisse.

"The Hag—she's making those moves by herself!" Leon held the doll stock-still to prove his point. "*See?*"

"Freaky," cried P.W. "The Hag's flying *solo!*"

Leon now felt as baffled as the rest of the crowd. Can the Hag actually be doing sizzlers *on her own?* he wondered. Did I shake loose some ancient double Dutch skills?

Leon sensed something different about his teacher. But what? He looked at Miss Hagmeyer closely.

Was it her ears? Nope, it wasn't her ears. This Leon easily confirmed, since all her antic jumping exposed them on each descent.

Was it her mouth? No, it wasn't her mouth either. It remained as pinched as it had been the very first day of school.

What about her panty hose? Her boots? Her dress? Her cape?

No, no, no . . . and no.

How about the eyes on her cape?

Again, no.

What about her own eyes?

Yes!

Normally so dull, Miss Hagmeyer's eyes now appeared to be *sparkling.*

"Show us some pop-ups!" Antoinette shouted.

Her request broke the spell. The inexplicable performance ended as abruptly as it had begun.

P.W. sounded the alarm when a jump rope grazed Miss Hagmeyer's wig. "She's losing control!"

"I'm on it," said Leon. He quickly trained his master piece toward the tottering teacher and smoothed out the faltering footwork.

"That was weird," said P.W.

"Nice save," said Lily-Matisse.

Leon shrugged off the compliment. "Tell me what pop-ups are," he said with renewed determination.

"Basically, you've got to make the Hag go as high as possible," Lily-Matisse explained.

Without missing a beat, Leon sprang Miss Hagmeyer three feet off the ground.

"You call that a pop-up?" teased P.W. "C'mon, let's see the Hag catch some *serious* air!"

Leon took the bait. He intensified his doll-enhanced gravity-defying exertions until it looked as if someone had slipped an invisible trampoline under Miss Hagmeyer's feet.

A new chant started up from the sidelines.

"Higher! Higher! Higher!"

Leon eventually brought Miss Hagmeyer nearly face to face with Henry Lumpkin and Principal Birdwhistle, both of whom were gawking out the second-floor window of the Birdcage.

"Uh, Leon," said Lily-Matisse nervously. "You'd

better bring her down. I think Birdwhistle and Lumpkin can spot us from up there."

"In a sec," said Leon. "I want to try one last thing."

Lily-Matisse persisted. "I'm telling you, Leon. We'll get caught."

"No way," said P.W. "They're totally fixated on the Hag. What's the move, Leon?"

"Remember the first time I showed you what the doll could do? On the jungle gym? You guys wanted me to have the Hag finish up with a special twist."

"A full-twisting double layout dismount," said Lily-Matisse. "You're not going to try *that*, are you?"

"No," said Leon. He smiled. "That's too simple."

To appreciate fully what Leon did next, it might be helpful to know something about freestyle double Dutch jump roping. As tricks go, a single complete gyration—commonly known as a 360—is considered a beginner's move. A *double* twist—a 720—is obviously somewhat harder. But it's only when a jump roper can master a *treble* twist—a 1080—that the professionals start to watch.

A *quadruple* twist will generate endorsement offers from sneaker manufacturers and soft-drink companies. (Simply *calculating* its numerical name—1440—is impressive.)

This brings us, inevitably, to the Holy Grail of double Dutch moves: the *quintuple*. If you can perform a quintuple twist then chances are your name is Hideyuki Tateda, since Hideyuki Tateda is the only person that the *Guinness Book of World Records* has ever recorded completing a five-twist turn.

It's too bad Leon didn't think to call the Guinness folks. If he had, a judge could have been on hand to document what happened next.

Watching the motion of the ropes with laserlike concentration, Leon pressed the master piece gently between his palms. At just the right moment, he snapped one hand forward and the other hand back and spun the doll like an old-fashioned top.

Once . . . twice . . .

By the time Leon caught the master piece, Miss Hagmeyer didn't just break Hideyuki Tateda's record. She *obliterated* it, executing *seven* full airborne revolutions, an unprecedented move called (mathematicians will confirm) a 2520.

TWENTY-TWO

SOV

Miss Hagmeyer wasn't the only one upended by Leon's dollwork. His playground stunts made the whole school flip. Nothing that nimble, nothing that wild had ever taken place at the Classical School—*ever*!

After Miss Hagmeyer landed back on earth, she teetered through the entryway and disappeared. The fourth graders all rushed back from recess to find their classroom empty. The only trace of Miss Hagmeyer was a note scrawled across the blackboard. It said:

Work on your master piecer until dismissal.

"Did the Hag write that?" Lily-Matisse asked Leon.

"Had to be her. Who else splits the word 'masterpiece' in two?"

"Well, her penmanship's looking awfully sloppy," said Lily-Matisse.

"Gee, I wonder why?" said P.W. "Maybe she's feeling a little dizzy. She probably went to see the nurse."

"Nah," said Lumpkin, who had overheard P.W.'s remark. "The Hag's with Birdwhistle. I saw her when

I left there." He snickered. "Now it's *her* turn to get caged."

Mr. Hankey, the janitor, stuck his head into the classroom and said, "Principal Birdwhistle told me to keep an eye on you wisecrackers. If I have to pick up one single solitary spitball after school, it'll be detention for the whole lot of you from now until Carnival."

"We would *never* waste spit on spitballs," said P.W.

"That's enough out of you, Mr. Wisenheimer," the janitor said. "Settle down and work on your projects."

Once Mr. Hankey had left the room, Leon, Lily-Matisse, and P.W. regrouped under the countinghouse tally.

"I *still* can't believe that final trick you did," P.W. marveled.

Lily-Matisse shook her head in awe. "Six complete turns!"

"Seven," P.W. corrected. "And *man*, that Velcro holds! I thought for sure the Hag's hair would whip off when she was spinning around!"

"*Fake* hair," said Lily-Matisse.

"Which was the toughest move?" P.W. asked.

Leon had to think a bit before he could answer. "Probably getting the Hag inside the ropes—that and the mumbles."

"The mumbles *were* amazing," said Lily-Matisse.

"Kid stuff compared to the pop-ups and the twists,"

said P.W. He grabbed Leon's hands. "These should be registered with the police as dangerous weapons."

Leon couldn't stop himself from smiling. "Well, you guys helped—a lot."

"Come off it," said P.W. "You were the one at the controls. Plus, when the doll lost power, who came up with the solution to the solution? That was a *very* sweet save."

"Maybe," said Leon. "But it was your idea to up the dosage, P.W. You were the one who realized that the spit worked like yeast. And you were key, too, Lily-Matisse," Leon added, sensing she was feeling left out. "I couldn't have handled those rope tricks without you. You were amazing!"

Lily-Matisse blushed. "Could you believe Antoinette's face when Miss Hagmeyer started doing kick-bys?"

P.W. began singing quietly. "Miss Hagmeyer had a hairpiece. . . ."

Lily-Matisse joined in. "The hairpiece had a smell. . . . "

Leon turned the duet into a trio. "The hairpiece went to heaven, Miss Hagmeyer went to—"

Leon suddenly stopped. "Where *does* the Hag go?"

"I can think of a few places I'd *like* her to go," said P.W.

"I'm serious," said Leon, turning pensive. "Where is she taking our animiles?"

"SOV," said P.W. "Wherever that is."

"Exactly," said Leon.

"What are you saying?" Lily-Matisse asked.

Leon took a deep breath. "I'm saying the fun and games are over. I'm *saying* we've got to find out where the Hag sells our animiles. And I'm *saying* we've got to get them back."

"Get them back?" said Lily-Matisse skeptically. "How? When it comes to animiles, she's totally unbendable."

"Oh, really?" said Leon. He patted his pouch. "She didn't seem unbendable during recess."

P.W. started giggling. "Awesome! Leon frees the animiles!" he said. "It'd be kind of like that palace revolt we just read about."

P.W. ran to his desk and returned with his *Medieval Reader*. "Hold on a sec." He flipped through the pages. "Here we go." He located the passage in question: "'And so did the knights errant liberate the prisoners and restore to them their livestock that were seized'— that's animals, by the way." He skimmed a bit more. "Blah, blah, blah. 'And then did the valiant knights hang the evil malefactor and spit upon the wicked tyrant's dismembered body.'"

"Let me see!" said Lily-Matisse. She grabbed the reader and scanned the section P.W. quoted. "It doesn't say anything about spit. You just stuck that in."

P.W. shrugged.

"I'm not sure about the hanging and dismember-ment," said Leon. "All I want to do is find out where the Hag is selling the animiles."

"Then we should probably get our hands on her SOV binder," said P.W. "It'll tell us where she's doing business. It might even give the name of the slimeball who is buying our stuff."

"But we don't know where she keeps the binder," said Lily-Matisse.

"Of course we do," said P.W. He glanced over at the metal cabinet with the heavy brass lock.

"You want us to break into the Hag's cabinet?" asked Lily-Matisse, aghast.

"No," P.W. said calmly. "I want the *Hag* to break into the cabinet for us." He turned to Leon. "Think your master piece can handle it? All you have to do is get the Hag to use her key. It would be a lot tougher if we were dealing with a combination lock."

Leon considered—and quickly rejected—P.W.'s proposal. "It's way too risky. Everyone would be watch-ing her—and me."

Lily-Matisse nodded. "Your desk is right next to the cabinet. You'd get nailed for sure. And you don't want that to happen—especially not so close to final inspection." She flicked the Sir Leon spool on the nearby chart. "One animile to go. And then that's it."

"*If* I pass final inspection," said Leon.

"You'll pass," said Lily-Matisse. "You've doubled your s.p.i.s."

"Yeah, but they're still borderline," said Leon.

"None of this gets us any closer to finding the animiles," said P.W.

Leon glanced around the room. He noticed that the finished bin was empty and that a bulging black plastic bag was now resting under the blackboard. "Looks like the Hag is about to make another delivery," he said with a meaningful smile.

When Napoleon arrived at pickup that day, Leon rushed over. "Bonjour, Monsieur Napoleon."

"Bonjour, Monsieur Leon. And how was your day?"

"A nine and three quarters," Leon said.

Napoleon smiled. "Is that so?"

"Yes," said Leon. "Want to turn it into a nine and *four* quarters day?"

"But of course," said Napoleon. "I would be very pleased to make your day perfect."

Leon waved Lily-Matisse and P.W. over to the cab. After a quick round of hellos, he said, "Guess what the Hag is about to do, Napoleon."

"What, Monsieur Leon?"

"She's about to sell some of our animiles. We want to tail her."

"Tailor?"

"He means, follow her," explained Lily-Matisse.

"Oh," said Napoleon. "Well, for that I am at your service." He opened the back door of his cab and tipped his imaginary hat.

The three detectives and their private driver had idled by the curb for about ten minutes when P.W. suddenly blurted into his wristwatch: "Grinch alert. Grinch alert."

Leon leaned toward the window and, spotting Miss Hagmeyer, said, "Suspect observed."

"Which one is she?" Napoleon asked.

"She's kind of tough to miss," said P.W. "Black cape, black boots, black hair."

"Plus she's got a black garbage bag slung over her shoulder," Leon added.

Napoleon spotted Miss Hagmeyer and he stepped on the gas.

"Don't get too close," Lily-Matisse warned. "The Hag's got super-sensitive hearing."

Napoleon lifted his foot off the pedal and trailed from a safe distance. Twice he almost lost her. Once when a large van cut him off. The second time because some tourists—all sporting leather shorts, green felt hats, and open-toed sandals with thick white socks—blocked the taxi at an intersection. Fortunately, Miss Hagmeyer's hunched silhouette was easy to relocate.

Eight blocks from the school, she pushed through the side entrance of a dilapidated warehouse.

Leon grabbed for the taxi's door handle.

"Wait!" said Napoleon.

"But we'll lose her!" said Leon.

"We promise to stick together, Monsieur Napoleon," Lily-Matisse said, in her most responsible-sounding voice.

"And we'll return straightaway," said P.W.

"How soon is straightaway?" Napoleon demanded.

"Ten minutes," said Leon. "Fifteen, tops."

P.W. made a show of pushing some buttons on his fancy wristwatch. "See. I've set my alarm."

"If you are not back in—"

But the backseat of the taxi was empty before Napoleon could finish his threat.

Leon was first through the warehouse door. P.W. followed. Lily-Matisse brought up the rear. They tracked Miss Hagmeyer to an elevator. A sign that said OUT OF ORDER forced her to take the stairs, so they did the same.

And so began the game of cat and mouse—a very quiet game of cat and mouse since the mouse (Miss Hagmeyer) had hearing that more closely resembled a bat's.

On the third floor, she stopped to catch her breath.

One flight below, Leon bent over the banister and peered up through the open stairwell. As he did, his sneaker made a faint squeak.

"Who's down there?" Miss Hagmeyer barked.

Leon flattened himself against the stairwell wall and waited until the clack of boot heels confirmed that Miss Hagmeyer had continued her climb.

She paused again, on the fourth floor. This time Leon was more cautious when he leaned out. He observed her boots, the hem of her cape, and the bottom of the garbage bag.

"Do you have a shot?" P.W. whispered.

"I think so," Leon whispered back. "But I want to wait until she's with the toy thief."

"I'd test the doll now—while she's resting," P.W. said in a low voice. "You don't want any nasty surprises when you're face-to-face with her and that slimeball."

"It makes sense," Lily-Matisse whispered.

Leon leaned over the banister and lined up a shot. He gave a couple of yanks on the doll. Nothing happened.

"Can't get the right angle," he said.

P.W. grabbed on to Leon's jacket so that he could lean out further. "Try now."

Leon stretched over the banister and extended his view: boots, body, bag . . . hand.

Bingo! With her bony fingers now visible, Leon hoped he could make Miss Hagmeyer release the bag of animiles.

But it wasn't Miss Hagmeyer who lost her grip. It was P.W.

Leon stumbled forward—over the open stairwell. To catch his balance, he had to grab the
banister, and to grab the banister he had to let
go of the doll.

It plummeted down the stairwell.

For a terrifying moment Leon waited to see if
Miss Hagmeyer would hurtle herself down to the
bottom of the stairs, forced to a grisly death by
the accidental release of the magic master
piece.

"I'm warning you," Miss Hagmeyer yelled
moments later—from above—"Whoever's
following me, I'm armed." It was clear
from the the eerie shadow on the wall
that she was gripping her instructional
needle like a dagger.

"You stay here," Leon whispered to Lily-Matisse
and P.W. "I'll go get the master piece." In the time it
took for him to rush to the bottom the stairwell,
retrieve the doll, and return, Miss Hagmeyer had continued on to the fifth floor, where she pushed through
a fire door.

Though winded, Leon followed close behind.
When he poked his head onto the landing, he
found himself in the middle of an ill-lit hallway with countless doors running off in both directions.

Miss Hagmeyer was nowhere to be seen.

"Think . . . we should . . . split up?" he asked, still breathing heavily.

"Negative," P.W. said.

"Not happening," said Lily-Matisse.

"So . . . then . . . which way . . . do we go?"

"Left," said Lily-Matisse.

"Right," said P.W.

"Shoot . . . for it," Leon told them.

They did rock paper scissors. P.W. won, so they turned right, inspecting every door they passed. None of the nameplates suggested a company that dealt in stolen stuffed toys.

At the end of the long, grim corridor, Leon peeked around the corner and discovered another corridor, just as long and just as grim as the first. The hunt continued, door by door, corridor by corridor. There was no trace of Miss Hagmeyer.

Then, some twenty feet from the spot where the floor search had first started, they hit pay dirt.

"Ohmigosh!" Lily-Matisse blurted out. "I *knew* we should have taken a left!" The door that prompted her I-told-you-so had the names of four businesses stenciled on the frosted glass.

SURELOCK HOMES

FAWN'S FLORA

DUNROAMIN' REALTY

ROYAL FLUSH PLUMBING SUPPLIES

Taped below the last of those names was a hand-lettered sign written in an all-too-familiar script.

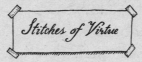

Stitches of Virtue

P.W. pressed himself against the door frame and grabbed hold of the knob. "Cover me," he whispered.

Leon positioned himself ten feet away, with Lily-Matisse directly behind his back. He gave the thumbs-up to P.W. and aimed.

P.W. tried to turn the knob. "Locked," he mouthed silently.

Leon motioned to check again. P.W. gave the knob a more vigorous twist, then rapped his knuckles against the glass.

No one answered.

"We blew it!" Lily-Matisse cried, once it was clear whispering was no longer necessary. "The Hag must have made her delivery while we were going in the _wrong_ direction!"

"At least we've found out what SOV stands for," said Leon.

"What do you mean?" said P.W.

"Look at the door," said Lily-Matisse. "Stitches. Of. Virtue. S-O-V."

"Oh," P.W. said, annoyed he hadn't made the connection on his own.

Lily-Matisse kicked the door in frustration. "We'll *never* get the animiles back."

"Sure we will," said P.W.

"How?" asked Leon.

P.W.'s wristwatch started beeping. It was time to return to the taxi. "I'll show you back at my place," he said.

"Show us *how?*" asked Leon.

P.W. smiled. "You'll see."

TWENTY-THREE
Plan B

P.W. lived in a five-story walk-up that housed his family's Thai restaurant on the ground floor and their apartment at the top. The restaurant was a cozy mom-and-pop operation called the Curried Elephant. It smelled of spices and orange peels and offered fourteen different kinds of curry, though none contained actual elephant.

"What took you so long?" said Ms. Dhabanandana, glancing up from a napkin she was folding into the shape of a tulip.

"We were doing something with Miss H," P.W. told his mother. She gave him a suspicious look, but before she could ask another question, P.W. said, "We're going upstairs."

Once inside the apartment, he guided Lily-Matisse and Leon straight to his bedroom.

"So what's this thing you want to show us?" Leon asked.

"Close my door," said P.W.

As Leon shut the door, P.W. cleared a path through the action figures, trading cards, and game cartridges scattered over the floor. He disappeared under his bed. Moments later, dirty clothes (T-shirts and socks mostly) started flying into the middle of the room.

"I had to hide this," P.W. called out between flings. "My sister is always messing with my stuff." Eventually he reemerged, legs first, grasping an object draped in a towel. "Ladies and gentleman," he announced. "Your attention, please."

"Can we get on with it?" Lily-Matisse said impatiently.

"Fine," said P.W. "Without further ado, I give you . . ." He whipped off the towel. "Plan B."

"The Hagapult!" Leon cried, his eyes widening at the sight of the actual Lego-and-rubber-band contraption proposed, in sketch form, the day of the food fight.

"Care to do the honors?" P.W. asked.

"That's a roger!" Leon said eagerly. He clamped the ankles and wrists of the master piece into the adjustable cuffs of the machine's launching arm. "Fits perfectly," he said. "Let's test her out."

"As soon as I recalibrate the counterweight," said P.W.

"Is all this really necessary?" said Lily-Matisse. "I still don't understand why you need a gizmo to get the Hag to fling stuff."

"I told you before," said P.W. "This is way cooler. Plus it

gives Leon pinpoint accuracy." He began filling a small crate at the front of the device with pennies.

"Why the coins?" Leon asked.

"It prevents tipping when we're in launch mode," P.W. explained.

"You guys are totally nuts!" Lily-Matisse exclaimed, retreating to the bed. "What are you two planning to do when the Hag *catapults* Leon's doll into the finished bin?"

"What are you talking about?" said Leon.

"I'm *talking* about final inspection," Lily-Matisse said. "You do remember that it's this Monday, right? How are you going to use that gizmo if the most important part—the doll—gets tossed into a garbage bag and taken to that warehouse where we should have turned left!"

"Can you give it a rest?" said P.W. angrily. He cocked the launching arm so that the doll bowed backward, head over heels. "Leon has all the ammunition he needs to take care of the Hag—speaking of which . . . " P.W. got up off the floor.

"Where are you going?" Leon asked.

"To get the ammo," he said. "I left it in the kitchen."

The moment P.W. left the bedroom, Lily-Matisse turned to Leon. "You're sure this is a good idea?"

"Why are you so worried?"

"I just told you. Final inspection is coming up.

Plus, there's Birdwhistle we've got to think about. What if she sees that thingy?"

"It's not a thingy, it's a trebuchet," said P.W., returning from the kitchen in time to catch the tail end of the warning. "And when did you get a brain swap with Antoinette?"

Lily-Matisse persisted. "All I'm saying is, strapping Miss Hagmeyer into a harness is risky."

"No, it's not," said P.W. "Not if it's properly loaded. I'll show you." He dumped a collection of small objects on the bedroom carpet. "We've got Legos in two-, four-, and six-notch varieties. We've got one of my dad's famous spring rolls and a fried dumpling—I stuck with the fried because they don't fall apart like the steamed ones."

Lily-Matisse picked up a small plastic doll's head by its long, golden blond hair. "What are you planning to do with *this*?" she asked.

"What do you think?" said P.W.

"You want to use the head of a Totally Hair Barbie for a *cannonball*?"

"Why not?" P.W. said matter-of-factly.

"Where's the rest of her?" Leon asked.

"In my sister's room," said P.W.

"Don't you think she'll miss this?" Lily-Matisse asked, jiggling the head.

"I'm planning to reattach it as soon as we're done," P.W. said.

Lily-Matisse watched in disbelief as P.W. snatched

the decapitated head out of her hand and squeezed it into the sling of the Hagapult.

"Lock 'n' load," he said.

Unfortunately, each time P.W. tried launching the head, its hair got tangled in the mechanism. He switched to the fried dumpling, then to the spring roll, then to the Legos. None of those projectiles worked well either. After a dozen misfires, P.W. started scrounging about for substitute ammo. He tried slinging a plastic cow ("they used cows in the Middle Ages"), a paperclip, a gum ball.

The results were uniformly dismal.

Lily-Matisse eventually grew tired of watching his failures from the sidelines. "Here," she said in a ho-hum way. "Try this." She held out something small and shiny.

P.W. went over to the bed and bobbed the proposed missile in his hand. The weight and size felt promising. "You know," he said, "this might actually work. Thanks."

Despite herself, Lily-Matisse smiled.

"What is it?" Leon asked from across the room.

"A glass eyeball," said P.W.

"I was going to use it on my master piece," said Lily-Matisse, "but it didn't look right. I should have returned it, but I kind of forgot—accidentally on purpose."

"I'm *glad* you forgot—accidentally on purpose,"

said P.W. "What is it? Mountain lion?"

"Close," said Lily-Matisse. "Lynx."

P.W. fitted the cat eye into the sling and reset the arm. He then cranked the doll backward until it was almost upside down. The tiny Victorian boots pointed in the air. The wig of black yarn brushed against the green Lego base plate that kept the mechanism stable.

P.W. was about to fire off the eyeball when Leon gave him a nudge. He understood immediately. "Hey, Lily-Matisse," P.W. called over. "Want to do the honors?"

"You sure?" she said.

"Definitely," said P.W.

She joined her friends on the floor. P.W. explained how the Hagapult worked, then brought his hand over hers to show her how to release the trigger. "When you're ready, let 'er rip," he said, removing his hand.

Lily-Matisse hesitated.

"Go for it," Leon urged.

"That's a roger," she said nervously. She launched the lynx eye. *Thwooosh!*

The sling hurled the glass eyeball with such force that it landed in the fish tank on the far side of the room. *Plink!*

"Yes!" P.W. shouted.

"Ohmigosh!" Lily-Matisse cried.

"Geez!" Leon exclaimed.

A buzzer sounded.

P.W. groaned. "Must be my mom." He went over to an intercom and pressed the button that said TALK. "Yeah?"

"Popcorn walnut, do you copy? Over."

"What is it, Mom?" P.W. said. "We're kinda busy."

"Leon's mother is on the phone. She wants him back home. Do you copy? Over."

Leon joined P.W. at the intercom. He pushed TALK and said, "Ms. D? Can you ask my mom if I can stay another hour?"

There was a long pause. "That's a negative. She wants me to put you in a cab right now. Do you copy? Over."

Leon again pushed TALK. "Ms. D? Can you ask her what's so urgent?"

After another long pause Ms. Dhabanandana said, "Something about an envelope from school. Do you copy? Over."

Leon's legs turned wobbly, his head began to throb.

An envelope! From school!

The news hit him with the force of a Lumpkin sidewinder.

"I bet you it's about the pop-ups," said Lily-Matisse. "Birdwhistle must have spotted us from her window."

"Don't jump to conclusions," said P.W. with a smirk.

"Don't try to be funny," said Leon. "Not now."

"Hey, relax," said P.W. "I'm just saying that if Birdwhistle *did* see us doing something, why didn't she haul us into the Birdcage, along with the Hag?"

"Because that's not how the school does things," said Leon. "Trust me, I know. They keep all the really bad stuff for the envelopes."

He uncuffed his master piece from the Hagapult and returned it to the pouch. Then he dragged himself down to the Curried Elephant. Passing through a field of tulips folded from napkins, Leon said good-bye to Ms. Dhabanandana and hailed a taxi back to the hotel.

TWENTY-FOUR

Another Envelope

Leon's nine-and-four-quarters day was plummeting fast. Nine . . . eight . . . seven . . . He was so worried about the envelope on the ride home, he didn't even think about his taxi-driver collection. The cabby could have come from Akron, Anaheim, or Antarctica. Leon would never know.

He tried to convince himself that the envelope was just a harmless reminder about the upcoming Carnival. (Only two days earlier Principal Birdwhistle had mailed out a memo on the mandatory bluntness of swords.) But that seemed unlikely. His mom wouldn't have called P.W.'s house unless the news from school was major.

Emma Zeisel was pacing back and forth when the taxi pulled up to the hotel. She had the dreaded envelope clutched tight against her breast.

Leon stepped out of the taxi and instantly had his worst fears confirmed. The envelope was an *exact* clone of the one that had torpedoed him the night before school started. It was identical, right down to the blood-red stamp that said CONFIDENTIAL.

"Mom?"

"We'll discuss it in the coffee shop," she said.

Frau Haffenreffer and Maria were seated at the counter as Emma Zeisel guided her son to their usual booth. Napoleon was standing beside them.

"What are you doing here?" Leon asked his friend.

"Your mother wished me to come, Monsieur Leon," Napoleon said as he scootched into the booth beside Emma Zeisel.

Leon couldn't make heads or tails of the situation. All he could do was stare at the envelope, which now rested, accusingly, on the tabletop.

"I've never burdened you with reports from the school before," Emma Zeisel told her son. "Teachers can be such terrible judges of character. Always blowing things out of proportion. But, well, this is different."

She pressed her fingernail against the edge of the envelope and gave it a flick. The envelope sailed across the table and poked Leon in the ribs like a needle.

"Could you read the letter out loud, sweetie? I want everyone to hear."

"*Fine*," said Leon bitterly. He grabbed the envelope and fumbled with the flap.

Was this about getting flunked? Or was Lily-Matisse right? Had Birdwhistle seen him performing dollwork? If Birdwhistle *had* seen him, would he be expelled?

Which is worse? Leon asked himself. Getting left back or getting booted?

"Sweetie?"

Leon removed the single sheet of paper from the envelope. After he squinched and clucked, he read the letter out loud.

THE CLASSICAL SCHOOL

"Where Nimble Fingers Make for Nimble Minds"

Office of the Principal

Dear Ms. Zeisel,

    When we met in my office last fall, I promised I would touch base later in the school year. At the time, there were concerns expressed about Leon's manual dexterity, and it was proposed that we consider allowing him to repeat fourth grade.

Leon stopped reading. They were *allowing* him to repeat fourth grade? That's like saying they were *allowing* him to stick sewing needles under his fingernails!

"Leon?" said Emma Zeisel.

He continued in an unsteady voice.

Since our meeting I have monitored
Leon's work. I am pleased to report that nearly
all of his teachers note remarkable improvement
in his fine motor skills. Only Miss Hagmeyer
has yet to get back in touch with me. (The poor
woman has been under a bit of stress recently.)
However, I have every confidence that she
will concur with her colleagues. In the
meantime I thought you should know that
all indicators point to your son satisfying
the requirements of fourth grade.

Cordially,
Hortensia Birdwhistle
Principal

Emma Zeisel reached over the tabletop and gave Leon a peck on the cheek.

"*Chapeau!*" exclaimed Napoleon, which is how French speakers say "hats off!"

"*Mazel tov!*" said Frau Haffenreffer.

"*Felicitaciones!*" added Maria.

The letter gave Leon some much-needed relief about his teacher. And it was clear Birdwhistle hadn't spotted him, which meant that the secret of the masterpiece was still safe.

Emma Zeisel signaled Frau Haffenreffer, who took her cue and disappeared into the kitchen. A minute later she burst back into the coffee shop carrying a very large platter.

Emma Zeisel said, "The Chip of the Month Club made a delivery today, sweetie. When I saw that shipment of chips and read the letter from school, well, I put two and two together and decided it equaled . . . *surprise party!*"

Leon beamed. It was turning into a nine-and-four-quarters day, after all. He gorged on pastries, potato chips, and praise for nearly an hour before an old concern crept into his thoughts.

Emma Zeisel picked up on her son's agitation almost before he did. "You okay?" she asked him.

"I guess," said Leon.

"What's the matter?"

Leon sighed. "I still have to pass final inspection."

"You will," said Emma Zeisel confidently.

"You don't know the Hag. She could *still* pull a fast one."

"Don't be silly, dear. What did she say about your master piece?"

"Nothing. I never showed it to her."

"Why not?"

"It's just that a lot's been going on," Leon said vaguely.

"Well, I'm sure when she gets a load of your master piece, she'll *flip*."

"We'll see on Monday," said Leon, wondering briefly if he could make his teacher do a somersault.

"Do you have the doll with you?" his mom asked.

Leon nodded.

"Well, show it to everyone—see what they have to say."

Leon unpouched the master piece and propped it on a bag of Hunky Dorys Buffalo Flavor Thick & Crunchy Potato Chips.

Emma Zeisel glowed with motherly pride as Frau Haffenreffer, Maria, and Napoleon oohed and aahed.

Maria poked the stain on the doll's dress. "You want me to take care of that, Leonito?"

"That's okay," said Leon.

"It's no problem. I've got this special solution. It works like magic."

"It's okay, Maria. Thanks anyway."

"Stain or no stain," said Emma Zeisel, "when the Hag comes face-to-face with that doll, she's going to go head over heels!"

"I hope you're right," said Leon.

Emma Zeisel picked up a glass of soda and held it in the air. "A toast," she declared. "To the master pieces we make." She tipped her glass at the doll pillowed on the Hunky Dorys. "And to the masterpiece we're raising." She redirected the glass at her son. "May they both give us joy forever."

Leon turned red. "Thanks, Mom. But I'm not sure about my master piece giving us joy forever."

"Why not?"

"Well, let's say it *does* pass final inspection."

"Which it will," said Emma Zeisel.

"Fine," said Leon. "I still don't get to keep it."

"Nonsense," Emma Zeisel said. "Miss Hagmeyer can't—"

"Mom, listen to me," Leon interrupted. "I know. For a fact. Once the Hag okays an animile, it gets binned, bagged, and sold."

TWENTY-FIVE

Carnival

As school events go, none generated more excitement among the Classical School fourth graders than Carnival. The year-end bash catapulted the normal day's schedule straight out the window, making room for medieval games, medieval foods, and—thanks to Leon—medieval hocus-pocus. He arranged to meet his two friends on the school steps before the start of the special day.

"Where's P.W.?" Leon asked Lily-Matisse when he arrived a few minutes late.

"No idea," she said.

Leon looked around. "Maybe he's testing the Hagapult in the playground. We'd better check."

They searched everywhere. No P.W.

"Now what?" Lily-Matisse asked fretfully.

"The bell's about to ring. Let's wait for him in the classroom."

Leon was the first to enter. "Wow!" he exclaimed the moment he poked his nose inside.

"Mom worked on the decorations all night," said Lily-Matisse.

Leon gazed about. "Wow," he said again.

Gone were Miss Hagmeyer's creepy sewing posters. In their place was a lush medieval landscape with rolling hills that nestled a turreted, crenellated, loopholed castle. "Kind of reminds me of something," Leon said.

"Mom copied it off a painting she showed you guys at the Cloisters," said Lily-Matisse.

"That's right," said Leon. He pointed to a bright yellow sun shining in the corner. "You think she used dried cow pee to paint that?" he asked.

"I doubt it," said Lily-Matisse.

"How'd she turn the windows all red and purple?"

"Mylar plastic. Mom's in love with the stuff."

Leon spotted one element of the room that hadn't changed—the countinghouse tally. He walked over to the chart and plucked the lowest yarn.

"The Hag better pass me," he said adamantly as he watched the Sir Leon spool quiver.

"Why should she pass your master piece . . . of *junk?*" a familiar voice demanded.

Leon turned just in time to receive a thwack on the shoulder with a wooden sword. It was Lumpkin.

Leon eyed the door.

"Looking for the Hag to save you, Sir Panty Hose?"

"No," said Leon, though that was precisely what he was doing. If he could bring Miss Hagmeyer, the doll, and Lumpkin within range of one another he could discipline His Evil Lordship. And who knew? With the proper dollwork, he might even get Miss Hagmeyer to grab her instructional needle and turn the class pinhead into a pincushion!

"Well, well," said Lumpkin. "What've we got in there?" He gave Leon's pouch a poke with his sword.

"None of your beeswax," said Lily-Matisse.

Lumpkin traced the lettering on the purple material with the tip of the blade. "L-E-O-N. Isn't that *cute*."

DRRRRINNNNNG!

"That pouch wouldn't be hiding your master *puke*, would it?" Lumpkin said, ignoring the bell. "I never did get to put that dumb thing in its place."

"Nor will you now, Mr. Lumpkin!"

True to form, Miss Hagmeyer strode into class right on time. "Lower that blade and take your seat *at once!*"

Miss Hagmeyer marched toward the front of the room, shaking her head and muttering under her breath about the kraft-paper landscapes and tinted windows.

"I'm putting everyone on notice," she growled as she hung up her cape. "I have very little patience for carnivals conducted during school hours." She began emptying her satchel but stopped when she noticed an empty desk.

"Where's Phya Winit?" she demanded. "I hope he

isn't using some trumped-up sickness to avoid final inspection."

No one said a word.

Miss Hagmeyer shook her head and went back to emptying her satchel. "Honestly, I don't know why schools squander valuable teaching time on end-of-year festivals. Greek Day. Sports Day. Farm Day. Science Fair. They're all the same. Ridiculous excuses for children to dress up and run around jabbing each other with sharp, pointy objects. Togas and spears. Sweat suits and javelins. Overalls and pitchforks. Lab coats and scalpels.

"And this medieval carnival takes the cake! How much time has been wasted turning out swords in Mr. Groot's woodshop? And why, I would like to know, is the banquet scheduled *before* I complete my inspections? That's not the way it would have happened in King Richard's time, I can tell you that! Banquets are supposed to *conclude* carnivals, not *disrupt* them.

"If I had my way, *this* is the only kind of pointy object that would occupy your fingers and your minds." Miss Hagmeyer held up her instructional needle. "If *I* had my way, you would be making animiles and nothing but animiles. Unfortunately, Principal Birdwhistle has other ideas."

Miss Hagmeyer put down the needle, picked up her chalk holder, and wrote out the Carnival schedule:

Medieval portrait
Tournament joust
Banquet
Final inspection of master pieces

"I want to be clear about this," she said. "As soon as the banquet is over, return here at once. No ifs, ands, or buts!"

"Except for ours," whispered Thomas.

"That is correct, Mr. Warchowski. I expect your miserable medieval rumps in their assigned seats by the time Mr. Hankey rings sext!"

"What's sext?" Lumpkin asked over the giggles of his classmates.

"It's explained in the *Medieval Reader*," Miss Hagmeyer said wearily. "Check in Fun Facts under Canonical Hours. Sext corresponds to twelve o'clock. Midday. High noon."

"I thought nones was noon," said Lily-Matisse.

"Well, you thought wrong," Miss Hagmeyer replied. "Nones is the ninth hour of the canonical day. It rings at three P.M. By which time we will know how many of you have mastered your craft."

Just then, P.W. burst into the room.

Miss Hagmeyer froze him in place with a beady-eyed glower. "So pleased you could join us, Mr. Dhabanandana."

"What did I miss?" said P.W.

"Not final inspection, if that is what you were hoping. In point of fact, what you *missed* was my tirade on the trouble with carnivals. But since that tirade is now over, you must be content with joining the others in preparing for the portrait."

As students were slipping medieval clothes over their modern ones, P.W. rushed over to Leon and Lily-Matisse.

"Bad news," he said. "My sister found her Totally Hair Barbie while it was still, um, totally headless."

"Let me guess," Lily-Matisse said knowingly. "She destroyed your Hagapult thingy."

P.W. nodded gravely. "I got most of it put back together, except for the winch and the rubber band, which the little weasel probably hid. Anyway, that's why I'm late."

"So what do we do now?" Lily-Matisse asked.

Leon quickly took charge. "If Plan B won't work, maybe Plan A will. P.W., are we set?"

P.W. smiled as he reached into the pocket of his blue jeans and pulled out the ragged toe of some really old panty hose. "That's a roger."

"Okay, then," said Leon. "We're in business."

Lily-Matisse gave him a puzzled look. "Are you dealing with Lumpkin or the animiles?"

"Both," said Leon.

"How?" P.W. asked excitedly.

"You leave that to me," Leon said. "Just be ready at

final inspection. When the Hag gets in range, I'll make a sign for you to toss the panty hose on the floor."

"And then?" Lily-Matisse asked nervously.

"And then," said Leon, "I suppose I'll just have to prove to Miss Hagmeyer that I have the discipline and diligence of a master."

A noise in the hallway put an end to the conversation.

Mr. Hankey paraded into the classroom swinging a bell the size of a bucket. "Let Carnival begin!" he declared. "Let Carnival begin!" The janitor glanced over at Miss Hagmeyer. "Everything's all set, Phyllis. Mr. Groot's ready with his camera on the steps of the school."

"Very well," she said with a sigh. "Class dismissed."

"Aren't you coming with us, Miss Hagmeyer?" Antoinette asked as she straightened her tiara.

"No, Your Majesty, I am not," Miss Hagmeyer replied stiffly. "I have my own snapshots to take care of."

Antoinette said, "What snapshots?"

Miss Hagmeyer ignored the question. "You're late," she said, fiddling with the key to the supply-cabinet padlock.

When the fourth graders gathered for the medieval group portrait, they confirmed Miss Hagmeyer's earlier observation. Carnival did indeed celebrate funny clothes and sharp pointy objects.

There were gauzy gowns and daggers, potato-sack tunics and swords, cardboard chest plates and rapiers, plus diamond-patterned tights and suits of sequined chain mail that glittered in the morning sun.

After a good deal of squirming and less-than-noble behavior, the students settled down.

Mr. Groot peered through the viewfinder of his camera and yelled, "Smile and say . . . LUMPKIN!" He suspended his picture taking. "Get over here."

Lumpkin loped down the front steps.

"I *saw* you," Mr. Groot said. "You were about to wallop Leon with that sword of yours. Such behavior violates the code of chivalry."

Lumpkin shrugged. "Whatever."

"Relinquish your weapon," Mr. Groot demanded.

That got Lumpkin's attention. "Why?" he whined.

"Because I wish to see it. Hand it over now." Mr. Groot dug into his pocket and pulled out a quarter. He lined up the edge of the coin with the tip of the sword. "Just as I thought," he said. "You know the rules. Principal Birdwhistle was explicit in the memo she sent your parents. No sword tip is to be sharper than the curve of a quarter. I am confiscating this weapon for the remainder of Carnival."

unacceptable   *acceptable*

quarter

"That stinks," said Lumpkin.

"So does your attitude, which is why you will swap roles with that scullery maid over there."

"But—"

"Do not argue, Henry. If you do, you'll be burned at the stake. Or at the very least sent to the principal's office."

Lumpkin tromped back up the steps in a vengeful rage, which Mr. Groot soon after captured on film. His medieval portrait of Miss Hagmeyer's fourth-grade class included a slingshot-toting master (P.W.), a

pillow-padded monk, a jester, three serfs with black-
ened teeth, a heretic, a bejeweled queen (Antoinette),
a tie-dyed lady (Lily-Matisse), a wizard, a page, a
prince, a pauper, two stable hands, and a cook. Also in
the group were an orange-haired scullery maid bran-
dishing a soupspoon like a battle-ax and a valiant
knight, clutching a purple pouch, staring straight at
the camera with a look of nervous expectation.

TWENTY-SIX

The Joust

As soon as Mr. Groot finished up, the fourth graders zipped toward the gym like eighteen arrows loosed from the longbow of a champion archer. The whole class was keen to see what Coach Kasperitis had planned for the tournament joust.

The coach did not disappoint his fans. He met them wearing a suit of armor cobbled together from old athletic gear. An ancient football helmet—embellished by a feather duster just like the one Maria used at the hotel—covered his head. A catcher's chest protector served as a breastplate. Around his neck he wore the clay jester's-head whistle he had purchased at the museum gift shop the day of the field trip. One of his hands gripped a gleaming shield, which looked suspiciously like the lid of a metal garbage can. The other hand, covered by a pitcher's mitt, grasped a pink foam "lance" more typically found around swimming pools.

"Settle down and listen up, lords and ladies and assorted rabble," the coach shouted through the faceguard of his helmet. "We've got a lot of ground to cover."

"Looks like you're covering a lot of ground all by yourself!" P.W. yelled.

"Knock it off," the coach said with a chuckle. "You know my rules. No teasing, no taunting, no trash-talk." After the laughs died away, he said, "Though it pains me to tell you this, I've been informed by certain so-called experts that dodgeball didn't exist in the Middle Ages."

Boos filled the gym.

"Not to worry," said the coach. "We'll be doing something *almost* as exciting. Does anyone know what that might be?"

"*Jousting!*" everyone screamed.

The coach's helmet bobbed up and down. "Now, before we begin, let's see if you know your stuff. Who can tell me the difference between a joust of peace and a joust of war?"

P.W.'s hand shot up.

"Go for it," said the coach.

"In a joust of war, the lance gets sharpened to a super-deadly point. A joust of peace is a lot tamer. It's about skill, not death."

"And which kind of joust do you think I've planned for you guys?" the coach asked.

"A joust of peace!" the class screamed.

"Bull's-eye," said the coach. He set down lance and shield and went into his office. Through the blinds, everyone could see him pull off his helmet and mitt.

While the coach was busy filling his pickle jar, Lumpkin taunted Leon. "Hey, Sir Panty Hose. Too bad it's *not* a joust of war."

"Just ignore him," Lily-Matisse said.

"I'm not worried," said Leon. "He'll get his joust of war back in class."

The coach reemerged, dragging the pommel horse. Cheers and laughs erupted as soon as the horse came into view. It had a papier-mâché head fitted to one end and a purple tail attached to the other. A coat of chain mail, made from the tops of soda cans, protected the areas in between.

"Mom did that, too," Lily-Matisse told her two friends.

"No kidding," said P.W.

The coach set the horse in the middle of the gym and arranged some floor mats around it.

"Listen up," he said. "The way the joust of peace works is like this. I'll be calling out your names, in pairs. The first name called starts out as Rider. Second name called gets to be Lancer. After sixty seconds, Rider and Lancer swap places. The scoring is simple. Only Lancers earn points. If the Lancer hits the Rider's shield, that's two points. If the Lancer knocks the Rider off the mount, that's immediate victory. *However*, if I see the lance hitting anything other than the shield— that's *immediate* disqualification. Everyone understand what I've said so far?"

"Yes!" the class shouted.

"Good. The joust requires me to modify the Kasperitis Code of Conduct. Specifically, that means no thrusting, no trampling, no pummeling, no decapitations, no looting, no marauding, no mayhem, and no bloodshed. I don't want Cranky Hankey complaining about staying late to clean your guts off the floor mats. And just so we're clear, none of those weapons you guys are holding can be used on the field of battle. All daggers and swords are to be left in the bleachers."

"What about soupspoons?" P.W. called out.

Everyone laughed but Lumpkin.

"One last thing," said the coach. "You've heard it before, but I'll say it again. No teasing, no taunting, no trash-talk of any kind." With that the coach tooted his jester's-head whistle and began the tournament joust.

The foam flew fast and furious as Lancers and Riders took turns on the pommel horse. Leon handled himself quite well as a Lancer. Matched against Thomas, he scored six points. But as a Rider, Leon proved less accomplished. Distracted by thoughts of Lumpkin and Plan A, he let Thomas unseat him twenty seconds into the second half of the bout.

Probably a good thing, Leon told himself as he watched the competition from the bleachers. It seemed unwise to risk life and limb—his own and the doll's—less than an hour before the classroom showdown.

P.W. joined him in the spectators' gallery at the end of the first round. "I messed up against Antoinette!" he grumbled. "I hit her stupid tiara."

"Tough break," said Leon. "At least you'll avoid Lumpkin."

"Yeah," said P.W. "But I know someone who won't."

"Who's that?"

"Take a look." P.W. pointed. "Lily-Matisse is kicking royal rump!'"

And it was true. Suited up for battle, Lily-Matisse proved to be a gifted jouster. Years of gymnastics training paid off unexpectedly. She ducked and rolled, tucked, arched, and jabbed her way into the second round. And the third. And the fourth. In fact, she made it all the way to the finals.

Unfortunately, so did Henry Lumpkin.

Jasprow vs. Lumpkin started with Lily-Matisse in the saddle. She fended off a ferocious lance attack by digging in her heels and bending her body like a wind-blown blade of grass. For nearly fifty seconds, Lumpkin could not touch her shield. Then, just as the first half of the face-off was coming to an end, Lily-Matisse let down her guard. Lumpkin glanced the shield rim and scored two points.

The coach blew his whistle. Rider and Lancer swapped places. It was now Lily-Matisse's turn to charge.

Time and time again, she aimed her lance at the shield of her orange-haired opponent. Time and again she missed. Lumpkin wasn't so much seated on the horse as *bolted* on.

"We've got to do something," P.W. said urgently.

"I know," Leon replied. "But what?"

With fifteen seconds left in the match, Leon cupped his hands around his mouth and called out a word he was pretty sure avoided the coach's prohibition on trash-talking: "*Soupspoon!*"

Lumpkin turned toward the spectators' gallery.

That was just the opening Lily-Matisse needed. She charged and, with a gentle tap, found the sweet spot on Lumpkin's shield.

"Two points!" the coach shouted. "All tied."

"That's not fair," Lumpkin protested.

Lily-Matisse spun around as her archenemy rose off his saddle to complain. She jabbed her lance tip hard into the dead center of his shield.

Lumpkin crashed onto the gym mats with a *thud!*

Over the shouts from the bleachers, the coach gave a blast on the jester's-head whistle. "Hear ye! Hear ye!" he called out.

"They didn't say 'hear ye' in the Middle Ages," Antoinette said. Her quibble was instantly drowned out by jeers.

The coach marched over to the pommel horse carrying a small trophy. After quieting everyone down, he said, "In recognition of her valor and victory in the tournament joust, I do bestow upon Lady Lily-Matisse the Kasperitis Chalice of Champions."

He handed her the chalice, which was actually a baseball trophy Mr. Groot had altered for the occasion. (The shop instructor sawed off the bat and reattached it under the player's armpit so that it would look like a lance.)

"Thanks," said Lily-Matisse.

"And with the Kasperitis Chalice of Champions comes the honor of assigning seats at the banquet," said the coach.

"*Thanks*," she said again.

"Way to go, Lily-Matisse," P.W. shouted. "You pulverized him!"

The coach leveled a harsh gaze at P.W. "What was that?" he bellowed.

Everyone, from beggar to queen, turned silent.

"Repeat the word you just used," the coach demanded.

"Pulverized?" P.W. said hesitantly.

The coach shook his head with apparent disgust. "And what's the most important rule in the Kasperitis Code of Conduct?"

"No trash-talk?"

"That's right. Do you think they even *had* trashtalk in the Middle Ages?"

"No," said P.W. nervously.

"Well, you're wrong!" said the coach, breaking into a big fat smile. "Hey, Queenie," he yelled to Antoinette. "Since you're such a stickler about what people did and didn't say in medieval times—go grab those wordlists off the bench and pass 'em around."

Wordlists—in *gym*?

Groans and grumbles spread through the spectators' gallery. But the grumbles and groans turned into giggles and guffaws when the students got a look at the handouts. They read:

Barnacle	Drone	Ruffian
Belch	Entrails	Scum
Blemish	Fetid	Toad
Buttock	Fool	Toothless
Carbuncle	Hag	Turd
Clod	Impudent	Villain
Cockerel	Mongrel	Vomit
Crone	Pig	Wart
Curd	Pimple	Worm

"Back in the Middle Ages, no tournament was complete without a flyting contest," the coach told them.

"What's a flyting contest?" Antoinette asked.

"According to Mr. Rattles—he's the one who made up the list—a flyting contest is an insult competition. The rules are simple. You guys have two minutes to come up with your best curse. You can use any word you want—as long as it's decent and medieval."

The joust of peace was fierce. The joust of words was fiercer. Slurs and slights filled the gym. And in the end, it was P.W. who carried the day by stitching together a nickname that described Henry Lumpkin perfectly. He called the bully a "pimple on the buttock of a toothless curd-turd."

Why did P.W. do something so obviously life-threatening? For the same reason Lily-Matisse had risked injury during the joust. Both felt confident that Leon and his master piece would protect them.

Moments after the end of the insult competition, Mr. Hankey stuck his head through the double doors of the gym and clanged his bucket-sized bell. "Banquet time," he announced. "Get thee to the lunchroom."

"You mean feast hall," Antoinette corrected.

Lily-Matisse installed herself at the head of the banquet table, in a throne covered with recycled tinfoil. She set down the Kasperitis Chalice of Champions and commanded Sir Leon and Master Dhabanandana to sit by her side. At Leon's suggestion she exercised her special rights still further by exiling Lumpkin to the opposite end of the room.

"Let's just hope that keeps him away until we get

back to class," Leon said as he surveyed the table. It was decorated like a medieval kingdom, complete with a gingerbread castle and vegetable forests. The banquet menu included cercles of oynon and fyngers of chicken and something called solana tuberosa in modo crispus fricta, which looked promisingly like curly fries.

Everyone was impressed. Well, almost everyone. "They didn't *have* curly fries in medieval Europe," Antoinette said. "They didn't have potatoes, *period*."

"Now there's a scary thought," said Lily-Matisse. "A world without curly fries."

"Or mashed potatoes," said P.W.

"Or potato chips!" Leon exclaimed.

P.W. grabbed a fistful of chicken. "Still, I could get used to eating this way. Food tastes a lot better without forks."

"Or soupspoons," said Leon. He gazed toward the far end of the table. "Where'd Lumpkin go?"

P.W. shrugged.

"I'm sure we'll find out," said Lily-Matisse nervously.

And she was right. Ten minutes before the end of the feast, after the fruit tarts and jellies had been served, after a jester had jested and a juggler had juggled, Leon felt a small tug. He looked under the table just in time to see Lumpkin crawling away.

"Yoo-hoo, Sir Panty Hose," said Lumpkin, as he

resurfaced at the far end of the table. "Missing something?"

Leon reached for his pouch. "It's gone!" he cried. "Lumpkin's got the master piece!"

Leon jumped up and raced toward the doll. Lily-Matisse and P.W. followed close behind. When they reached Lumpkin, he was tapping his soupspoon against the pouch, like a musician playing the triangle.

Tap . . . tap . . . tap.

"Give it back," Lily-Matisse said.

Lumpkin kept tapping.

Tap . . . tap . . . tap . . . clink!

Lumpkin raised a brow. "Hmm."

Leon tried to grab for the pouch, but Lumpkin fended him off with a vicious swipe. The soupspoon caught the back of Leon's hand.

"Now, now, Sir Panty Hose. None of that." Lumpkin tucked the spoon under his arm, opened the pouch, and dumped the contents. Doll and juice bottle tumbled onto the banquet table.

Leon watched helplessly as Lumpkin brought the bottle to eye level and inspected the murky liquid inside. "What's this?"

"Mead," P.W. said quickly.

"Huh?"

"It's a kind of medieval drink," said Lily-Matisse. "Very tasty."

Lumpkin unscrewed the bottle and took a sniff.

Leon wasn't sure what to do. Much as he would have loved to see Henry Lumpkin drink teacher's spit, it didn't make sense to waste the powerful potion.

Lumpkin brought the jar to his lips. . . .

"That's not mead!" Antoinette shouted seconds before he was going to take a swallow. "It's not clear enough to be mead."

Lumpkin put down the jar and scowled, then turned his attention to the other item that had fallen from the pouch.

"Well, well," he said, looking straight into the eyes of the doll. "So we meet again."

"*Please*," Leon cried.

Lumpkin ignored him. "What was I going to do with you?" he said to the master piece. "Oh, that's right." He brought his hand back.

"Stop!" cried Leon.

Lumpkin hurled the master piece. It flew over the banquet table with such force that it knocked a sugar-cone roof off the north tower of the gingerbread castle and kept on going. It hit a stack of trays and kept on going. It ricocheted off a wall and kept on going. It only ended its flight after it glanced off the side of the salad bar and dropped into a garbage can.

"Hank the Tank for two!" Lumpkin shouted boastfully.

Leon raced over to the crash site and retrieved his master piece. Lily-Matisse and P.W. arrived seconds later.

"The wig!" Leon cried. "It's missing!"

Where the hairpiece should have been, there was now only a sparse Velcro stubble. Leon rooted through the garbage can while Lily-Matisse and P.W. searched for the wig along the doll's flight path.

"Found it!" Lily-Matisse yelled, emerging triumphantly from behind a stack of trays. She handed Leon the hairpiece. He reattached it and gave the doll a once-over.

The clothing was a little rumpled, but otherwise everything seemed okay. Then Leon straightened out the cape.

"Oh, no!" he blurted out.

"What's wrong *now?*" said Lily-Matisse.

"Look!" Leon cried. He pulled back the cape to expose the doll's legs.

P.W. and Lily-Matisse understood at once the severity of the situation. The force of impact had ripped through the doll's panty hose and had opened a seam on one of the legs. And leg seams, all three knew, were where Miss Hagmeyer usually conducted the stitch counts that determined whether animiles passed—or failed.

Twenty-Seven

Final Inspection

Miss Hagmeyer heard the door creak before Leon set foot inside the classroom.

"You're early," she snapped. She was kneeling before the supply cabinet, her arms shoved deep inside the panty-hose drawer.

What is she fishing for? Leon wondered as he watched her root through the tattered, tangled hose.

All of a sudden she pulled something to the surface. It was the black binder!

"Why aren't you still at the banquet?" Miss Hagmeyer demanded.

"Just wanted to check over my master piece," Leon said. And while I'm at it, get a look at that binder, he thought to himself.

"A bit late for that, isn't it?" Miss Hagmeyer grumbled. She reached into another drawer and removed some translucent white cloth, which she pinned to her wig.

Leon now had two reasons to stare at his teacher.

"It's a wimple," Miss Hagmeyer clarified, touching the delicate head cover. She shut the cabinet doors and replaced the padlock. "My one concession to Carnival clothing."

"Looks good," said Leon.

"Skip the flattery, Mr. Zeisel. If you have things to check, get checking. Final inspections begin in exactly seven minutes." Miss Hagmeyer walked to the front of the room.

Leon sat down and pulled a needle and thread from the cubbyhole of his desk. Before he tended to the doll, he propped up his *Medieval Reader*, like a castle wall, to block out unwanted attention.

The leg gash was worse than he feared. Lumpkin's sidewinder had destroyed a seam that stretched from boot to buttock. The damage penetrated all three layers of the doll's leg: the liver-colored stocking, the skin of pale white cotton below it, and the panty-hose core. In fact, the wound went so deep that it exposed a small length of coat-hanger bone.

The doll wasn't the only one harmed. Leon had a nasty welt on his hand, compliments of Lumpkin's soupspoon. He ignored his own injury, however, and focused on the doll's—it was far more serious.

Leon rewrapped the exposed leg bone, folded one edge of the white cotton skin over the other, made a few overcast stitches just above the boot, and checked his work.

Not good enough, he decided.

The panty-hose stuffing was pushing against the seam, spreading the stitches to unacceptable widths. Standard overcasting, Leon concluded, would never meet the Hagmeyer minimum of four s.p.i. That meant figuring out a different method of repair. Leon cut through the thread with his string ring and started over.

He was just pressing the two edges of cotton together—they reminded him of a pair of lips—when Mr. Hankey passed by clanging his bell.

"Finally," said Miss Hagmeyer. "He's three minutes late."

Lily-Matisse and P.W. were the first to return from the banquet. They rushed straight over to Leon.

P.W. placed the pouch and spit bottle behind the *Medieval Reader*. "You ran out of the lunchroom so fast you left these behind," he said.

"Thanks," said Leon distractedly. He shoved the bottle into his desk.

"So?" said P.W. "Have you lost power?"

Leon bent the arms of the doll a couple of times and glanced over at Miss Hagmeyer.

"She's not responding," said Lily-Matisse.

"I know," said Leon. "For the moment, I'm getting zero reaction."

"But that could change, right?" said Lily-Matisse anxiously.

"Of course it could change," said P.W.

Leon finished off a stitch and looked up. "We'll know for sure after I've fixed the rip."

"Will you be done by inspection time?" Lily-Matisse asked.

Leon sighed. "Not if I have to keep answering questions."

"Got it," said P.W.

"Ditto," said Lily-Matisse.

They let him get back to work.

Pinching the material together with one hand while working the needle with the other, Leon tackled the repair with the intensity of a crackerjack surgeon performing a life-saving procedure. In fact, he was so busy tending to his patient he didn't hear the class being called to order.

Miss Hagmeyer silenced the students with a wave of her needle.

"Apprentices and potential masters," she said, brushing the gauzy see-through wimple away from her face. "Our year together began when I wrote out the motto of a medieval master. 'A place for everything and everything in its place.' Nine important words for nine important projects."

She aimed her needle at the countinghouse tally. "That timeline tells the story of those projects—as well as my efforts to use them to turn all of you into masters. Today we will see if a year of discipline and diligence has paid off. When I call your name, approach the desk with your submission. If you wish, you may describe it—*briefly*.

"I will then conduct my inspection, which will conclude in the usual manner—by the measurement of a seam. *If* the seam satisfies my s.p.i. standards, I will declare you a master of the guild and will send you to the countinghouse tally with these snagglers." Miss Hagmeyer tapped a giant pair of scissors. "Advance your spool to the end of the tally, and use the snagglers to snip it free. Once you have done that, return the scissors to me and sit down with your spool and submission."

"Does that mean we get to keep our master pieces?" Lily-Matisse asked.

"I said no such thing, Miss Jasprow," Miss Hagmeyer said. "Now let's begin. Brede, Antoinette."

Antoinette stood up and faced the class. "My Master Piece, by Queen Antoinette. My master piece is an Irish Wolfhound." She held out a stuffed dog with a glittery rhinestone collar. "Irish Wolfhounds are the most regal dogs in the world. 'Gentle when stroked, fierce when provoked.' That's their motto. They were introduced . . ."

Leon tuned out. For the first time all year—for the first time in his entire life!—he was happy his last name started with Z. It gave him more time to work.

Antoinette's wolfhound passed with a stitch count

of seven s.p.i. P.W.'s master piece, a three-headed dragon, got approved with a respectable six. Lily-Matisse presented a jazzed-up winter rabbit with tie-dyed lavender ears. Miss Hagmeyer criticized the bunny's "flamboyance" but felt compelled to okay it since its stitch count measured a nine—more than twice the minimum. Even Henry Lumpkin earned the title of master—for a five s.p.i. pit bull made from material that matched his olive drab army jacket.

Seventeen animiles passed under the tape measure. Seventeen masters entered the Guild.

One submission remained.

"Zeisel, Leon," said Miss Hagmeyer.

Leon slipped his master piece into its pouch, lowered the *Medieval Reader*, stood up, and approached the front of the room.

He was unsure whether the doll's loss of signal power was temporary or permanent, but he decided not to take any chances. He gingerly loosened the drawstring on the pouch and pressed up from the bottom until the head of the doll poked out like a Push Pop. Then he peeled down the pouch—careful not to touch the doll inside.

As soon as he deposited the master piece on Miss Hagmeyer's desk, he cleared his throat and said, "We've been told that it's the job of an apprentice to make a master piece worthy of a master. Well, that's what I've tried to do."

The *big* Miss Hagmeyer took one look at the *little* Miss Hagmeyer and instantly started to shake.

"B-b-but Leon . . . It's-it's-it's . . . ME!"

"No, Miss Hagmeyer," Leon corrected firmly. "It's your spitting image!"

The doll knocked the stuffing out of Miss Hagmeyer as effectively as Lumpkin had knocked the stuffing out of the doll. It took her nearly a minute to recover. Once she had, she inspected the master piece with an odd, almost greedy silence. Her bony fingers and beady gaze traveled over every nook and cranny of the doll, from wig to boots. The eyes on the doll (all four of them) attracted her attention first, and then the cape. But it was the black lace-ups that most intrigued her. She was impressed that Leon had tied the laces just like hers—with double rabbit ears, and a safety knot added for good measure.

Naturally her fascination fascinated the class. Everyone leaned forward to watch Miss Hagmeyer inspect . . . Miss Hagmeyer! Would she lift up the hair and check out the mushroom-shaped ears? Would she remove the miniature wig?

The life-size Miss Hagmeyer disappointed her students by avoiding both noteworthy features of the masterly work.

But was it masterly?

Leon *still* didn't know.

Miss Hagmeyer said nothing—not a word—after

her initial stuttered outburst. She focused all her attention on the doll. That made Leon antsy. Eventually she placed the doll faceup on the desk and said, "I suppose it is time to take a measure of the master piece—and its maker." She fiddled with the doll's stockings, to expose the seams.

Hey, Miss Hagmeyer! Get your nose out of my panty hose! Leon yelled, if only in his head. He looked on silently, relieved she was ignoring the spit stain on the clothes. Still, he knew he wasn't off the hook.

As the whole class watched, Miss Hagmeyer pressed her tape measure against the freshly repaired leg. Recording the results on her clipboard, she muttered something Leon couldn't quite catch. It sounded like she had called his work "uneven."

"Huh?" he said.

"We do not say 'huh' in my class, Mr. Zeisel. We say 'excuse me.'"

"Excuse me?" said Leon. "Did I do something *uneven?*"

"Uneven?" Miss Hagmeyer gave him a puzzled look.

What's she trying to pull *now?* Leon asked himself before he said, "Didn't you just say my seam is uneven?"

"No," Miss Hagmeyer replied. "I did not."

"Oh."

"I *said* 'eleven.'"

"Eleven what?" Leon asked quizzically.

"Stitches, Mr. Zeisel. Your seam—or should I say *my* seam?—measures eleven s.p.i."

"*Eleven?*" shouted Leon.

"Yes," Miss Hagmeyer said, as the class erupted in cheers.

She picked up the snagglers and presented them to Leon, tips down. "Now go and claim your spool."

So it was official. The class klutz had passed inspection. And he had done so with top marks!

Leon couldn't wait to tell Napoleon and Frau Haffenreffer and Maria. He especially couldn't wait to tell his mom.

He marched over to the countinghouse tally. Seventeen sliced strands of yarn hung to the side, like a mop of orange hair. One strand still stretched across the chart.

Leon pushed his spool to the far right of the yarn and cut it free with the snagglers. He caught the spool, dropped it into his pouch, and headed back for his doll.

"May I please have my master piece, Miss Hagmeyer?" he said as politely as possible.

Miss Hagmeyer didn't respond. She was still marvelling over it.

"Miss Hagmeyer?"

Still no reaction.

Leon decided to take charge. He tugged the doll

out of Miss Hagmeyer's hands and gently clutched it in his arms.

Then, before Leon knew it, Miss Hagmeyer was clutching . . . *him!*

At first Leon thought the embrace was intentional. By the time he realized what actually was happening—that the doll had been reactivated—it was too late.

The whole class oooooohed as Leon struggled to free himself. It wasn't easy. To peel Miss Hagmeyer off his body, he had to wrench the doll away from his chest. But to wrench the doll away from his chest, he had to peel Miss Hagmeyer off his body!

After a good bit of squirming, Leon managed to pry the doll away. Miss Hagmeyer let go of him moments later.

The class quickly figured out that their teacher was out of commission, though not the reason why.

"Hey, Haggy!" Lumpkin shouted. "Wanna wrestle?"

"Shush," Antoinette told him, "She'll hear you."

But of course Miss Hagmeyer didn't hear Lumpkin, or anyone else—not while Leon was holding the doll.

Lumpkin's challenge tempted Leon. It would have been sweet to make Miss Hagmeyer body-slam him against the supply cabinet. But Leon resisted the impulse. He had other plans.

Chaos reigned supreme in the classroom. Master

pieces flew through the air. Swords smacked against shields. Even Antoinette misbehaved, humming all four stanzas of "Miss Hagmeyer Had a Hairpiece" while waving her tiara in the air.

Leon took advantage of the medieval mayhem to check in with P.W.

"Looks like we're back in business," he said.

P.W. grinned. "Looks like it." He tapped his pocket. "The crowning apparatus is fully operational. Commence launch sequence whenever you're ready."

TWENTY-EIGHT

The Binder of Bonding

Leon released Miss Hagmeyer from her trance once he was safely in his seat.

After she regained control of her mind and body (and the instructional needle), she instantly took hold of the class.

"Now that all of you have finished your presentations," she said, "I wish to make one of my own. It concerns the business of animiles."

"We know all about *that* business," P.W. muttered, rubbing his fingers together like a miser.

Miss Hagmeyer chuckled ruefully. "You don't actually *believe* those rumors, do you, Mr. Dhabanandana? About the evil hag who sells her students' animiles for vast sums of money?"

The class exchanged looks. Miss Hagmeyer had never chuckled before, not even ruefully. Then again, she had never done a lot of things she was doing now. Resting her needle on the desk, she reached for the binder and, with both hands, raised it in the air. Even from the back of the room Leon could see that the cover had the letters SOV exactingly chain stitched across the front in light blue thread.

"This," said Miss Hagmeyer, "is what the monks of the Middle Ages would have called a codex of connection. I will spare you the Latin. It is a book that ties together the work of master and apprentice. It is, in other words . . . a binder of bonding."

"Binder of *bondage* is more like it," Leon whispered to Thomas.

Miss Hagmeyer heard the remark. "Bondage, Mr. Zeisel? So you think you're my slave?"

"No, Miss Hagmeyer," Leon replied. Just the opposite, he thought to himself.

Miss Hagmeyer lowered the book. "You went from two s.p.i. to eleven. From the bottom of the class to the top. From apprentice to master. From making a lumpy, lifeless snake to an animile with perfect seams. Don't you think that was worth a bit of bondage?"

"I guess," said Leon.

"Perhaps you will be better convinced after you have examined the *Hagmeyer Codex*." The first thing that caught Leon's eye, after he lifted the cover of the binder, was a photo.

Item: Snake
Animile No. 1
Maker: Brede, Antoinette
S.P.I.: 5
Completion Date: 9/14
Recipient: "Artemis"
Destination: Petra

Who is Artemis? Leon wondered. Where is Petra?

Leon made a mental note to check the map in his room. Then he flipped ahead until he found one of his animiles.

Leon was still staring at the terry cloth towel snake when he felt the tap of the instructional needle on his shoulder.

"Time to let the others take a gander, Mr. Zeisel," Miss Hagmeyer said. "And since I've broken with protocol by beginning at Z, we'll work backward. Take the binder to Mr. Warchowski." She looked over at Thomas. "When you're done, pass it along."

Before obeying Miss Hagmeyer's directive, Leon scanned the statistics that accompanied the picture.

Item: Snake
Animile No. 1
Maker: Zeisel, Leon
S.P.I.: 2
Completion Date: 9/30
Recipient: "Danielle"
Destination: Paramaribo

"Paramaribo!" Leon cried. "That's the capital of *Suriname!*"

"I am very impressed by your command of geography, Mr. Zeisel, but that is not what we are studying at present." Miss Hagmeyer closed the binder. "Take this over to Mr. Warchowski and return to your seat."

As the binder passed from student to student, Miss Hagmeyer explained its significance. "Stitches of Virtue, or SOV—contrary to what Masters Zeisel and Dhabanandana seem to think—is *not* a commercial venture. It is an enterprise based on the medieval principle of *caritas*—a term you can find in the glossary of the *Reader*."

There was a fluttering sound at the front of the room.

"Got it," Antoinette chirped. "*Caritas*, or charity. The word dates from 1137. Says here it means 'benevolence for the poor.'"

"Thank you, Miss Brede, for that speedy elaboration. Now if I might continue. I send your handmade toys to orphaned tots all over the world."

"SOV is a *charity?*" P.W. cried out.

"That is correct," said Miss Hagmeyer. "A charity—and a crusade."

Murmurs filled the room.

P.W. exchanged puzzled glances with Leon and Lily-Matisse. They'd been dead wrong about Miss Hagmeyer. She had no Grinchy scheme to *sell* their animiles. She was *giving* them away.

"How did you get all the pictures?" Thomas asked.

"I include a disposable camera with every shipment," said Miss Hagmeyer.

Lily-Matisse raised her hand. "Why didn't you tell us before?"

"Simply put, the *Hagmeyer Codex* is reserved for the eyes of masters. None of you was ready to see it. None of you was a member of the guild."

Antoinette held up her wolfhound and said, "Now that we are, can you tell us where you'll be sending our master pieces?"

"Ah," said Miss Hagmeyer. "That raises an important matter. Masters must decide the fate of their work for themselves. You may deposit your final animiles in the finished bin or, if you choose, you may keep them."

Eyes widened. Jaws dropped. The news floored everyone, Leon most of all.

He could keep his master piece. *He could keep his master piece!* HE COULD KEEP HIS MASTER PIECE! It suddenly felt as if Miss Hagmeyer had spun *him* in the air seven times.

"*However,*" she continued, dragging Leon back to Earth, "I must point out that though all of you are masters, you are also fourth graders—fourth graders about to receive final reports. I earnestly hope I can document the spirit of *caritas* in each and every assessment I send home." She eyed the finished bin. "I trust you will make the right choice."

Leon felt trapped. He could keep the master piece and guarantee himself yet another negative report. Or he could deposit the master piece in the finished bin and kiss his magic powers good-bye.

He didn't know what to do, but one thing was certain. If he did have to part company with the doll, he would give it a worthy send-off.

"Right," said Miss Hagmeyer. "When I call your names, approach. The choice you face is simple. You can embrace the virtue of charity or give in to the sin of greed."

The procession began, as usual, with Antoinette, who did what was expected and donated her wolfhound to Stitches of Virtue. Leon watched and waited. After four of five students had relinquished their master pieces in similar fashion, he stood up and said, "I can't believe you would *plan a* surprise like that, Miss Hagmeyer."

While everyone stared, Leon winked at P.W. But P.W. didn't get the cue.

"I beg your pardon?" said Miss Hagmeyer, perplexed by the outburst.

Leon repeated himself, this time more forcefully. "I *said*, I can't believe you would PLAN A surprise like that!"

All at once, P.W. understood. Plan A! The scheme to unite Miss Hagmeyer and Lumpkin—and a pair of really old panty hose. He tapped his pocket to let Leon know he was set.

"Thank you for sharing your shock with the class, Mr. Zeisel. Now please sit down."

Leon took his seat and prepared for Plan A. It required four discrete steps. Miss Hagmeyer had to:

1. Reach down and pick up a pair of panty hose.
2. Stretch open the waistband of said panty hose.
3. Raise said panty hose in the air.
4. Thrust said panty hose, in a swift downward motion, over Lumpkin's head.

After that, Leon figured, things could take care of themselves.

When Miss Hagmeyer said, "Lumpkin, Henry," Leon reached for his doll, careful to avoid direct contact. (The last thing he needed was another accidental hugging.)

As Lumpkin lumbered forward, Leon gave the signal. P.W. withdrew the panty hose and tossed them on the floor. The hose landed some four feet from Miss Hagmeyer's boots.

Perfect! Leon told himself.

"So, Mr. Lumpkin, have you decided to join the crusade or—"

Before Miss Hagmeyer could finish her sentence, Leon bent the doll at the waist and extended one of its arms toward the floor. Miss Hagmeyer fell into a trance and reached for the panty hose.

So far, so good, Leon told himself.

Lumpkin watched with growing concern (while the rest of the class watched with growing excitement) as Miss Hagmeyer straightened up, stretched open the waistband of the hose, and raised her arms until the hose hovered less than a foot from Lumpkin's head.

Only step four—the thrust—remained.

Leon lined up the shot and, with the arms of the doll perfectly positioned, executed the swift downward motion. . . .

All of a sudden Miss Hagmeyer began making odd, jerky motions—motions completely unrelated to Leon's fluent dollwork.

The panty-hose plan had clearly hit a snag.

Leon repeated step four, but Miss Hagmeyer kept jerking about, refusing to crown Lumpkin with the brown-gray hose.

When the class started tittering, Leon had no choice but to suspend his dollwork and free Miss Hagmeyer from her trance. As soon as he did, she completed her unfinished sentence, unaware of the bizarre interlude.

"—will you be keeping your pit bull?"

"I'll join the crusade," said Lumpkin timidly.

Lily-Matisse and P.W. looked at Leon, desperate to know what had gone wrong. All he could do was give them a confounded shrug.

P.W. made a pouring motion. Leon understood

instantly. He reached into his desk and grabbed the spit bottle, reapplied some of the solution to the site of the original splotch, and hastily revived his dollwork.

It was no use. Miss Hagmeyer refused to attack. It was as if Lumpkin was protected by some invisible force field.

Leon watched helplessly as the bully slam-dunked his pit bull into the finished bin.

"Hank the Tank for two!" Lumpkin yelled before lurching back to his desk.

While Miss Hagmeyer continued the roll call, Leon struggled to diagnose the reason for the failure. It wasn't a distance issue. The master piece was definitely in range. Nor did the sight-line present problems. Leon was *sure* he had a clear, direct shot. And the supplemental spit should have taken care of any potential signal weakness.

So what was it? *What?*

Leon slumped in his chair. Why, he wondered despairingly, does something always go wrong when I'm using the doll against Lumpkin?

He recalled having the exact same difficulty in the lunchroom. Twice he had tried to get Miss Hagmeyer to launch cottage cheese at Lumpkin. Both times, inexplicably, the cottage cheese had veered off course.

Suddenly Leon understood why the master piece wasn't working properly. Why it had messed up in the lunchroom. Why it had messed up now.

It hadn't attacked because it *couldn't* attack. Plan A and Plan B (and every other anti-Lumpkin plan from C to Z) were doomed to failure.

Master pieces only worked on their spitting images.

Once Leon realized that the Hagmeyer doll would *never* neutralize Lumpkin, he had an easier time accepting the possibility of giving it away and avoiding a negative home report. After all, fourth grade was almost over. The doll wouldn't be of much use once he entered fifth grade.

It was at the moment that Miss Hagmeyer was saying "Warchowski, Thomas," that the idea popped into Leon's head. Actually, "popped" is the wrong word. It smacked into his brain like a medieval battering ram. *Whoomp!*

Shaking with excitement, Leon glanced at the padlocked supply cabinet. He had to gain access. But how? Leon briefly considered using his master piece to make Miss Hagmeyer open the doors. He nixed that idea. Even if he succeeded in guiding Miss Hagmeyer to the back of the room, he didn't think he could get her to insert her key into the lock. And even if he could do that, everyone would see him, since his desk and the cabinet were right next to each other.

No. He had to come up with another way to get the stuff he needed.

TWENTY-NINE

The Crusade Continues

"**Z**eisel, Leon," Miss Hagmeyer said.

Leon pouched his doll and walked to the front of the room.

I can do this, he told himself.

He approached his teacher.

"So what does the newly minted master wish to do with his master piece?" Miss Hagmeyer asked. "Is he keeping it for himself, or will he be embracing the spirit of *caritas*?"

I *can* do this, he repeated.

"Well?" Miss Hagmeyer pressed. "Are you depositing your master piece in the finished bin?"

"No," said Leon firmly.

The room fell silent.

Leon could see the muscles in Miss Hagmeyer's face, pinched under normal circumstances, draw in even tighter. But before she said a word, Leon held out his pouch and pushed from the bottom. The head of the master piece popped up like a jack-in-the-box.

The full-size Miss Hagmeyer first glowered at the mini-Miss Hagmeyer, and then she glowered at Leon.

"Mr. Zeisel," she said. "A place for everything and—"

"—everything in its place," Leon said. "I know. Which is why I'd like *you* to have my master piece."

Miss Hagmeyer jerked backward, as if yanked by an invisible thread.

"What?" she gasped.

The *proper* response is "excuse me," Leon said to himself before repeating his offer. "I want *you* to have my master piece."

Whispers spread through the classroom as Miss Hagmeyer plucked her likeness from Leon's pouch. No one could believe he was giving his animile to Miss Hagmeyer—not after all the trouble she had caused him.

But it was Miss Hagmeyer herself who was the most flabbergasted. "Are you p-p-positive?" she stammered.

"Yup."

Miss Hagmeyer suddenly leaned over and gave Leon a hug. For a moment, he thought he had accidentally reactivated the doll. But he hadn't. He wasn't touching the master piece. This hugging was entirely voluntary!

Oooooooohs again filled the room.

After Leon broke free, he noticed that Miss Hagmeyer's eyes were sparkling the way they had the time she did sizzlers in the playground. She daubed a tear from her cheek with her wimple and said, "Thank you, Leon, I will cherish her."

This is it. It's now or never, Leon told himself.

"Miss Hagmeyer?" he said.

"Yes?" she sniffled.

"I was wondering. . . .Would it be okay if I made another animile?"

"*Another* animile?" Miss Hagmeyer's mouth curved into a shape that resembled a smile.

"To carry on the crusade," Leon said.

A few students starting hissing. It wasn't like Leon to suck up.

"Quiet!" Miss Hagmeyer snapped.

"The thing is," said Leon, "I'll need a few supplies."

"Of course," said Miss Hagmeyer.

Leon pointed at the countinghouse tally. "That yarn would come in handy."

"The yarn?" said Miss Hagmeyer.

"It's just the right color," said Leon.

Miss Hagmeyer handed him the snagglers. "Help yourself."

Leon walked over to the chart, snipped off the yarn, and tucked it into his pouch. "And actually," he said when he returned the snagglers, "there are a few other things I could use, too." He glanced at the supply cabinet.

Miss Hagmeyer pressed the brass key into his hand. "You take whatever you need."

Leon undid the padlock, opened the cabinet doors, and filled his pouch with cloth, panty hose, and glass eye-balls.

"What are you making?" Thomas asked, gawking from his desk.

"An animile," Leon said vaguely.

"Well, duh. I mean what *kind*? A gargoyle?"

"Nastier," said Leon.

"Nastier than a gargoyle?" said Thomas approvingly. "A dragon?"

Leon shook his head. "Nastier," he said. He closed the doors, replaced the lock, and returned the key.

"I hope that Leon isn't the only one making animiles over the summer," Miss Hagmeyer told the class. "Diligence shouldn't stop with the end of the school year. After all, spool work can be *cool* work!"

Snickers greeted Miss Hagmeyer's feeble attempt at humor.

Mr. Hankey stuck his head into the classroom and clanged his bell. "It's nones, Phyllis."

Miss Hagmeyer looked at the wall clock. "It most certainly is *not* nones, Mr. Hankey."

"Well, I was told to get the fourth graders out to the playground. Principal Birdwhistle wants to see 'em."

"Is something wrong?" said Miss Hagmeyer over the groans of her students.

"Not a thing," the janitor said with a laugh. "Principal Birdwhistle had me set up a dunking pool. She should be sitting down in it right about now."

The mood in the classroom suddenly turned boisterous. All eyes locked onto Miss Hagmeyer. "Fine," she told the class. "Consider yourselves banished."

As the students broke for the door, Miss Hagmeyer thwacked her instructional needle against the table. "Stop!"

Everyone froze.

"One last thing," Miss Hagmeyer said. "When you have Principal Birdwhistle in your sights and a bean bag in your hand, make sure you prove to her that your year with the Hag has made your fingers *nimble!*" And with that she released her students. They galloped toward the playground like tournament steeds.

On the way, Lily-Matisse and P.W. cut Leon off and demanded an explanation for his curious classroom behavior.

"Have you gone completely insane?" said P.W. "How could you give her the doll?"

"It's no biggie," said Leon.

"No biggie?" said Lily-Matisse. "That's like Merlin saying, 'Here. Take my wand!' I had some tumbling moves I wanted you to test out! Now we'll never get to see the Hag do a full-twisting double layout dismount!"

P.W. scoffed. "Who cares about gymnastics? No more doll means no more Hagapult. I could've replaced the winch and rubber band. It could've been all systems go. We could've *owned* Lumpkin."

"No," said Leon. "We couldn't have. Not with the Hagmeyer doll. I finally figured out what the problem was. Master pieces can't attack."

"What are you talking about?" said P.W. "What about the food fight?"

"The food fight was an accident, not an attack. I was aiming at Lumpkin, but signal disturbance sent the cottage cheese off course—twice. And you just saw what happened with the panty hose."

"Still," said Lily-Matisse, "you could have put the master piece in the finished bin like everyone else. Giving it to the Hag was *so* Antoinettey."

"Hey, I needed stuff from the cabinet," said Leon. "Sucking up seemed like the fastest way to get it."

"You should have dollworked the Hag over to the cabinet," said P.W.

"I thought about that," said Leon. "There wasn't time. And getting her to unlock the door would have been tricky. Besides, everyone would have seen me."

They entered the playground. Lily-Matisse shook her head. "I still can't believe you're thinking about sewing projects."

"Yeah," said P.W. "We've got more important things to deal with."

"Such as?" said Leon.

"Such as a certain toothless curd-turd."

"I'm not worried about Lumpkin," said Leon.

"You're not worried about the sidewinders?" said Lily-Matisse.

"Nope."

"Or the dead-arms and noogies?" said P.W.

"Nope."

"Then you're nuts," said Lily-Matisse.

"After all that's happened today, Lumpkin's going to *pulverize* us!" cried P.W. "It's just a matter of time."

"I don't think so," Leon said confidently.

Lily-Matisse gave him a sideways glance. "All right. What gives?"

"Yeah, Leon. What's this *project* of yours?" P.W. demanded.

"Before I tell, I want the needle pledge."

"Isn't it kind of unnecessary?" said Lily-Matisse. "You don't have the doll anymore."

"The pledge," Leon insisted.

"Fine," said Lily-Matisse. "Crossmyhearthopeto-diestickaneedleinmyeye. There. Satisfied?"

"Aren't you forgetting something?"

"Sheesh!" Lily-Matisse sealed the oath with a feeble pretend *ptooey*.

"P.W.?"

P.W. said the pledge and spat without complaint. "Okay, so let's hear it."

Leon pulled a strand of orange yarn from his pouch. "Remind you of anything?" he said, wiggling it.

P.W. and Lily-Matisse exchanged confused looks.

"I'll give you a hint," said Leon. He pointed at Lumpkin, who was jostling his way to the front of the dunking-pool line.

Lily-Matisse stared at the yarn, then at Lumpkin, then at the yarn. She abruptly cupped her mouth with her hand. "Oh. My. Gosh."

"What's gotten into you?" P.W. asked.

"Lumpkin's *hair*!" Lily-Matisse blurted out.

"What about it?" said P.W.

"It's the same exact orange color as the yarn!"

"It is?" said Leon. A giant smirk stretched across his face.

P.W. looked at the yarn more closely.

"Un-freakin'-buhlievable!" he suddenly shouted.

"What?" said Leon with fake innocence.

P.W. gave an excited poke at the pouch. "What else do you have in that goody bag?"

Leon removed a scrap of green cloth.

"That's a perfect match for Lumpkin's army jacket!" P.W. cried.

"Really?" said Leon, grinning more than ever.

All at once Lily-Matisse, P.W., and Leon began laughing uncontrollably. When they finally stopped, P.W. said, "We'll be totally noogie-proof!"

"And sidewinder-proof!" said Lily-Matisse.

"Basically, we'll be Lumpkin-proof," said Leon.

"Freaky!" P.W. exclaimed. "Our very own Henry

Lumpkin doll! Think of the possibilities!"

"Knowing Leon," said Lily-Matisse, "I bet he has."

When Mr. Hankey clanged the final bell, Lily-Matisse, P.W., and Leon piled into Napoleon's taxi and headed for the Trimore Towers.

"And how was your day, Monsieur Leon?" Napoleon asked. "One a scale of one to ten—"

"Eleven!" all three classmates shouted.

"Jinx!"

"Jinx!"

"Jinx!"

"Eleven?" said Napoleon. "Is such a thing possible?"

"Absolutely," Lily-Matisse said. "Just ask the Hag. Leon got the highest grade in the class—*eleven* stitches per inch!"

The news pleased Napoleon immensely. "*C'est magnifique!* We must alert Madame Zeisel." He grabbed his car phone and placed a call.

By the time the taxi reached the hotel, Leon's mom and Maria were waiting out front.

"Terrific news, sweetie! I *knew* you'd pass. But top marks?" Emma Zeisel planted a big kiss on her son's cheek. He blushed.

"Way to go, Leonito," said Maria. "You showed that Miss Panty Hose!"

"Thanks," said Leon.

A van pulled up to the hotel.

"Penguins!" shouted Lily-Matisse, pointing to the exiting passengers.

"Must be the Antarctica Society," said Emma Zeisel matter-of-factly. "I better get back to Reception. Oh, Frau Haffenreffer is setting up some pastries and chips for the three of you in the coffee shop."

"Want me to go change the signboard?" Leon asked.

"Not necessary, sweetie. Already taken care of."

And indeed it was.

When Leon and his friends pushed through the revolving door, they were greeted by the following notice:

**CONGRATULATIONS
MASTER LEON!!!!
11 S.P.I. !!!!**

"Went a little crazy with the exclamation marks, didn't you, Mom?"

"Not at all," said Emma Zeisel. "That's all there

were in the letter box. Otherwise I'd have used tons more."

A penguin waddled toward the revolving door.

"Uh-oh," said Maria. "I better get the Poop-B-Gone."

"I have it covered," said Emma Zeisel. She held up a diaper.

Maria laughed.

"So what are you kids going to do now that you've finished all those silly sewing projects?" asked Leon's mother.

"Oh, they're not *all* done, Ms. Z," said Lily-Matisse.

"Really?"

"Really," said P.W. "We've got a huge project we're just about to start. Isn't that right, Leon?"

Leon tapped his pouch and looked at his friends.

"Yup," he said with a smile.

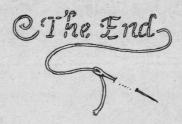

The End

Leon's adventures continue in

Leon
AND THE
Champion
Chip

CHAPTER ONE

The Purple Pouch

The evening before the start of fifth grade, Leon Zeisel was feeling unusually chipper. He sat on his bed in Trimore Towers—the six story, wedding cake-shaped one-star hotel he called home— and prepared his things for school.

Three-ring binder? Check.

No. 2 pencils? Check.

Pens? Check.

Lab notebook? Check.

After reassuring himself that all *required* materials were present and accounted for, Leon reached under his bed and pulled out the *unre-*quired item that was making him so chipper.

Keen though he was to peek inside the large purple pouch that protected the item in question, Leon worried about jinxing things, so he resisted temptation. He placed the school supplies—plus the pouch—into his backpack, hung the backpack on the doorknob, and pushed the pouched item out of his mind.

For a while.

But in the middle of the night Leon awoke with a start. A single word pulsed through his head.

The word beat quietly at first: POUCH! POUCH! POUCH!

But soon it got louder: POUCH! POUCH! POUCH!

Then louder still: POUCH! POUCH! POUCH!

Leon couldn't stop the tom-tom of temptation. Eventually he hopped out of bed and padded over to the bedroom door, dragging his blanket behind him. He placed the blanket across the doorjamb to make sure no light would seep into the living room. Once the blanket was properly positioned, he grabbed the backpack off the doorknob and switched on the lamp by his bed.

As soon as his eyes adjusted, Leon unzipped the backpack and removed the purple pouch. He took a breath. Then he squinched his eyes and clucked his tongue, a good luck ritual performed to ward off worry. And Leon Zeisel *was* feeling worried—*and* thrilled and antsy and eager.

After the squinch and cluck, he got down to business. With great care, he unpuckered the pouch by loosening the braided drawstrings, and he removed two objects: a small glass bottle filled with tarry brown liquid and a nine-inch-long handmade rag doll.

He set the bottle aside and directed his attention to the doll. It was a stocky figure of a boy dressed in an olive drab army jacket. The boy had bright orange hair, a surly looking mouth that curved downward, and beady eyes made out of actual beads. The beady bead eyes glowered at Leon.

Leon glowered back. "You staring at me, Pumpkinhead?" he whispered sternly.

Pumpkinhead remained silent.

"Wipe that look off your face *now*, soldier!" Leon commanded.

The doll failed to obey the order.

"Okay, lamebrain, you asked for it." Leon dispensed a disciplinary noogie to show Pumpkinhead who was boss.

Actually, he made Pumpkinhead give *himself* a noogie—bunching up the figure's tiny cloth fingers and grinding them into the soft, stuffing-filled skull.

"And there's more where that came from, Pumpkinhead," said Leon. "You'll find that out for yourself tomorrow, bright and early."

Reassured by the one-way exchange, Leon began packing up. As he reached for the bottle of tarry brown liquid, he felt a slight tug on the leg of his pajamas. He didn't think much about it until his bed lamp came crashing down. A wire had wrapped around his shin.

Almost at once, Leon's mother called out from the living room. "Sweetie? You okay?"

"Fine," Leon managed, as he groped about in the dark.

"What are you to up to in there?"

Leon could hear the springs of the pullout couch in the living room creaking, a sure sign that his mom would soon burst in. "Just organizing stuff for school," he shot back, as fumbled to re-pouch the bottle and rag doll.

The doorknob turned. "What's blocking the door?" Emma Zeisel demanded.

Leon zipped up his backpack seconds before his mother pushed the blanket aside. She entered the bedroom and flipped on the wall switch.

Sniffing the air, she said, "I smell something fishy. You've been going through that collection of yours, haven't you?"

"No, Mom. It's just back-to-school jitters," said Leon, his heart pounding.

"Well, jitters or no jitters, now's no time for

mischief—not the night before the start of fifth grade. Get it?"

"Got it."

"Good," said Emma Zeisel firmly. "Now get your behind back into bed."

Leon crawled under the sheets. His mom then waved the blanket back over her son, tucking in the edges with the expert hand of a seasoned hotel professional. "There we go," said Emma Zeisel. She gave her son a kiss and returned his bed lamp to the nightstand. "I'd tell you, 'Lights out,' but you seem to have taken care of that all by yourself."

"I was just—"

"Hush now, and get some shuteye," she scolded gently. "You have to be up by six thirty to walk the poodle in 309."

"Six *thirty*?" Leon whined.

"At the latest, sweetie. You're the one who told Napoleon you wanted to get to school before the first bell. Remember, he's picking you up at a quarter to eight on the dot."

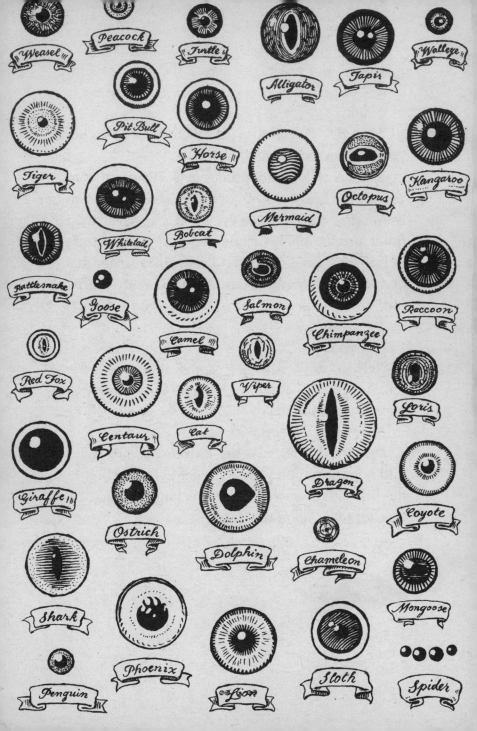

Weasel

Peacock

Turtle

Alligator

Tapir

Walleye

Pit Bull

Tiger

Horse

Mermaid

Octopus

Kangaroo

Whitetail

Bobcat

Rattlesnake

Goose

Salmon

Chimpanzee

Raccoon

Red Fox

Camel

Viper

Loris

Centaur

Cat

Dragon

Giraffe

Ostrich

Dolphin

Chameleon

Coyote

Shark

Mongoose

Phoenix

Sloth

Spider

Penguin

Lion